53.894

DEAD CENTER

A   H E N R Y   H O L T   M Y S T E R Y

Collin Wilcox

A HENRY HOLT MYSTERY

DEAD CENTER

HENRY HOLT AND COMPANY
NEW YORK

Published by Henry Holt and Company, Inc.,
115 West 18th Street, New York, New York 10011.
Published in Canada by Fitzhenry & Whiteside Limited,
91 Granton Drive, Richmond Hill, Ontario L4B 2N5.

Library of Congress Cataloging-in-Publication Data
Wilcox, Collin.
Dead center / by Collin Wilcox.—1st ed.
p.   cm.—(A Henry Holt mystery)
I. Title.
PS3573.I395D43   1992   91-31076
813'.54—dc20   CIP
ISBN 0-8050-1615-5 (alk. paper)

Henry Holt books are available at special discounts
for bulk purchases for sales promotions, premiums,
fund-raising, or educational use. Special editions
or book excerpts can also be created to specifications.
For details contact:
Special Sales Director, Henry Holt and Company, Inc.
115 West 18th Street, New York, New York 10011.

First Edition—1992

Designed by Lucy Albanese

Printed in the United States of America
Recognizing the importance of preserving the written word,
Henry Holt and Company, Inc., by policy, prints all of its
first editions on acid-free paper. ∞
1   3   5   7   9   10   8   6   4   2

*This Book Is Dedicated
to the Six of Us.*

DEAD CENTER

A HENRY HOLT MYSTERY

1

"Sir?"

Frazer put the half-filled martini glass aside, turned, let a deliberate moment elapse as he looked the waiter up and down.

"You're—?" Another moment, this one inquiring.

"I'm Taylor. Bruce Taylor."

"You've been working here how long?"

"It'll be a week tomorrow."

"And?"

Taylor frowned. "Sir?"

"And how do you like it?"

Still in his twenties, slim, sandy-haired, open-faced, the waiter smiled. It was an engaging smile, an all-American smile.

1

Conclusion: Charles, the manager, had exhausted the supply of available continental types and was recruiting college boys. To test the premise, Frazer said, "You've been to college."

Pleased, the young man nodded. "That's right."

"Where?"

"U.C.L.A."

"Ah—" Satisfied, visibly bored now, Frazer nodded. "Good." Then, cryptically: "So?"

"There's a man—a gentleman—in the lobby. Carlton Wallace. You're old friends, he says."

The name's evocation was instantaneous: The frat house. The booze. The girls. Four years at U. of M., where it had all started. How many years was it now? He'd been twenty-two when he graduated; he was forty-two now. Twenty years. Was it possible?

"How's he look?"

Puzzled—cautious—Taylor frowned again. "Sir?"

"Wallace. How's he look to you? All right?"

"Oh . . . sure." Once more the all-American smile surfaced. "Sure, I'd say so. Good clothes, a fifty-dollar tie." The smile broadened affably. "I always look at the ties. Then I look at the shoes. Three hundred–dollar shoes, I'd say. Minimum."

"Okay." Frazer consulted his watch: ten minutes after eight. For a Thursday night, the restaurant was busy. Could it be the review Bea Pixa had written in the Sunday paper?

"Okay, bring him in."

"Yessir." Taylor nodded, turned, made his way among the tables to the lobby entrance. A moment later he reappeared, followed by Carlton Wallace.

Yes, the waiter's instinct had been accurate: Wallace made an acceptable appearance. But the Carlton Wallace following Taylor between tables was no longer slim, no longer lithe. Only the face was the same: smooth, self-satisfied, self-confident. For Carlton Wallace, the gift of grace had come easily, effortlessly.

2

In the Lambda Phi house, Wallace had been an insider. Always.

Frazer rose, smiled, extended his hand. Wallace spoke first. "Tony. I read about you in the airline magazine." As their hands disengaged and Frazer motioned the other man to a seat, Wallace looked appreciatively at his surroundings. "This is the place to see and be seen. That's a quote."

"What'll you have, Carl? Order dinner, if you'd like. Except that I can't stay." Frazer shrugged apologetically, waved gracefully, an explanation. "It's Valentine's Day, you know."

"I've already eaten." Wallace turned to the waiter. "Hennessy, please. Straight up."

The waiter nodded, smiled, looked inquiringly at Frazer, then withdrew.

"And," Wallace said, continuing, "and, according to the article, this restaurant is just a hobby—so you always have a table, someplace to drop in when you're bored."

"I'll have to look up this article." As Wallace continued his appraisal of the restaurant decor, the diners, the rhythms and cross rhythms, Frazer scanned the other man's face, searching for the visual relationship between the twenty-year-old Wallace and the forty-year-old Wallace. Plainly—predictably—it was a success story: everything complemented the fifty-dollar tie.

"So—" After the waiter placed a half-filled crystal brandy snifter on the table, Frazer watched the other man drain most of the contents. Was Wallace a drinker? Something in the long, single gulp of brandy begged the question. "So—" Frazer repeated. "What? You're married, I imagine. Gainfully employed, obviously. A father?"

Wallace's smile was unreadable, but then twisted wryly. "Married, yes, right out of college. And a father, yes. Two kids. But—yes—we got divorced. Pamela Ames. Remember?"

"Ah—" Frazer nodded. Yes. Pamela Ames. Sigma Alpha Phi. Daughter of Walter Ames, advertising tycoon. Ames, Blanchard and Weston, based in Detroit, tapped into automobile advertising. Pamela had been blond and sullen, with no visible breasts. "Remarried?"

Wallace nodded. "Right." He drained the goblet and, without benefit of invitation, signaled for another. Yes, something suggested a drinker's mannerisms, perhaps a hint of arrogance, of defiance. After all, one of them sold liquor. And sellers needed buyers.

Frazer drew back a gleaming white cuff, consulted his watch. Ignoring the pointed gesture, Wallace tossed off half the second brandy before he said, "I don't have to ask about your marital status, Tony. All I had to do was read that article." The remark was edged with irony. Or was it thinly veiled contempt, the price he had accepted so long ago? Wallace's eyes gave no clue; his gaze had gone flat.

"Where d'you live, Carl?"

"Chicago. I started out in Detroit, working for Pam's father." Wallace grimaced. "Big mistake."

"So you were in advertising."

Wallace nodded, drained the second snifter. "Still am. But not working for my father-in-law. Jenny—my wife—is twenty-six. Believe me, that's the way to go." Wallace winked. Yes, it was the Lambda Phi wink. Significantly, Wallace contemplated his empty glass. Frazer looked away.

"I don't have to ask about your marriage," Wallace said again. "I read all about it. How does it feel, seeing your life spread out in four colors?"

Frazer shrugged. "It goes with the territory."

"The gold mining territory, according to the article. Your wife's—what—great-grandfather was tapped into the mother lode. Right?"

"Right." It was a dead-level response. Frazer pushed back his chair.

"So you didn't marry the boss's daughter." A malicious beat

4

passed, another frat-house evocation: Carl Wallace, the cool one—the cruel one, after a few drinks. "You married the granddaughter. Or is it the great-granddaughter?"

"Speaking of whom—" Frazer rose. "I'm off. Nice to have seen you, Carl." He decided to smile, decided to offer his hand.

A little unsteadily, Wallace rose, took the outstretched hand, saying: "You always knew how to please the girls, Tony. And now look." With his free hand, he gestured expansively. "All this. All yours."

"That's right. All mine." He caught the waiter's eye, nodded to the empty brander snifter.

"Is she older than you, Tony? How much older?" It was a soft, sibilant question: the slender knife, expertly wielded.

Frazer smiled, disengaged his hand. "Fuck off, Carl. Have another drink. And then fuck off." He turned, walked to the checkroom, where Amy waited with his coat held ready. He slipped into the coat, smiled at her, dropped a five-dollar bill in the silver tray, and left.

At the intersection of Franklin and Geary, Frazer stopped for the red light, turned up the collar of his topcoat. The night was cold and foggy and windy, with rain forecasted before morning. At home, Constance was waiting. At noon, pleading an essential business appointment that only he could fulfill, suggesting problems with an unnamed government agency, solemnly promising to return by cocktail time, he'd succeeded in getting out of the house, getting away from her, a reprieve. Then, at four o'clock, he'd called, ready with the elaborate excuse that would move back the deadline to nine o'clock, usually the final dispensation. Constance had been in the bathroom, the maid had said, and he'd left the message with her, an unexpected stroke of good fortune, no more lies required, no cajoling.

Every year the leash got shorter.

After the portable cellular phone, was the omnipresent mini-camera next, Big Brother's ultimate surveillance device.

Big Brother, Big Constance.

Grimacing at the bad pun, he saw the traffic light turning green.

Is she older than you, Tony?

Ah, but he must turn the painful incident to show a profit. Today's lesson: next time, tell the waiter to keep the Carl Wallaces of the world in the lobby.

After checking for traffic, Frazer stepped off the curb. Across the four-lane street, he saw the slight, scarecrow-ragged figure of a street person, loitering on the sidewalk in front of the parking garage. Frazer made the slight correction that would allow him to angle past the beggar with a six-foot margin before he resumed his progress toward the parking garage.

In America, the population of street people—derelicts—was increasing every year. One solution, someone at the club had said, was to get them hooked on heroin, then restrict the supply of needles. Ergo: AIDS, the final solution. Johnny Lynd had said it. And he hadn't been joking.

Almost at the far curb, in his peripheral vision, he saw the beggar move, coming closer.

Yes, Johnny Lynd's solution had merit. It—

"Tony."

With his right foot on the curb, his left foot still in the gutter, he faltered. *Tony,* the beggar had said.

Tony?

The light was bad. The beggar was stooped and wore a shapeless hat that shadowed his face.

Was it a joke? A tasteless practical joke, see Tony run?

Aware of a sudden flutter of fright, an instant's regression to childhood's earliest fears, he was momentarily immobilized, his eyes fixed on the shape of the face beneath the hat.

"This is for you, Tony."

The voice. The memory, stirring. The hate, hidden so long. Yes, it was—

From the folds of the coat a shape gleamed: a metallic cylinder.

From the cylinder a small tongue of bright-yellow flame exploded. Something struck him in the solar plexus. He staggered back, regained his balance, raised both hands, a supplication. But a second explosion followed the first. The explosions were muted, strangely muffled. Was he falling? Yes, his knees had struck the concrete sidewalk, the position of prayer, of supplication. Had he torn his suit? Kneeling, had he forgotten his prayers? Had he . . . ?

The third shot exploded inches in front of his eyes. Everything shattered, all of it gone.

Except for the void descending.

He must walk, not run. He must not look back. At the corner
of the parking garage, as he'd planned so carefully, so meticulously, he must turn to his left—here. Allowing himself, therefore, a glance to his left, as he'd also planned. Yes, two people—
men—were bending over the body. One man was looking down
at Frazer. The other man's head was up. He was looking.
Searching. Probing. Now, as another pedestrian ventured
closer, the second man raised his arm, pointed.

"Police," the second man shouted. "Call the police!"

Three steps took him to the corner of the three-story garage.
Another step and he was liberated, invisible to those who clus-
tered around the body now. A narrow walkway separated the

garage from the building next to it, a large warehouse, storage for new cars arriving from Japan. The walkway was about fifty feet long, with a gate at the far end. The gate was secured by a padlock and chain. The first phase of his plan had included cutting the chain with bolt cutters. The bolt cutters, he was surprised to learn, had cost more than two hundred dollars. But, the clerk had assured him, the tool was the best of its kind available. Japanese, of course. Makita.

The pistol, made long and cumbersome by the silencer, was still in his hand. Without breaking stride he verified that, yes, he'd set the automatic's safety catch, one precaution he'd most particularly rehearsed. Now, with his left hand, he drew open the shapeless beggar's overcoat. With his right hand, he slipped the pistol into the long leather sheath slung beneath his left arm. The gate was coming closer—closer. The chain was draped over the latch, as if it were locked. He removed the chain, lowered it gently clinking to the concrete walkway. Cautiously he swung the gate open. Yes, the car was still there, parked a half block away. In the backseat, he'd left the garment bag. The garment bag was ready to receive the beggar's clothing—and the executioner's gun. The leather sheath would remain beneath his sports jacket until he was home, safe.

As he walked toward the car, he felt it beginning: his body responding. Was it terror? Ecstasy? Had he come alive—finally come alive? When would he begin to feel, to know?

He draped the garment bag over the back of a lounge chair and went to the hallway door. Yes, the door was double locked, and bolted. And, yes, the drapes were tightly drawn. He turned to the garment bag, unzipped it, took out the pistol wrapped in a large towel. A year ago he'd known nothing about guns, had never fired one, never handled one. Now, with assurance, he released the clip, placed it on the towel beside the pistol. Of course, a cartridge remained in the pistol's chamber, the safety penalty the gas-operated automatic weapon exacted. Carefully he drew back the slide, tracked the ejected cartridge as it spun to the carpet at his feet.

Then, about to retrieve the cartridge, he felt himself go rigid, suddenly immobilized.

The shell casings.

Three ejected shell casings.

Just as most bullets bore distinctive marks from a weapon's rifling, so did brass shell casings bear telltale marks from a gun's receiver and its ejector.

As he bent to pick up the unfired cartridge, he was conscious of the effort required, as if his muscles were locking, resisting his will to move. It was, he knew, the hand of fear.

This, then, was the beginning, the first test. Leaving the scene, walking to his car, taking off the beggar's overcoat and hat, putting everything in the garment bag, thus transforming himself into a member of the establishment, then driving the two miles to his home, all this had been accomplished according to plan, according to foot-by-foot, minute-to-minute rehearsal. During the time—fifteen minutes, no more—he'd felt as if he were apart from himself, as if he were disembodied, a random bit of flotsam adrift on the sea of his own consciousness. He'd expected to feel terror, or desperation, or even ecstasy. He'd expected either complete control or complete confusion, abject helplessness, no more, no less. Instead, he'd felt nothing.

Until now, staring down at the cartridge cupped in the palm of his hand, he'd felt nothing.

But now it was beginning.

Soon he would know. As only those who crossed over from life to death knew what lay on the other side, so would he know fate's design. Whatever was stirring deep beneath the surface of his consciousness, whatever emerged, he was either its master or its slave. Terror or triumph. Soon he would know.

Some were slaves of the law—perpetual servants. Fear was their master, subservience their fate.

But some men mastered fear. First they mastered themselves, then they mastered fear. For these men—this handful of superior beings scattered across the face of history—law was their servant, their handmaiden. While the goddess held her scales extended, these men ripped open her bodice to expose her breasts.

At the thought, even with the cartridge in his hand, he felt himself begin to smile. Later, in bed, he would allow his thoughts to linger on the lady with her breasts exposed, the blushing goddess of justice.

His goddess, this night.

3

Grimly, Hastings shook his head. "The crazy son of a bitch. For a couple of hundred dollars, he'd take me to *court?*"

"It isn't the money," Ann said. "You know that, Frank. We've *talked* about it. You've threatened his manhood. You've *always* threatened his manhood."

"I hit his goddam Porsche with the flat of my bare hand. And he says I'm harassing him. His lawyer—what were they, college roommates? He'll work up the case for a twenty-five-dollar lunch. It'll cost me twenty-five *hundred.*"

"To be fair," she answered, her voice measured, "you did damage the car door. You said yourself that the stop broke and the door hit the side of the car."

He grinned conspiratorially. "No comment."

"It's ten-thirty," Ann said. "Let's go to bed."

"Will you comfort me, if we go to bed?"

She smiled—that special smile. "I'll sure give it a shot." She rose from the couch, went to him, stood before him. She wore jeans and a much-worn fisherman's sweater; her thick tawny hair fell loose to her shoulders. As he rose from his favorite armchair, she lifted her head to him, solemnly joined her eyes with his. Deliberately she moistened her lips with the tip of a small pink tongue. For tonight, then, their long-running struggle with Ann's ex-husband would be forgotten.

He put his hands on her waist, drawing her slowly, steadily close.

Just as, in the hallway, the telephone warbled.

Touching him with the full length of her body now, beginning to move with him, a promise, her violet eyes gone gravely muzzy, she whispered, "Do you have the duty?"

"Afraid so. My tour started yesterday. I forgot to tell you." He kissed her, felt her deep, urgent response. "Think positive," he whispered. "It could be a salesman."

"Mmmm." As the phone's second ringing concluded, she kissed him again. Boldly.

"Stay there." He moved her back, steadied her firmly. "Hold the thought." Aware that, yes, he was aroused, deeply aroused, he stepped quickly into the hallway, lifted the phone. With his free hand, covertly, he arranged himself more comfortably inside his trousers.

"Yes."

"It's Canelli, Lieutenant."

"Ah—" As he spoke, he turned toward Ann. Apologetically. Ruefully. Then, speaking into the phone: "What can I do for you, Canelli?"

"Well, jeez, Lieutenant, we've got one dead on Franklin Street, corner of Geary. It happened about an hour and a half ago—a little before nine o'clock. I called the lab and the coroner, and both of them got here maybe ten minutes ago. Geary and Franklin, that corner is pretty heavily traveled, you know. Although because the weather's so cold and wet, there were only about three witnesses. But one of them is a parking attendant at the garage where it looks like the victim was going when he got shot. Chris, that's his name. The attendant, I mean. Chris Jeffrey. Nice kid, with one of those baby faces. He's a law student, it turns out. So he was real—you know—interested. So anyhow—" As Canelli paused for breath, always a feature of his reports from the field, Hastings sighed. His partial erection had subsided. From the kitchen, he heard water running. Also resigned, Ann was tidying up the kitchen after the disorder always left when her two sons washed dishes. One more night of love had been left in limbo, the homicide detective's fate.

"So anyhow," Canelli was saying, "this kid Chris saw the whole thing. The victim had just crossed Franklin in the crosswalk and was apparently making for the garage to get his car. The entrance to the garage is on Franklin, maybe fifty feet, give or take, from the Geary intersection. So then, from the opposite direction, on the same side of the street, there's this bum coming. And they meet when the victim's maybe twenty-five feet from the entrance to the garage. Well, naturally—" Another deep breath. "Naturally, the victim was going to ignore the bum, take evasive action, you might say. That's when the bum must've said something."

"Did this kid—Chris—hear what was said?"

"No," Canelli answered. "At least, I don't think he did. But he wasn't close enough to hear anything. He saw the whole thing, though, and the bum *acted* like he was saying something."

"Okay. Go ahead."

"Well, anyhow, whatever the bum said, it must've rung a bell. Because the victim hesitated and turned. I guess words were exchanged. But, anyhow, whether or not words were ex-

14

changed, Chris said he saw something shiny in the bum's hand. And he thought he heard the sound of shots, even though there was a lot of traffic on Franklin right then. And the shots, Chris said, sounded real muffled. But, whatever, the victim falls. First he falls to his knees, and then he falls forward, on his face. So then the bum, calm as anything, according to Chris, walks back the way he came. Chris, meantime, went to the victim and turned him over. And that's when he saw the blood. The victim, it looks like to me, must've been shot in the head, maybe the forehead. There's so much blood it's hard to tell."

"So what'd you think? Should I come out there?" In the shading of the question, Hastings tried to convey his reluctance. As, in the kitchen, Ann was turning off the water. The kitchen light went out, and Ann came into the hallway. They exchanged a shrug, both of them sadly shaking their heads, resigned.

But if he got the job done quickly, he could return in an hour or two. He would get into bed, stroke her, bring her sensuously awake.

"Well," Canelli was saying, "the thing is, Lieutenant, Chris knew the victim. And it turns out the guy is Tony Frazer."

Canelli waited expectantly.

Tony Frazer . . .

The fragmentary images began to coalesce: the society column clips, pictures of the beautiful people at opera openings. Money. Money. Money.

"A society guy," Hastings said.

"You got it, Lieutenant," Canelli said cheerfully. "And it just so happened that there was a big article about him and his wife in last Sunday's paper. Did you see it?"

"No."

"Well, reading between the lines, it's pretty clear that Frazer was one of these real good-looking guys who live off their wives, who's always older than the guy, and real rich. You know, parties all the time. So then, maybe a year ago, Frazer decides he's going to open a restaurant. The restaurant doesn't make any money—loses money, probably, if you read between the lines. But who cares? Not Tony Frazer. See, he's got a place to hang out. That's why he bought the restaurant. He's got—had—his own private table put on a kind of a raised platform, I remember that part from the article. You know, like a king or something, sitting on a throne."

Hastings turned to a fresh sheet in the notepad that was always beside the phone. Since he'd come to live with Ann and her two sons, one of his few demands was that there always be a notepad beside the phone, along with a drinking glass containing an assortment of pens and pencils.

"Do you have names and addresses?" Hastings asked.

"Yessir, I do." There was a rustle of paper. Then: "The name of the wife is Constance Frazer. The restaurant is Anthony's. It's on Van Ness, right near—"

"I know where it is."

"Yeah. Well, by the time I got here—maybe a half hour after the event—there were a lot of people on the scene. Including a guy from Anthony's, I guess he was the manager, who gave me Frazer's home address—" Canelli read off the address. "That's in Pacific Heights, where else?"

"So someone from Anthony's sure as hell notified Constance Frazer." Signifying by-the-book admonishment, Hastings's voice was flat. According to departmental guidelines, a homicide victim's next of kin, if nearby, was always notified in person, preferably by a homicide detective. As the homicide officer in charge, notification had been Canelli's responsibility.

"Yeah—well—" Canelli cleared his throat apologetically. Hastings could visualize Canelli's broad, swarthy, amiable face, now registering deepest chagrin. Never had Hastings known a policeman more sensitive to criticism than Canelli. "Well, I'm afraid that's right, Lieutenant. See, people from Anthony's got here before the uniforms did. Two, three minutes after the shooting, no more. So, by the time I got here, everyone who worked at Anthony's knew what happened. And, in fact, there was a real hysteria, I guess you'd say, at Anthony's. Lots of Frazer's society buddies were there, and they all left their meals and went out to see for themselves. And about half the staff, too. It was a real mob scene. But the uniforms, they did a great job, I'm not knocking them. It's just that there wasn't any way we could put a lid on things."

"So we're assuming that Constance Frazer knows. But we aren't sure."

"That's about it, Lieutenant."

"And the witnesses—do they all agree on what happened?"

"They sure do. That's the good news, you might say."

"This Chris, the parking attendant. You say he *thought* he heard shots. How close was he to the victim when the victim went down?"

"About forty feet, give or take."

"And he only *thought* he heard shots?"

"Yeah, well, that occurred to me, too. Except that there's always a lot of traffic on Franklin, you know."

"No bullets found? No shell casings?"

"No, sir. The casings could be lying in the gutter, maybe, in a bunch of debris. But I sure didn't see them. We've got floodlights now, though. And I passed the word that Frazer was a heavy-duty socialite who gets his name in the papers. So everyone's on full alert, you might say."

"No one heard shots but Chris. Is that right?"

"Yessir, that's right."

"Okay . . ." As he spoke, Hastings heard the sound of the shower, from the rear of the flat. Since the first days of her marriage, even before she'd had her children, Ann had lived in the same large, long, three-bedroom Victorian flat. The ceilings were wonderfully high and coved, the turn-of-the-century detailing of the woodwork was superb, and the location was vintage

17

San Francisco. But there was only a bath and a half. So, after some discussion, it was decided that Hastings would shower in the morning and Ann at night. Result: she always smelled wonderful when she came to bed.

"Okay," he repeated. "The guy lived about ten minutes from here. So I think I'll talk to the widow, then go on down to the scene."

"Shall I hold the body until you get here?" In the question, Hastings could hear the predictable faint note of hope. Occasionally, increasingly more often as the years passed, he allowed Canelli to take full charge at the scene of a homicide, signing off the body to the coroner and securing the scene after the lab crew was finished.

"Don't bother to hold the body," Hastings decided to say. "You close out at the scene. Your responsibility. Okay?"

"Well, jeez, sure, Lieutenant. Thanks."

"You're welcome. I'll see you in an hour, probably."

4

"*Dead?* Did you say he's *dead?* *Tony?*"

"Grace. Are you drunk?"

A short, bitter chuckle. "I'm afraid so, Mother. Or, if you prefer, I'm drowning my sorrows. So now—" A hiccup. "So now we can both drown our sorrows. Are *you* drunk?"

"For Christ's sake, Grace. Didn't you hear what I *said?* Tony's been killed. They called me from the restaurant more than an hour ago. I've been trying to get you ever since."

"Yeah—well—" Bitterly—brutally—Grace lingered over the single word. "Well, Grant and I were having dinner tonight. It was a beautiful dinner. Michael's in Malibu. Spectacular ocean view. But it turned out to be our last dinner. Because

19

the purpose of the dinner, you see, was to tell me that Grant's moving out. His lawyer will be in touch, he said. Grant hopes I'll be reasonable. That's when I started to drink. Seriously."

"Grace. I—we—"

"You did the right thing, Mother, marrying a lapdog. Was Tony wearing his rhinestone-studded collar when he died? Or are they diamonds?"

"For Christ's sake, Grace, he was killed on the street by a beggar. A street person. He—" Suddenly she sobbed. "He was coming home. It's—it's Valentine's Day."

"Ah, yes, Valentine's Day. I pointed that out to Grant over dinner. He admitted that it was bad timing. He had an excuse, though. He's been seen with the lady in question all over town. So he was being kind, you see. He didn't want me to hear about it from a third party. Wasn't that—" Another hiccup. "Wasn't that considerate of him? Grant's very considerate, you know. Very polite. Not in bed, he's not very polite. But—"

"You haven't heard anything I said about Tony. My God, he's in the morgue by now. And my only daughter doesn't have the decency to—"

"What am I supposed to say, Mother? Am I supposed to say I liked him? Christ, you didn't even invite me to the wedding. Remember?"

"That's unfair, Grace. It was on shipboard. You know that."

"Oh, yes. Excuse me. Incidentally, which number was Tony? Was he husband number four?"

"That's hurtful, Grace. That's—"

"Ah. Sorry. Number three. But the point is, you see, that Grant is number one for me. Of course, I'm only twenty-eight. So by the time I'm your age, Mother, I suppose I'll—"

"I'm not going to listen to this, Grace. When you sober up, call me. I'd appreciate that. And I'm sorry about Grant. I can't say I'm surprised. But I'm sorry."

20

"Oh, fuck off, Mother. Just fuck off, will you?" In Los Angeles, the phone slammed into its cradle.

Slowly, as if it were too heavy to hold, Constance Frazer cradled her own phone. Wearing a floor-length silk robe, she sat at her mirrored dressing table. Conscious of the effort, she raised her eyes from the telephone to the mirror.

Who was it—which queen—who'd ordered all the mirrors in the palace smashed? How old had she been, that queen? How lonely? How unhappy?

How desperate?

In the mirror, remorselessly, her own likeness returned her stare. Without makeup, the flesh of her face was lumpy and flaccid. Beneath her small chin, despite Elizabeth Arden, the muscles sagged. Beneath her clear blue eyes, her best feature, the flesh was dark and raddled, crosshatched by countless tiny lines and creases.

Fifty-three years . . .

Each one of those years had left its imprint on this reflected image that—

From the small communications console mounted on the wall beside the door, a signal warbled: the front door. She glanced at her wristwatch: eleven-twenty. Was it a neighbor, who'd heard the news? The police? A reporter, the first one on the scene, the leader of the pack? Expectantly she rose, faced the console. Downstairs, Katherine would be crossing the entry hall toward the front door. John, Katherine's husband, would be stationed nearby, out of sight. In his hand, a large, lethal handgun would be ready. Born in the ghetto, John feared nothing, nobody.

In another few moments, then, on the intercom, she would hear—yes, Katherine's voice, speaking softly, in her husky black-ethnic voice: "Mrs. Frazer?"

Standing in front of the console, she felt the heaviness of

her body, felt the effort required, just to stand erect. When she'd been a girl, in the summertime, she'd run for hours across the fields of her grandfather's ranch: she'd felt light and free and happy then.

Constance depressed the console's TALK button. "Yes?"

"There's a police officer here, Mrs. Frazer. His name is Frank Hastings. He's a lieutenant."

"Does he want to see me?"

"Yes, ma'am."

Constance looked down at the silken sheen of the robe that clung so closely to the thickness of her thighs. She'd never received a stranger dressed like this, looking like this, without her makeup. But the effort required to change, to make up her face, would be enormous, requiring more strength than she possessed.

Fuck off, Mother . . .

Somehow the words—the flare of hatred behind the words—had taken away her strength, left her helpless.

"All right," Constance said, speaking into the perforated disc of the communications console. "Bring him up to my sitting room."

"Yes, ma'am." A pause. "You okay, Mrs. Frazer?"

Suddenly the kindness of the question combusted with the hatred in Grace's voice, momentarily choking her reply. Finally: "I'll be all right, Katherine. But thanks. Thanks very much."

"So me and John'll stay tonight. Is that what you want?"

"Oh, yes, Katherine. Please. *Please.*"

"No problem. I'll bring the lieutenant up."

"Give me a few minutes, though."

"Yes, ma'am."

"Sit down, Lieutenant." She gestured to a chair, watched him as he sat facing her. He was in his middle forties, a big, muscular man with a squared-off face. His manner was deliberate, his movements measured. His eyes were watchful, revealing nothing. His brown hair was thick, graying at the temples. He wore running shoes, corduroy trousers, and a leather jacket. He needed a shave.

"I'm here because we always try to notify the next of kin in person," he said. "But you already know, your maid said."

"Jim Masters called. That was an hour ago. Or more, maybe, by now. He's the manager of the restaurant."

"Ah—" He was nodding. "Yes. I see."

"How did it happen, Lieutenant? Who did it? Why?" Asking the questions, she realized that her voice was unsteady, uncertain.

Fuck off, Mother.

Why did those words reecho? Why not Jim Masters's words, telling her that Tony had been killed?

"Apparently," Hastings was saying, "it was a robbery that went wrong. There were witnesses. They all agree that a street person approached your husband and said something, probably demanded money. Then, probably, your husband refused. Then there were the shots." As he described the scene, the detective's voice was uninflected, as if he were reading from a prepared speech for which he had no enthusiasm. Like his voice, his face gave no hint of his thoughts or feelings.

"My God, it—it's something that happens to someone else." Her voice, she knew, was thin and bleak. Somehow she couldn't keep her eyes focused. Would she faint? In her whole life, she'd never fainted. She'd never lost consciousness, except under anesthetic. "It—it's something you read about in the papers."

"I know . . ."

In the silence she heard muted voices from downstairs. Was it Katherine and John? Or was it someone else? Was this the beginning—the reporters, the undertakers, the lawyers? When would the curious begin trampling the flower beds, hoping for

23

a glimpse of her? Once, humorously, Tony had said he'd like to make the move from the society pages to the main news section. How sad that he would never know he'd done it.

"Do you have someone to stay with you, Mrs. Frazer? Relatives? Friends? Someone to help you?"

"I've got friends, I suppose. And I've got relatives. But whatever help I get, Lieutenant, I'll pay for." Exhausted by the bitterness, by the bleakness, she spoke in a voice that was hardly more than a whisper. "That's what happens, you see, when you're very rich. You only get what you pay for."

Shifting in his chair, Hastings made no reply. Now, for the first time, his eyes registered something that might be sympathy. Or was it embarrassment?

But, even though this stranger in her house might pity her, she realized that something compelled her to go on. To speak— to confess—to accuse—there was nothing else left for her now.

"A lot of people—my daughter, for instance—thought that Tony was bought and paid for. My friends—my so-called friends—thought so. And my daughter, just a few minutes ago, she called him a lapdog. Of course, I can excuse her. She was drunk, you see. Her marriage is coming apart, so I can excuse her. Besides, she was always jealous of Tony, because he was in my will. And Grace is very materialistic. Very greedy, really. She—" Suddenly her throat closed, choked by a deep, wracking sob. Not a pretty, ladylike sob, eyes batting, lace hankie poised. But an ugly, fishwife's sob. As she turned desperately away from him, she was aware that he was rising, saying something polite, excusing himself.

5

As if he were emerging from a hypnotist's trance, he lifted his head, blinked, focused finally on his surroundings. Yes, he was still sitting in his favorite chair, placed to face the dark, empty fireplace. Yet somehow time had advanced a half hour since he'd last looked at the clock, since he'd last been conscious of himself. Had he ever before lost himself in time? What had changed in the last half hour? Against the window, rain was hissing, the first squall in a storm that had been predicted before morning. The wooden windows rattled in their frames; water began to gurgle in the gutters and drainpipes. From the fireplace, the moan of wind began.

On the sidewalk, at Franklin Street near Geary, the rain

would begin to wash the blood away. Tony Frazer's blood, at first running in rivulets down the sidewalk to the gutter, then down the gutter to the sewer grate, mixing with debris from the city's streets, swept into the sewer mains, flowing finally out to the ocean.

Would the waterborne debris carry the shell casings away? Would the rain correct the error he had made?

But, really, had an error been committed? Or was there a contrary case to be made, himself absolving himself?

Had there been an alternative? If there was no alternative then there was no error, it was simple logic. Silencers were effective on automatic pistols but not on revolvers. Automatics ejected shell casings; revolvers didn't.

Should he, therefore, have remained at the scene, searching for the three casings? The thought was ludicrous. Therefore, so long as he used the Woodsman, an automatic, then no error would be committed.

Should he have chosen a revolver, not an automatic? Again, the answer was "no." He had decided on a silencer. That had been the primary consideration: the flexibility, the margin of safety, that a silencer offered. The shell casings were a risk factor only if the gun was found in his possession. And, unless he willed it, that would never happen.

Signifying, therefore, that no error had been made.

Case closed.

Allowing him, after the last half hour's inexplicably out-of-body reverie, to return to himself, let himself go back . . .

Go back?

Go back to where? To the killing of Tony Frazer? Was he meant to re-create in his thoughts that precise moment when Tony Frazer fell to his knees after the first two bullets to the chest, then fell on his face when the third bullet entered his brain, the executioner's coup?

No.

The killing of Tony Frazer was the second beginning, not the first beginning.

Yet the killing of Tony Frazer allowed him to pull back the curtain of consciousness, himself observing himself. Allowing him finally to begin the long journey back into time, liberated, allowed to search for the moment when he'd first known the others were the murderers.

Them, not him.

Never him.

Because executioners were rewarded. Not punished.

6

"Somebody must've stepped on one." Apologetically Canelli handed over the small clear-plastic evidence bag. Hastings took the sealed bag, held it up to light from the lobby of the parking garage, looked at the two brass cartridge casings.

"Twenty-twos," Hastings said.

"I know."

Protected against the worsening rain that had begun less than an hour ago, they stood beneath a concrete overhang outside the entrance to the parking garage. Three hours had elapsed since the murder. The official vans had come and gone, along with a TV team and one newspaper reporter. The witnesses had been questioned and requestioned, and had been excused.

The rain had scattered the curious and washed away the blood on the sidewalk. Only a single strand of yellow tape remained, strung between Canelli's unmarked car and a black-and-white patrol car. Hastings's aging Honda station wagon was double-parked parallel with the tape.

Taking back the small evidence bag, Canelli offered a larger, heavier bag, the one with the victim's effects: a billfold, a card case, a ring of keys, a slim gold pocket knife, a small leather-bound notebook, a matched gold pen and pencil set by Cross, a gold wristwatch, miscellaneous small change, and two business-size envelopes, both torn open. The alligator wallet was sized to be carried in an inside jacket pocket, not a hip pocket. Conclusion: either the victim always wore a jacket, or else he went to the trouble of transferring the contents of the wallet to a smaller one when he chose not to wear a jacket.

"Did you look at the contents of the wallet?" Hastings asked.

"Sort of," Canelli answered. Adding: "You know: fingernails. There's about a hundred dollars, and I couldn't see that anything was disturbed."

"And nobody got a look at the assailant's face."

"Not a real good look." Canelli pointed to the spot where the body had fallen. "There's not much light. Plus, the guy was wearing a big hat—a fedora, like that. And, besides, he wore a great big overcoat that kind of slapped around him, so it was hard to figure what kind of a build he had. I mean, he could've been a hundred fifty or two hundred, take your choice."

"It sounds like he could've been trying to disguise himself," Hastings said thoughtfully.

Canelli shrugged. "Who knows?"

"What's the ME say?"

"There were three entrance wounds, no exit wounds, at least nothing apparent with the guy still clothed, with only his shirt opened. Two wounds to the center of the chest and one shot to the face, right at the bridge of the nose." Canelli shook his head ruefully. "His face was a mess. Not a terrible mess, like it'd been a bigger bullet. But still—" Lips compressed, Canelli shook his head again. He was a big, awkward man. His swarthy face was round and guileless, his eyes were a dark, soft brown, perpetually puzzled. His expression was often anxious, his manner often uncertain. "Still, I figure it'll be—you know—a closed casket."

"As I understand it," Hastings said, "the gunshots were muffled. Right?"

Canelli nodded. "Right. Everyone seems to agree on that."

"There were—what—three witnesses?"

"Yeah, well, it sort of depends on how you rate them, the same old story. There was this kid Chris, that I told you about, he was the closest—" Canelli turned, gestured to a spot just inside the open entrance to the parking garage. "He was standing right there, and he saw the whole thing, like I told you. The other two—" He gestured to the intersection of Franklin and Geary. "They were there, crossing Geary. They didn't really see anything until Frazer actually went down. And then they thought he'd tripped and fell, or was drunk, like that."

"Did they hear the shots?"

"Well . . ." Canelli frowned earnestly. "Well, they sort of *remembered* them, I guess you'd say. They weren't aware of them at the time. But then they remembered hearing what sounded like a couple of pops. Or maybe *pfftts*, like that. But there was enough traffic on Franklin that they didn't think anything about the pops, or *pfftts*, or whatever. Not until afterward."

"But they weren't more than thirty feet from the victim." His eyes measuring the distance, Hastings spoke speculatively.

"So what're you thinking, Lieutenant? A silencer?"

"It could be. A twenty-two pistol with a silencer, you'd hardly hear it."

"Hey—" Canelli smiled, nodded amiably. "Hey, Lieutenant, a silenced twenty-two, the hit man's favorite weapon." The

30

smile widened. "What if it was a professional job? Like—you know—this society restaurant guy was in with the mob. Maybe it was—you know—loansharking. Maybe he was in over his head, with this recession and everything. And he didn't want his wife to know, whatever. So he decides to stiff the mob, play it snooty, maybe. So he got hit. How about that?"

Hastings looked at his watch, then took his keys from his pocket. "Let's see what the lab says. What we've probably got is a bum who stole a gun somewhere and decided to become a robber, and the traffic noise covered the sound of the shots. So maybe—" He looked Canelli over elaborately. "Maybe we should dress someone up like a bum, let him go undercover around here for a few days, see what he hears. What'd you think?"

Canelli's face fell. "Hey, Lieutenant—" He gestured to the rain, now pounding the sidewalk and sluicing down the gutters. "Hey, they're saying it's going to rain like this for a week. Maybe more."

"Just a thought, Canelli. Just a thought."

7

"According to Ballistics," Friedman said, "there might be something to Canelli's theory that it could've been a professional job. The lab says the cartridges were high-speed twenty-twos, and the bullets were jacketed hollow points. According to the scratches on the shell casings, they say the gun was an automatic."

"The hit man's favorite weapon—a silenced twenty-two-caliber automatic firing hollow-point bullets that can't be identified by the rifling." Hastings nodded thoughtfully.

"Plus," Friedman offered, "the ME says two of the three shots were fatal. The shot to the bridge of the nose penetrated the brain, and another shot penetrated the heart. The third shot lodged in the spine."

"Good shooting."

"Very good shooting. So what now?"

Hastings smiled. "I'm the field man. You're the coach."

"Canelli says you want him to dress up like a bum and go undercover."

"I was mostly kidding. Besides, if it really was a professional job, going undercover obviously wouldn't help."

"If it was a bum, though, undercover could be the way to go. Street people usually pick a territory and stay there."

In reply, Hastings nodded.

"I read an article on Tony Frazer in last Sunday's paper," Friedman said. "Did you see it?"

"No. Canelli read it, though."

"Well, I'll tell you—" Friedman shook his head. It was a mannerism heavy with irony and contempt, a mannerism Hastings knew well. In his fifties, cheerfully overweight, Friedman was the squadroom sage, an amiable, inscrutable gadfly with the face of a Buddha and the body to match. Friedman kept them all guessing, both the good guys and the bad guys. Friedman revealed nothing, not fear or anger or outright pleasure. During all the years they'd co-commanded Homicide, Hastings had discovered only two things that could rankle Friedman: city hall politicians and the idle rich.

"I'll tell you," Friedman repeated, "this guy must've been a real horse's ass, one of those guys who lives off a rich wife and doesn't mind if the whole world knows it. He was a—a gigolo. He probably started out working for a male escort bureau."

"You got all this from an article in the Sunday paper?"

"I read between the lines. Besides, there were pictures of him. All you had to do was look at him. He was—" Friedman broke off, searching for the word. Finally, indignantly: "He was *pretty*. Rosy cheeks, even."

"Mmmm."

"You talked to his wife. This can't come as a surprise to you.

33

What is she—sixty-five, or something? With a half-dozen face-lifts and body tucks and boob bulges?"

Amused, Hastings said, "I've got to admit, she reminded me of an over-the-hill Barbie Doll."

"There. You see?"

Hastings pointed to Tony Frazer's personal effects, scattered across one side of Friedman's outsize desk. "Anything there?"

Friedman shrugged. "The usual. Except that everything is the most expensive money could buy, naturally—either alligator or solid gold. Just a driver's license and some credit cards and membership cards in the wallet, plus money. He probably didn't want any bulges under his clothes, to spoil the drape. He belonged to all the right clubs, of course." Friedman picked up the small address book, riffling the pages. "I'll have Sigler check this out on the phone. Then I'll see if I can get some idea of Frazer's connections, whether he was in trouble financially, or was playing around, had a girlfriend on the side, whatever."

Agreeing, Hastings nodded. Then: "What else?"

"Well," Friedman said judiciously, "unless we turn up any heavy-duty skeletons in Frazer's closet, and notwithstanding Canelli's Mafia hit man scenario, I guess we've got to assume that it's what it appears to be. Which is that some bum tried to stick Frazer up, and panicked, and pulled the trigger. God knows it happens. So often, in fact, that if Frazer was also a bum, or a bus driver, or whatever, we probably wouldn't even be having this little chat."

"Three perfectly placed shots—two to the chest, one to the head, for insurance." Hastings spoke quietly, speculatively.

In response, Friedman shrugged. "Even bums can get lucky, you know."

"So what's the plan?"

"The plan," Friedman said, "is that you get in touch with the grieving widow and persuade her to offer, say, a thousand dollars reward. We publicize the reward in the papers. We also have flyers printed, which we'll post in a three-block radius of Geary and Franklin. We'll also distribute them among the street people in the area. I'll leave it to your imagination what kind of kick we'll get for a thousand dollars."

"What we'll get are a hundred bums with lice coming in to turn whoever screwed them out of a drink from last night's muscatel bottle."

"I'm willing to listen to alternate plans." Friedman said it complacently, amiably. Having invested his wife's inheritance in the stock market with spectacular success, Friedman could afford to ply his policeman's trade with a light, whimsical touch.

"I'll give it some thought."

"Good. How're you and Ann and her two strapping sons getting along?"

"*We're* getting along fine. It's her goddam ex-husband."

"The society psychiatrist who specializes in the sexual frustrations of newly divorced women."

Hastings nodded grimly. "He gives Ann a lot of shit about us living off his alimony checks. Plus he doesn't think I'm a good influence around the house. So a couple of weeks ago, I decided to have a little talk with him, after work." He spoke ruefully, admitting: "I waited for him in his parking lot. In about thirty seconds, he got me so steamed that I hit the goddam door of his Porsche with my hand. The stop on the door broke, and the door slammed into the fender."

"So he won. You lost."

"He's going to sue me, for God's sake. And he's constantly threatening to sue Ann for custody of Dan and Billy."

"Of course, he's remarried."

"Of course."

"To one of his glamorous patients, naturally."

"How'd you know?"

"I guessed."

"Hmmm."

35

"The answer, of course, is for you and Ann to get married. You'll never find a better woman. Take my word for it."

Hastings nodded. "I know. Th—that's what makes it so hard."

"If you were in your twenties, not your forties, it wouldn't be so hard." Friedman smiled puckishly. "No pun intended."

"It's not my age. It's just that—"

"It's just that you got divorced a long time ago. And you've got a long, inconvenient memory."

"Inconvenient . . ." Hastings snorted softly. Then, reflecting: "Inconvenient—yeah. I guess so."

"Come to think about it," Friedman speculated, "you and Tony Frazer were dancing to the same tune. Both of you married socialites. You got the shaft, and he got the swag."

"Except that I'm alive."

"True."

8

"For Christ's sake, Gerald. We're *friends.*"

"Of course we're friends," Manley answered. "We both have good forehands, and our wives seem to get along. But this is business, Randy. This is business, and there's a recession out there. A very deep, very nasty recession. Everyone's taking hits. I've taken hits, God knows. Is there any reason you shouldn't take a hit?"

"You're playing word games with me."

The two men sat facing each other across a small conference table. On the variegated walnut and ebony table, an attaché case was open in front of Randall Bates. In his own office, his own turf, Gerald Manley required no papers, no props. This conversation concerned survival, not facts or figures or charts or graphs.

Dropping his voice to a low, resonant note that projected gravity and regret, and, yes, reproach, Manley slowly shook his head. "I'm not playing word games, Randy. You know me better than that." Tanned and trim and confident, Gerald Manley was conscious that, at age sixty, in the prism of his ambition, the objectives he'd set for himself were finally coming into clear alignment. For two years he'd called every major turn of the economy. For this recession, having sold the market short, he was now perfectly positioned. So that now—here, and now— payday was beginning. Regrettably, his first victim was Randy Bates, one of his favorite tennis partners. But Randy was young, only forty-five. Randy would recover.

"I thought I knew you, Gerald. For God's sake, give me three months more. I'll—Christ—I'll give you another point. What could be fairer?" As he spoke, Bates could clearly hear the tremor in his own voice. His face, he knew, was failing him, revealing the desperation that, only an hour ago, had been no more than misgivings. Across the table, Manley's lean, squared-off centurion's face revealed nothing beyond a hint of impatience that the meeting was dragging on, taking valuable time.

Once more Manley was shaking his head. "The problem is, I don't need points. I need lump sums. If you miss a payment, that means I miss making a payment."

"You've got cash, Gerald." Bates grimly sought to lock eyes with the other man. How had it happened that, until now, this moment, he had never realized that Manley's eyes were colorless, as if they were transparent? Had it happened because, until now, he'd never searched these eyes for some sign of compassion?

"You've got cash, Gerald," he repeated. Then, all hope suddenly gone, unaware that he'd meant to say it: "I've had you checked out. You're loaded with cash, goddam you. You're loaded, but you're going to put me under because of one missed payment."

"You read the contract, Randy. You signed it. We've made money together. And we'll make money again. But I can't take your marker." Manley's voice was without inflection. He raised his wrist, consulted his watch, lowered his arm, spread his hands on the table palms down, as if he were about to rise.

"I won't forget this, Gerald. And, by God, you won't forget this either. I'll promise you that. I've spent years getting to where I am now. And you're going to take it all away."

Still with his hands spread wide on the conference table, Manley made no response.

"Last hand." Manley shuffled the cards. "Five-card draw. Jacks to open."

Ten minutes later, with the chips redeemed and the drinks finished, the six men said their good-byes and left the game room, bound for a bathroom, or the bar, or the lower lobby and the checkroom. One of the players, Nick Ames, fell into step with Manley as they walked to the elevators.

"So how'd you come out?" Ames asked.

"Twenty-seven dollars to the good."

Ames smiled ruefully. "That's about what I lost. Buy you a drink?"

"No, thanks."

One of the two elevators opened its doors, and the two men rode down to street level. They stood together in the spacious lower lounge that opened both on the bar and the lobby. Paneled entirely in walnut, with parquet oak floors and a vaulted ceiling that soared more than twenty-five feet, the lounge was furnished to fit precisely the classic men's club convention: leather chairs and sofas, massive oak library tables, Oriental rugs scattered on the floors, a baronial fireplace.

"You're, ah, sure about that drink?" Ames asked.

As the subtleties in the other man's inflection registered, Manley reflexively made his debit-credit assessment of the motivation underlying the question. Ames was a corporate lawyer, a quiet, reflective, precise man with an impeccable reputation. Probable income, mid to high six figures; probable net worth, seven figures. Conclusion: whatever Ames was about to say, listening would be time wisely invested.

"Have you got a minute, Gerald?"

"Of course." As he said it, Manley turned with the other man so that they faced away from the others gathered in the lounge. Thus, by common consent, privacy was assured.

"I—ah—don't know whether you're aware of it," Ames began, his manner uncharacteristically tentative, "but Randy Bates and I are married to sisters."

Manley was satisfied with the expression he was able to achieve: interested but noncommittal, revealing nothing, admitting nothing, promising nothing.

"I guess—" Plainly vexed with himself, Ames cleared his throat, frowned, began again. "I guess this is the first time I've ever done this—interceded with someone in connection with a business deal. In fact, it's against my principles. After all, I guess we're talking about influence peddling here." He attempted a smile, unsuccessfully. Manley, holding the high hand, chose not to respond to the smile. But neither did he frown or otherwise express displeasure. Unlike Randy Bates, Nick Ames had clout.

"Well, in any case," Ames went on, "the fact is that, a couple of hours ago, Janie called. That's Randy's wife. My wife's sister. In fact, that was the call I took during the poker game." Once more Ames tried a smile, this time more successfully. "I don't usually take calls when I'm playing poker, as you know."

This time Manley decided to smile in return. But he would give the conversation five additional minutes, no more.

"Well—" Ames gestured. It was an expression of his own displeasure, having been put in this position. Translation: basically, they were both discomfited by Randy Bates's impending financial collapse. "Well, you know where I'm going with this, Gerald. After your meeting today, I gather that Randy was pretty shattered. Otherwise, I couldn't imagine him letting Janie call me here, at the club. But, anyhow, she did—asked me to speak to you, intercede with you, on Randy's behalf."

Manley nodded sympathetically. His expression was grave. "I can understand how you'd feel uncomfortable, Nick. And, frankly, I'm surprised at Randy, too."

Holding his gaze steady, Ames spoke quietly, compellingly. "Is there any way for Randy to dodge the bullet, Gerald? Any way at all? I don't know the numbers, of course, but if there's any way we could work out something—guarantees, deferred credits, something like that, I'd be more than happy to act as an honest broker. Pro bono, of course."

Projecting deep, helpless regret, Manley shook his head. "I don't see how, Nick. I honest to God don't. I don't have to tell you the problems out there. Thank God, so far I've stayed liquid enough to keep all the balls in the air. I'm sure you're okay, too. But if I gave Randy an extension, I'd have to do the same for the next guy. Otherwise—" He offered a fraternal smile, deeply regretful. "Otherwise, I come out looking like more of an s.o.b. than I do now."

"Is this—what—a quarterly payment due on a limited partnership? Is that it?"

"That's it."

"It's a commercial real estate deal, I understand."

Manley nodded. His silence was meant to suggest that the conversation should come to a close.

"Can I ask you the amount of Randy's payment?"

"It's about a million three."

"Ah—" Thoughtfully Ames nodded. Then: "That's a sizable chunk of money, no question."

"No question."

Against the cold, wind-whipped fog Manley turned up the collar of his trench coat, pulled his hat down more firmly. A half block ahead, at the intersection of Mason and Post streets, the traffic light was against him. Two blocks ahead, a block beyond the parking garage, the dark, dangerous streets of the Tenderloin began. The block ahead, therefore, was no man's land, let the pedestrian beware. Only a week ago, leaving the club, there had been a—

From the dark, narrow entrance to a dead-end alleyway just ahead, a figure materialized. It was a street person: a man wearing a big, baggy overcoat and a shapeless fedora, low across his face. The sidewalk was narrow, deserted except for the two of them. Now the stranger was turning toward him, doubtless about to make his spare-a-quarter pitch. In the right-hand pocket of the trench coat, Manley fingered the paper money for the parking garage ticket that he'd transferred from his wallet to his coat pocket before he'd belted up the coat. The coat, Burberry's best, was a pleasure to wear, an actual tactile pleasure. But, bound by its ever-so-English tradition (since the early nineteenth century), Burberry outside coat pockets offered no access to inner jacket and pants pockets. Accounting, therefore, for the unaccustomed wad of money in his coat pocket. Should he give the derelict a dollar? How long had it been since . . . ?

Now unpredictably the derelict made an abrupt movement that placed him squarely across the sidewalk. The distance between them was no more than ten feet. Annoyed, Manley broke stride, gave way. He was moving to his right, toward the curb. He had never been mugged, never been robbed. In grade school he'd never lost a fight. Next month *Fortune* would run a story on him: a profile headlined GERALD MANLEY, PACIFIC COAST PRESENCE. Why, then, was he giving way to this shadowy figure, this lower form of life? Behind him was the security of the club, a safe haven, a mooring. Ahead, in the parking garage where he was well known, the Mercedes awaited. But here, now, on this deserted sidewalk, in this cold, wind-whipped rain, he was alone, unmoored. Ignominiously, he was about to step off the curb, yielding to this creature of the night who might—

"Gerald."

It was the creature's voice. *Gerald?* How was it possible? Should he break stride? Was it a prank, a grotesque joke, shades of the fraternity house? Should he run, escape? Would pride allow a craven retreat?

"Gerald." Louder now. More insistent. Was this voice known to him, an echo from the past?

Without conscious thought, balanced on the curb, actually teetering, he was turning to face the presence, an involuntary response. Yes, his hands were out of his pockets, fists bunched, the primitive man emerging, mere millions an irrelevancy, *Fortune* forgotten, another irrelevancy. Survival was—

Pale light glinted on a metallic cylinder. Was it a gun? Was it possible?

His wallet. Credit cards, membership cards, all lost. And the money. A didactic voice came back, a fragment of memory, sound advice: *Give them the money. It's only money. It's your—*

"Good-bye, Gerald."

Yes, from the face shadowed by the outsize hat, the voice was familiar. Was it . . . ?

A flash. A concussion. Slowly cartwheeling, the universe was inexplicably revolving with him at its center. His eyes tracking across the sky, he felt himself falling. The curb—he'd fallen from the curb. On his face he felt the cold, cruel wind. But he must turn, face his antagonist. He must—

The money . . .

Yes, it was the money. For the money in his pocket, he would die. Not the stocks, or the CDs, or the skyscrapers, but the few dollars in his pocket. Was it a joke? Had he remembered to cry out for help? At the club, would they hear? The *Fortune* article, a milestone. Money. Finally, fame. How could he—

Once more, a flash. A crash.

Finally nothing.

9

As he had done before, he was sitting in his favorite chair, staring into the dead fireplace. Earlier, just as he'd done before, he'd cleaned the gun, put it away in its hiding place, along with the underarm holster he'd fashioned. With its six-inch barrel and five-inch silencer, the pistol was more than a foot long. And the silencer, he knew, was fragile. Alignment was essential; a single slight blow could be critical. He'd worked on the holster for three days. Constantly, working with awl and needle and shoemaker's thread, he'd thought of his mother. She'd always done her sewing in the morning, when the light was best in the dining room, where she kept her sewing basket. When he was only six years old, she'd taught him to sew. His father had disapproved, frowning and shaking his head and pursing his lips. But his father had said nothing. Ever.

After he'd put the pistol away, according to plan, he'd put the overcoat and hat in the clothes hamper in the bathroom, with a layer of dirty clothing on top. Then, very thoroughly, he'd washed his hands. Twice, three times he'd washed his hands. Then he'd gone to the kitchen, where he'd drunk two large glasses of water. Then, finally, he'd come into the living room, and sat where he sat now, in front of the fireplace.

A pattern, then, was emerging. He'd expected it, but not so soon.

Did it matter?

Could murder, the ultimate human experience, the final ecstasy, be so soon reduced to rote?

Or was it, rather, a function of practice, of the endless hours preparing himself? Pavlov's dog, was that the highest truth? Did everything come down to habit, an animal salivating when a bell rang, expecting a morsel of food that seldom materialized?

Did it matter?

The first time, when Tony Frazer had died, he'd followed blindly where sensation led, no more than an animal himself.

Himself an animal—an animal himself. Yes, the line scanned, the equation balanced. How else to explain the surge of sensation, the rush that both illuminated and blinded, himself soaring in another dimension, both apart from himself and united with the innermost essence of himself?

In pagan cultures, priests presided over sacrifices, decreed who should be executed. The priests were God's instruments on earth. Exalted. Fulfilled. Transported.

Just as he, sitting here in this darkened room, could expe-

46

rience exaltation. That was Gerald Manley's gift to him: confirmation that, yes, fulfillment awaited, the final ecstasy. Frazer's execution had been the test; Manley's execution had been the promise.

At the thought, he realized that, in the darkness, he was smiling.

10

Across the desk, Friedman yawned deeply as he unwrapped the day's first cigar. According to long-standing tradition, he sailed the wadded-up cellophane wrapper toward Hastings's wastebasket, missing by a wide margin. Then Friedman began the process of rummaging through his pockets for a match. Finally finding one, he lit the cigar, then sailed the smoking match squarely into Hastings's wastebasket. As Hastings grimly followed the match's trajectory, Friedman drew on the cigar, then sent a smoke ring across the desk. Hastings promptly destroyed the smoke ring with a long-suffering wave of his hand.

"While you were tucked in bed last night," Friedman announced, "and I therefore had the duty, a guy named Gerald

Manley got killed, on Mason Street. Our boys in blue missed these, but a rubbernecker found them about ten feet from the body." As he spoke, Friedman opened one of the file folders he'd placed on the corner of Hastings's desk and produced a small transparent evidence bag. "Take a look at those."

Inside the bag, Hastings saw two .22-caliber brass cartridge casings.

"Hmmm . . ." Intrigued, Hastings nodded, handed the evidence bag back. "So?"

"So we could be on to something here. Like, what would you say to tracking down a serial killer? As opposed to the usual drug pushers, and pimps who hit their hookers too hard, and sidewalk creeps who pop people because they only had ten dollars to rob. How about some real classy homicides for a change?"

"Tony Frazer. Is that what you're thinking?"

Friedman blew another smoke ring, this one in a different direction. Then, the sage about to make a pronouncement, he nodded deeply. "You've got it. Tony Frazer and Gerald Manley." Satisfied, he drew again on the cigar. "This could be the start of something big. I've got a feeling. Maybe a whole string of dead millionaires. How's that sound?"

Hastings pointed to the evidence bag. "Do the ejector marks match? Is that what you're saying?"

Friedman shrugged airily. "Who knows? The lab hasn't seen them yet. But the victims match. Practically exactly."

"How do you mean?"

"They were both high rollers. Okay, Frazer, I guess, was pretty much your garden-variety pretty boy who married the lady for her money. Lots of money, as you know. And Gerald Manley, last night's victim, was a very big bore venture capitalist, the way I get it. The point is, though, that both of them were rich. And both of them were murdered at night, on the street. In both cases, the assailant got away clean. And, in both cases, the weapon was a twenty-two-caliber pistol—odds on, the same pistol, an automatic firing jacketed high-speed hollow points. As you observed, the hit man's favorite weapon."

"Except that hit men aren't serial killers. You're getting your scenarios mixed up."

"Nevertheless, I'll lay odds—long odds—that the same gun killed these two guys." Friedman looked across the desk owlishly. "Care to make a wager? Say, five to one?"

"No, thanks." Hastings slipped on a pair of reading glasses, pulled out the lower drawer of his desk, searched through a formidable collection of file folders, frowned, muttered a lukewarm obscenity, and finally found the Anthony Frazer folder, misfiled in the "G's."

"Is that Frazer's file?" Friedman asked.

Hastings nodded.

"And? Anything we didn't know the day after he was killed?"

"Of course there is," Hastings answered, his voice irritably edged. "It's been two weeks."

"Who's doing the workup?"

"Sigler. I told him to put Frazer at the top of his list, because of the publicity." As he spoke, Hastings riffled through a half-dozen reports.

"Ah—good." Satisfied, Friedman nodded. "Sigler's the best report writer on the squad. Present company included. So what's he say?"

Continuing to consult the reports, Hastings began to recite: "As nearly as I can tell, Frazer was exactly what he appeared to be. He was forty-two years old. Grew up in Chicago, started college at Northwestern, finished at the University of Michigan. Married right out of college, to an heiress to a publishing fortune, in fact." As he said it, Hastings realized that he was wincing. Until now, this minute, the similarities between his own story and Frazer's hadn't registered. Substitute "Stanford" for "the University of Michigan," substitute "automobile radiators" for "publishing," and the match was remarkable. Aware of the other man's reaction and the reasons for it, Friedman dropped his eyes, examined his cigar ash. The ash almost long enough to flick into Hastings's wastebasket, another feature of their little game.

"They were divorced after a few years," Hastings said. "No children. Frazer came out to San Francisco, sold a little real estate, some stocks and bonds. He never made much money, I gather, but he invested it wisely—in clothes and cars and theater tickets. He married Constance Nash. Her grandfather was Donald Nash, who owned thousands of acres in the Central Valley, plus about half of downtown Fresno. Constance is a— a—" He broke off, searching for the word. Finally: "She's an absolute prototype."

Friedman's eyebrows came up. "Prototype? I thought prototypes were cars, or airplanes, or maybe toasters."

Ignoring the comment, Hastings said, "She's got to be in her fifties, but she thinks she's twenty. Overweight, overdressed, too much makeup. Vain as hell. You know the type."

"Sure. She's the type that'd marry a type like Tony Frazer."

"Right."

"So there's nothing in Frazer's background that'd get him killed," Friedman said. "No connection with the bad guys, no drugs, no gambling, no stock swindles, no insanely jealous floozie who might hire someone to kill him."

"Absolutely nothing. Everything about Frazer seems to be right at the surface. He was that kind of a guy. What about Manley? What's his story?"

"A multi-, multimillionaire venture capitalist, as I said. He's very big down in Silicon Valley, that's where he started. Lately, the past few years, he's been into big-ticket real estate. Office buildings, shopping centers."

"This recession is hitting real estate hard," Hastings said.

"I doubt that it bothered Manley, not according to one of his poker-playing buddies." As he spoke, Friedman slipped on reading glasses, scanning his notebook as he said, "There's another thing about the similarities between the two murders. In both cases, the victim was leaving posh surroundings and going to get his car, which was parked in a nearby parking garage." Emphasizing the point, he fixed Hastings with a significant stare. Then: "Frazer was leaving his upscale restaurant, which his wife bought for him. And Manley had spent the evening at the Rabelais Club, eating dinner with his fellow multimillionaires and then playing cards. That's how I happened to find out so much about him. His poker-playing buddy, also rich and powerful, happened on the murder scene soon after Manley got whacked. One of our boys in blue managed to hold on to him until I got there, and the crony gave me the whole rundown on the victim." Still consulting the notes, Friedman said, "Manley was about sixty, married a couple of times. Two or three kids, a couple of airplanes, a showplace house in Belvedere, the usual."

"What about enemies?"

"I'd guess," Friedman said, "that he was the type that made enemies. He played the game fair, but he played hard. It's conceivable, I suppose, that he got killed in the line of duty. But somehow I doubt it."

"Why d'you doubt it?"

"Probably because I'm assuming that the two murders are connected. If that proves to be the case—if the same gun was used in both murders—then, if it was murder for gain, or for revenge over a shady business deal, or whatever, we'd have to connect Frazer and Manley. And so far, there doesn't seem to be a connection. Which brings me back to my serial killer theory. Or, in this case, call it random murders with a pattern."

"So you're saying that someone with a twenty-two automatic is going around town killing millionaires. Just because they're millionaires. Is that what you're saying?"

"That's what I'm *theorizing*. There's a difference."

"You always start out assuming some exotic motive. It's a thing with you. Do you realize that?"

"This time," Friedman said, "I'm on the right track. Believe it."

"Hmmmm."

11

Just before Hastings switched off the cruiser's engine and set the hand brake, the cellular phone warbled. The caller would be either Friedman or Ann.

"I just heard from Ballistics," Friedman announced. "Sure enough, all four casings came from the same gun. It was a Colt Woodsman."

"Ah."

"Also, the four cartridges came from the same manufacturer. Which, of course, isn't a very big deal. In court, though, the DA'd get points."

"What about the wounds? Anything from the coroner?"

"An excellent question. In fact, physically, the MO's were identical. Two bullets to the chest and one into the head, the coup de grâce. In Manley's case, though, all three were lethal. That's to say, the two shots to the chest both hit the heart. Now what d'you think of my serial murderer theory?"

"It's looking better," Hastings admitted.

"Where are you?"

"On Mason Street. I'm going to look at the scene. Then I'll see what they have to say at Rabelais."

"Have you ever seen that place on the inside?"

"No."

"Well, you'll be impressed."

"Were you impressed?"

"Yes."

"Then I'll probably be impressed."

"It figures."

As he introduced himself and showed the shield, Hastings watched the other man's face for a reaction. Wearing a dark three-piece suit, black shoes, and a conservative tie, gray-haired, slim and tall and handball-fit, the man might have been a banker or a butler, possibly an undertaker. The tall man glanced down impassively at the gold shield, then turned his attention to a group of four men just entering the lobby of the Rabelais building. The man's greeting was both warm and remote, a measured smile coordinated with a grave inclination of a meticulously barbered head. The arriving men greeted the host cheerfully as they passed through the lobby, bound for the nearby cloakroom. The host called each man by name, each name prefaced by "Mr." One of the arriving guests asked whether the dining room was crowded.

"There're tables, I'm sure," the host answered. He spoke

easily, equably, without subservience. Then, turning to Hastings, he said, "I'm Paul Butler, the assistant manager here. Is it about Mr. Manley?"

"Yessir."

"Just one moment, please." Striding easily, moving gracefully, the man went to a small reception desk, spoke briefly into a telephone, then gestured for Hastings to follow him down a short corridor to the door of a small office. Butler closed the office door behind them and gestured Hastings to one of the office's two chairs. Sitting behind an uncluttered desk, Butler asked, "Any idea who killed him?" Asking the question, Butler's manner was informal, almost casual. This, Hastings realized, was Butler's real persona, no longer the man with the forced smile, deferring to his betters. As he spoke, Butler took a cigarette from an inlaid box. "Mind?"

"No." Hastings decided to smile. "They're your blood vessels."

"I've quit three times," Butler said ruefully. "The last time it was almost a year. Then my dog got hit by a car, a goddam drunk driver. And I just had to have a cigarette. I don't plan to quit again. The hell with it."

"Did you get another dog?"

Butler nodded. "We got a golden retriever. Great dog. Are you a dog person?"

"I used to be. But my—ah—life-style isn't right for a dog now. They need a routine."

"I don't know about a routine. They need company, though. Human company."

"You're married, I gather."

Butler nodded. "Thirty years next month."

"How long've you worked here?"

"Two years." It was a flat response. Plainly, Rabelais wasn't Butler's favorite topic.

Intrigued, Hastings decided to ask "What'd you do before you came here?"

"I had a restaurant. It was a seafood restaurant and it was very successful, at least initially. So I decided to take in a partner and open another restaurant in Marin County. That's when the last recession hit. The worse business got, the more my partner drank." He shrugged, then frowned, then ground out a half-smoked cigarette in a crystal ashtray. "So now I'm fifty-five." Once more his voice had turned flat, perhaps bitter. Then, visibly collecting himself, Butler said, "But you didn't come for my story."

"You're right. I came for Gerald Manley's story."

"I gather you haven't caught the one who did it."

Once more Hastings smiled. "We don't answer questions, Mr. Butler. We ask them."

Butler's answering smile was complex. Finally he nodded, admitting: "Yeah, I can see that."

"So what can you tell me about Gerald Manley?"

Butler shrugged. "I can't tell you anything that isn't in the newspapers. He was about sixty years old. He'd been a member here for about fifteen years, I understand. In the context of Rabelais, there wasn't anything remarkable about him. He was very rich, very personable, and he was always ready to buy a round of drinks. I believe he was married for the second time."

"He doesn't sound like a man who made enemies."

Butler shrugged. "He didn't make any enemies here that I know of. What he did in his private life, or in business, I wouldn't know."

"Guess."

Butler's expression turned quizzical, then mischievous. "In his private life, I'd guess he was a smooth-talking, egocentric, two-timing son of a bitch. In business, he was probably an egocentric, smart, ruthless son of a bitch."

Also quizzically, Hastings studied Butler. The other man's answering stare was don't-give-a-damn bold, a subtle challenge. After a long moment's silent assessment, Hastings decided to say, "It doesn't sound like you're real happy in your work."

"You're right, I'm not. I'm sick of these people. When this recession bottoms out, I'm going to open another restaurant, the hell with it."

Hastings nodded thoughtfully. "Sounds like a good idea." Then, recalling something Friedman said, he asked, "Is it true that there're more presidents and cabinet members and CEOs in Rabelais than in any other men's club in the country?"

"That's right," Butler answered.

"I'm amazed. I grew up in San Francisco. I've always heard about Rabelais. But I had no idea it was such a big deal."

"The reason for that," Butler said, "is that Rabelais spends a lot of money keeping itself and its members out of the papers. When big shots get together, unwind, they don't want to go public. Aside from the food and the service, which is excellent, what Rabelais really offers is anonymity, when the good times start to roll."

"Still, I'd think New York or Washington would be a more logical place for a club like this."

"New York and Washington have many clubs like this. They cancel each other out. Besides, everyone wants to come to San Francisco and party. San Francisco's everyone's favorite city. And then, of course—" A brief, significant pause. "And then there's Seascape."

"Seascape?"

As if he'd expected the question, Butler nodded indulgently. "Now, that's very interesting," he said. "You're a man whose job involves getting out in the great world. But you've never heard of Seascape."

"I'm waiting."

"Seascape is up on the coast just above Jenner. It's a retreat. Very rustic. And very, very secluded. It's—"

"Wait a minute." Hastings sat up straighter, his eyes sharpening. "Didn't a woman die up there a few years ago?"

Butler nodded equably. "You got it, Lieutenant. I was sure you would."

"A hooker, flown up from Las Vegas for the weekend."

"No comment."

"Ah—" Pleased, Hastings settled back in his chair. A hooker who'd died in the line of duty, this was familiar territory. "What was it? A drug overdose?"

"That's my understanding."

"Covered up. Instantly."

"Still no comment."

"I remember hearing—"

On the desk, Butler's phone warbled. "Excuse me." He answered, listened, frowned. Saying into the phone: "All right. Jesus, I'll call the plumber." He banged down the phone, saying apologetically "There's a goddam toilet stopped up on the fourth floor. It's a mess, I guess."

"No problem," Hastings said, rising. "Thanks. I'll be in touch." He put his card on the corner of Butler's desk. "Call me if anything occurs to you."

"I hate this goddam job."

"I know."

12

Sitting at his desk in his glass-walled office, Hastings saw Canelli enter Homicide's squadroom from the outside corridor. Canelli wore scuffed, run-over shoes, baggy pants, and a quilted down ski jacket. The shapeless red jacket was torn and dirty. Canelli's dark, thick hair, worn long, was greasy and tangled. A day's stubble of black beard covered his face. Under one arm, Canelli carried a folded newspaper. He went directly to his desk, one of twelve in the squadroom, and put the newspaper on his desk. Still standing, frowning, he began shuffling through the contents of his in-basket. When he'd finished, he stood still for a moment, obviously lost in thought. Finally he picked up the folded newspaper and turned toward the rear corridor, and the commanders' offices. When he saw Hastings looking at him, he waved. When Hastings crooked an invitational forefinger, Canelli smiled, nodded, made his way among the desks of the squadroom and finally into Hastings's office.

"I was half-kidding," Hastings said, "about going undercover on the Tony Frazer thing."

"Well, I know *you* were half-kidding, Lieutenant. But Lieutenant Friedman, he thought we should give it a shot, what the hell. So he called the Salvation Army, and they fixed me right up."

"Did they delouse that stuff?"

"Oh, sure." Canelli nodded vigorously. "It's all been cleaned. Everyone down at the Salvation Army, they really got into it. There was this volunteer, an old guy named Claude, a real interesting guy. He used to be a costumer for the opera, if you can believe that. And, Christ, he really went to work, just like old times, Claude said. He got a knife and started ripping up the coat and pants. Then he got some eye makeup, or something, from a couple of women who work down there, and—" Spreading his pudgy hands, himself on display, Canelli grinned. "And here I am. What'd you think?"

"I'm impressed."

"Actually," Canelli said, "I should've picked up on going undercover when you first mentioned it, even though I knew you were half-kidding. And, of course, it rained pretty steady there for almost a week after Tony Frazer got killed. But then, like I said, Lieutenant Friedman talked to me this morning after they figured out that Frazer and Gerald Manley were killed with the same gun. I mean, it looks like we're in a whole new ball game here. It looks like— *Oh!*" He interrupted himself, spread the newspaper on Hastings's desk. "Here's the *Sentinel*, just hit the streets. Wait'll you read Dan Kanter's piece. Christ, it's like he's got a mike planted in here or something."

Frowning, Hastings took the paper, nodding as Canelli

pointed to the page-one story, bottom of the page. Dan Kanter was the *Sentinel*'s prize-winning crime reporter.

Hastings scanned the story quickly, continued on page six. Yes, somehow Kanter had learned that the same gun had killed both Manley and Frazer. The *Sentinel*'s final edition was locked up at noon, a little more than four hours ago. Meaning that Kanter had learned about the ballistics match no later than ten o'clock that morning, less than an hour after Friedman had learned of the matching ejector scratches.

Hastings turned back to the front page, reread the three-column headline:

ARE MILLIONAIRE PLAYBOYS MURDERER'S TARGETS?

Marveling, Canelli shook his head. "I don't see how Kanter does it, I honest to God don't. I mean—" He pointed to the newspaper. "Jeez, he knows as much about the goddam murders as we do, it looks like. And Manley was just killed last night, for God's sake. Less than twenty-four hours ago."

Skimming the story again, Hastings said, "Except that when you say he knows as much as we do, that's not saying much. So far there isn't a single witness to the Manley murder. And we don't even have a plausible theory, much less a credible suspect."

"Yeah, but this gun thing—the same gun for both murders— that's a big deal. And, jeez, Kanter, he—"

Hastings's phone warbled; the intercom indicator blinked.

"Lieutenant?" It was Millie, receptionist for the Inspectors' Bureau.

"Yes?"

"Dan Kanter's here to see you."

Amused, Hastings shook his head, resigned. "Tell him to come in." And to Canelli: "Surprise. It's Kanter."

"Speak of the devil, eh? Should I leave or what?"

"Stick around." Hastings smiled. "He'll want to see your costume." As he spoke, Kanter came striding briskly down the hallway to Hastings's door, which he immediately opened. In his sixties, slightly built, Kanter was wiry when he moved, wry when he smiled, and wily on the scent of a story. Totally bald, Kanter was a natty dresser who, Friedman had once pronounced, would once have worn spats, a derby, and a pearl stickpin—and who yet might. In San Francisco, no one knew the location of more skeletons than Dan Kanter.

"Ah—" Kanter nodded, moved briskly to the only vacant chair, and sat down. He adjusted his trouser creases, checked his gleaming white cuffs, touched the knot of his tie. "Two birds with one stone. You look like a bum, Canelli. I hope that was the intent."

Canelli nodded cheerfully. "You got it, Dan."

"I understand you're both working on the Millionaire Playboys' case."

"I think you've got your labels screwed up," Hastings said. "Frazer, maybe. But Manley—" He shook his head. "He wasn't a playboy."

Kanter was unruffled. "Your job is to catch 'em, Frank. My job is to sell papers. And labels are what it's all about in my business. Phrasemaking. Then we worry about the nits."

"How the hell did you find out about that ballistics match so soon?"

Behind thick, black-rimmed glasses, Kanter's blue eyes lit up. His face, Hastings decided, made him look a little like one of the Seven Dwarfs: round and ruddy, with rosy cheeks and mischievously twinkling eyes. Did Kanter exercise? Did he take megavitamins, like Robert Cummings? Did he drink? Smoke? Screw?

"Surprised you, didn't I?" Kanter said cheerfully. Then: "Ask yourself—in the normal course of things, how long would it've been before you'd've told me that those two guys were killed with the same gun?"

"No comment."

Kanter spread his hands. "I rest my case. By the way, were

63

the bullets jacketed high-speed twenty-twos, the hit man's favorite cartridge?"

Hastings sighed.

"Meaning," Kanter said, "that they were."

Rather than reply, Hastings studied the small, dapper, quick-talking crime reporter. They'd known each other for more than ten years. Did they like each other? Dislike each other? Until now, had he ever wondered?

"The way I figure this," Kanter said, "there's got to be some connection between the two victims. Find the connection, and you'll be on the trail of the murderer."

"I agree," Hastings said. "Are you here to give us the connection?"

Kanter smiled mischievously. "All in good time, Frank. All in good time."

"You should've checked with us before you wrote that." Hastings gestured to the newspaper, still on his desk. Repeating grimly: "You should've checked."

"There wasn't time to check. If I had I would've missed today's paper."

"Next time, check."

No reply. But, behind his black-rimmed glasses, Kanter's eyes were steady, unyielding.

"I'll make a deal with you." Hastings dropped his voice to a low, uncompromising note. "If you print something that helps us on this case, doesn't hinder us, we'll be glad to go along with you. Otherwise you won't get shit. You got lucky today. But I can guarantee that it'll be harder next time. I can also guarantee that, first thing tomorrow morning, I'm going to be up on the sixth floor at the lab. And I'm going to be kicking ass."

"From which I deduce," Kanter shot back, "that you don't have a damn thing more than the gun on this thing. You're sucking air."

"What I'm sucking," Hastings said, "doesn't concern you."

13

"The only thing we've got," Friedman said, "is the gun."

Resigned to the truth, Hastings nodded reluctantly. "Did you read Kanter's story today?"

"How could I miss?"

"Do you think it'll help? Or hurt?"

"It's too early to tell. Until Manley got whacked, we were looking for a street person—when we were looking, let's be honest. Now it's a new ball game, and we don't even know who's playing." Friedman shrugged. "Sometimes publicity helps, sometimes it doesn't. It all depends on the case." He looked at his watch. "It's almost six. Gotta go. Clara's mother is in town, and we're going to the theater, of all places." He pushed himself back from his desk as he said, "Sigler's done a good, thorough workup on Tony Frazer, and I've told him to do the same thing on Manley. Tomorrow I'm going to start feeding stuff on Frazer and Manley into a computer."

Puzzled, Hastings frowned. "A computer? Why?"

"To see if there's any connection between the two of them. Maybe they were involved in a diamond smuggling operation, who knows? Maybe the head smuggler decided to get rid of his partners. These goddam computers, you know, if you've got a good programmer the sky's the limit. Let's say we give a programmer Frazer's credit card vouchers for the last five years— and Manley's vouchers, too. The programmer assigns a symbol to every item and puts everything into the computer. There could be hundreds of items. Thousands, maybe. But the programmer hangs in there, and pretty soon he's got two parallel lists in the computer. He presses the 'matchup' button, or whatever it's called. And, surprise, both guys had lunch at the same time in the same place in Antwerp last May with The Dutchman, who's the third guy in the diamond smuggling ring—the guy who eventually decided to get rid of Frazer and Manley. Maybe The Dutchman wanted to keep all the loot. Or maybe Frazer, let's say, was going to bug out. So The Dutchman decided to have him killed. Then Manley started to shake, so The Dutchman had to have *him* killed. Naturally, The Dutchman's hit man used his favorite handgun."

"That," Hastings said, "is a typical Pete Friedman theory, you know that? Otherwise known as blue sky. You're a romantic, for God's sake. Every case that has any pizzazz to it, you automatically go for the most exotic motives you can imagine. *Always.*"

A benign smile spread on Friedman's large, round face as he nodded. "A romantic. Yeah, I guess so." He nodded again as the self-satisfied smile widened. Repeating: "Yeah, that's right, I suppose."

"The fact is, the only solid connection we've got between the two killings is the gun. The other connection—between the two victims—that's theoretical. Otherwise known as fantasy."

"Okay," Friedman countered, "granted. But someone pulled the trigger of that gun. The question is, why did he pull it?"

"He could be a wacko—a bum who's decided he's going to start killing rich guys. In other words, it could be exactly as it appears. Face it."

Friedman shrugged, stood up, tightened his tie, and began brushing futilely at the day's dusting of cigar ash on his vest. He finger-crombed his thick, graying hair, buttoned his jacket across his paunch, and switched off his desk lamp. "Are you leaving now?" he asked.

Also rising, Hastings nodded.

"How about dropping me downtown at the restaurant? It'll give me a chance to catch up on your love life."

"How about the mess in the Middle East instead? Or the recession?"

"Whatever."

14

"I won't do it, Bruce. You can call Dad if you want to. But not me." She spoke in a low, tight voice. Seated across the coffee table from him—a cobbler's bench, circa 1800—Julia's clear blue eyes had gone cold and hostile. She sat on their leather Chesterfield—Parsons' in London—every line of her high-styled body registering a quiet, ladylike contempt, exquisitely calculated, infinitely cruel. No, not ladylike. Rather, civilized: the jungle-bred cat, watching and waiting. Big-game hunters, Carr had once read, sometimes mistook immobility for docility—once.

"Okay." Carr banged the empty highball glass down on the cobbler's bench. "Then don't call him. Forget it." He rose from his chair—a companion piece to the Chesterfield—and went to the side table, and the Scotch. Already the liquid in the bottle was a third down for the evening. Would he ever be reduced to watering the Scotch, the final indignity? Sometime he must address the question seriously. It was important, after all, to plan for the future.

Carrying the half-filled glass back to the chair—his favorite chair, there was that—he sat down, sipping the drink as he looked at Julia over the rim of the glass. From upstairs, he heard Justin, age twelve, talking on the phone. His son, talking on his own phone. Last month, Justin's phone bill had exceeded a hundred dollars, half of it for porno calls at premium rates.

And yet his son loved him, he was sure of that. Together they had laughed, he and Justin. Still they laughed. Now, though, the laughter was less frequent; the smiles were guarded. He'd been thirty years old when Justin was born. Therefore, he would always be thirty years older than his son. Somehow the thought was a comforting one.

"Are you going to talk, Bruce? Or are you just going to stare at me like that? If you are, I should tell you that the pose doesn't suit you. The glass hides your mouth and chin, which are two of your best features, don't you think?"

He drank from the glass again—a gulp, this time—then set the drink aside. Saying: "My best features—yes. Thank you, darling. You're very generous."

As they stared silently at each other, he heard a siren wailing. Close by someone was injured. Or had committed a crime. Or a house could be burning. Tragedies, big and small, some terminal, some transitory.

Soon, in the next several seconds, he must speak to her seriously, substantively. Otherwise she would rise and tug at her skirt, a habit of hers when she was angry. Then she would go into the library. She would close the door. He would hear her on the phone. It was, after all, eight-thirty in the evening, the optimum time to confirm appointments for tomorrow, not too early, conflicting with the dinner hour, not too late.

Tomorrow, playing tennis and shopping and having lunch, she would spend more than a hundred dollars. Just tomorrow.

He cleared his throat, steadied his gaze on her remarkably clear blue eyes. Saying: "It's the eighth of the month, Julia. The day after tomorrow is the tenth. There's almost twelve thousand dollars due to be paid out, excluding the mortgage payment. And there's about six thousand dollars in the bank. I won't even tell you about the business, about those problems." As he spoke, he was aware of movement across the room. Max, the family standard poodle, was stirring from sleep. As always, the dog was reacting to tension he sensed developing.

"You're referring, I guess, to that real estate deal Dad tried to warn you about."

"I'm referring to the deal your father backed me up on. If he hadn't vouched for me, I'd never have gotten involved."

"Do you realize what you're saying, Bruce? Listen to yourself. You're blaming Dad because he tried to help you. Very much against his better judgment."

"Oh, Jesus . . ." As he shook his head, he was aware that he was again reaching for the highball. It was as if his hand were moving of its own volition, an interesting phenomenon. Upstairs, rock music was playing. Justin was finished on the phone.

"All right—" Carr drank half the Scotch, stared at the liquor remaining in the glass, then willed his hand to return the glass to the side table. The glass was cut crystal; they'd bought the side table at Southeby's. "All right," he repeated, "then we'll have to go into bankruptcy. That's all that's left, Julia. Unless your father co-signs for a loan, we'll go under. Do you think your Radcliffe friends could handle that?"

"If I were you," she retorted, "I'd worry about your so-called yachting buddies, or your so-called drinking buddies, at all those clubs you belong to. They turn on their own, you know. They're like wolves, Dad says. One of them gets injured, and the rest tear him to pieces."

"Please. Spare me quotes from your father. Things're bad enough without that." He took up the glass again, stared at her for a long, final moment, then drained the glass. In response, he saw her perfectly drawn lips part in a smile of frozen contempt. A year ago, only a year ago, she'd merely pitied him. Now she despised him. He could see it in the smile, read it plainly in her eyes.

She rose from the sofa and adjusted her skirt. She spoke very quietly, very precisely. "You're becoming an embarrassment, Bruce. Especially when you drink." She turned, strode across the living room to the hall. Moments later he heard the door to the study open, then close. In the silence, the click of the latch was magnified, louder that he'd ever heard it.

15

This time, the third time, he was able to use his car. Therefore, he'd decided to leave the tattered overcoat and the shapeless felt hat in the black plastic garment bag hung neatly in his bedroom closet, behind the garment bags that contained his summer clothing. A derelict driving a car would, after all, surely seem incongruous, and would therefore be remembered.

In the two daily newspapers, no mention had been made of a tramp, a street person seen leaving the scene of the murder. The police, then, were withholding information, since surely he'd been seen during the moments following Tony Frazer's death. Or, more probably, the police had asked the papers not to print the information and the newspapers had complied. They were, after all, both part of the establishment: the propagandists and the storm troopers.

But if the propagandists were concealing the description of his clothing, his costume, why had the police instructed them to reveal that the same gun had been used to execute both Frazer and Manley? There was, certainly, a plan. But what was its purpose? It was a life-or-death question. His life. Conceivably his death.

It had taken him more than a week to discover where Bruce Carr lived. How remarkable that it had taken so long. Their lives, after all, were linked. Yet, in another sense, their lives never intersected, just as two parallel lines never met. It was elementary geometry, signifying that the rules still obtained.

But not always. Because, quite casually, they'd ruined him. Without intersecting, their lives a world apart from his, they'd ruined him. They'd consigned him to a very particular hell, then left him to burn.

Just as now, one by one, he was sending them to hell.

Until now, predictably, parking garages had been the controlling factor. Inevitably, the modern American man homed in on his car. Find the car, therefore, and one always found the man.

So he'd known that Tony Frazer would eventually walk from his restaurant to the Franklin Street parking garage. Just as Manley, through habit, would go from Rabelais to the garage on Mason Street.

And, yes, when he'd finally found Bruce Carr's car—a pun—he'd had only to wait for Carr to appear. Then, ergo, he'd followed Carr to his home. He'd had to run a red light at the intersection of Jackson and Van Ness, but otherwise he'd had no difficulty tracking Carr to his home, a tasteful three-story brown shingle house on Cherry Street. In the normal course of things Carr, still in his early forties, could expect to live here in Presidio Heights, biding his time before making his final assault on Pacific Heights, the bastion of San Francisco society.

For more than a week, in different guises, from different vantage points, sometimes in his car, sometimes on foot, he'd observed Carr and his family. Predictably, the mornings had been routine. Driving the dark-green Mercedes, Carr left for his office early, usually by seven-thirty. At eight-fifteen, in the station wagon, the wife drove the son to his private school. The school was a mile away, on Lake Street. Sometimes the wife returned directly home, sometimes she did errands, shopped. Whenever she returned directly home, she wore her hair wrapped in a scarf. Otherwise, she went bareheaded. Thus did she reveal her plans for the morning.

If the mornings were routine, the afternoons and evenings— and the nights—had no pattern. Sometimes the lights in the house went out at ten o'clock, sometimes at midnight, or later.

But, at the end of the day—every day—one habit never varied.

Every night, before the lights went out, Carr took the dog, a standard poodle, for a walk. Every night they walked two blocks up the hill to a tiny park no larger than a single city lot. There, as all dog owners must, good weather or bad, Carr stood patiently waiting for his dog to relieve itself. Then, briskly, dog and man would return to their home, this time on the opposite side of the street.

The side where he now waited, parked.

He sat on the passenger's side of the car. Meaning that when Carr walked down the sidewalk, returning home, it would only be necessary to shoot through the open window, a point-blank shot.

In his lap, careful of the silencer, he cradled the Woodsman. The gun was uncocked, with no cartridge in the chamber. Therefore, when Carr and the dog crossed the street from the park, homeward bound, that would be his cue. He would pull back the slide, cocking the pistol and jacking a cartridge into

74

the chamber. After that—for ten shots, if necessary—it would only be necessary to press the trigger.

It was remarkable, the unity he now felt with the gun. At first the touch of the cold steel on the warmth of his flesh had been repugnant, revulsion mixed with fear—and with something indefinable, a force that pierced the center of himself, where fear and exultation existed together, both evoked by the gun, first the feel of it, then the elemental power, the finality. The judgment, finally executed.

So that now, the touch of his fingers on the machined steel was a caress, warming the cold metal with his flesh.

Standing on the sidewalk, Carr strained to see the poodle. The dog was black, as dark as the shadows of the park's trees and shrubs. But there was no chance that Max would run off, even though the tiny park wasn't fenced at the rear property line. Max was a well-behaved poodle.

As a young man, Carr had privately scorned those who chose to live part of their lives through their pets. Now, forty-two years old, he understood how it could happen. Julia, age forty, moved away from his touch. Justin, age twelve, had just begun to look at him with veiled suspicion, as if he suspected fraud.

Only Max sought out his company. Only Max offered love without reservation.

Max, who was materializing out of the shadows. Max, coming when he was called, faithfully wagging his aristocratically sculpted poodle tail, courtesy of Perfect Paws, pickup and delivery, a hundred dollars a shot.

Carr bent down, ruffled the dog's ears, began walking, swinging the leather leash. The time would be almost eleven. At home, upstairs, in her bathroom, Julia would be removing the day's makeup, then creaming her face and neck, that inexorable female ritual. In the first years of the marriage, living in a small apartment on Green Street, it was a ritual they'd shared, one ritual among many, his rituals and her rituals, the fabric of their life together. They'd made love several times a week in that apartment. During one night of love, they'd conceived Justin. Julia had been twenty-eight, he'd been thirty. When they'd told Julia's father that she was pregnant, he'd announced that he would buy them a "starter" house.

Announced—yes. J.D. Farrell, tycoon, never simply spoke. Always, J.D. announced. Or, if the subject was politics, J.D. pronounced.

At the intersection just ahead, Max had stopped at the curb and was waiting for him, expectantly looking back over his shoulder, waiting permission to cross the street. Carr smiled wistfully. Who depended more on this time they always shared together? He, a mature human male? Or Max, also mature, a male dog who'd come to live with them when he was only six weeks old, a ball of squirming, yipping, wetting fluff so small that he could be lifted in one hand?

"Okay, Max."

The dog bounded across the street, made straight for his favorite tree, a huge sycamore that was bulging the sidewalk, cracking it. Carr would walk slowly ahead, passing the sycamore, giving Max all the time needed to sniff, pee, sniff, pee, in whatever order his genetic imprint decreed.

The nightly ritual called for them to walk to the park on the north side of the street and return home on the south side. On a cold, raw Thursday night in March, at eleven o'clock, only four cars were parked on this side of the street. Tomorrow night and Saturday, the street would be crowded with cars. After two months of recovery from the constant round of holiday parties, the city's beautiful people and their imitators were once more eyeing their guest lists, conferring with caterers, reserving crucial time blocks with their favorite hairdressers. Next Saturday they were dining at the Indonesian Consulate. The night before, Friday, *La Bohème* opened.

From behind him, headlights flashed; a car was turning into Cherry Street, coming toward him. But, trust Max, the dog was safely away from the street, still industriously sniffing at the base of the sycamore. The car was approaching slowly, coming abreast of him—passing. It was a Jaguar XJ, twelve cylinders. Price: fifty-five thousand, with tax and license.

Ahead, in a sedan parked at the curb, the Jag's headlights had fragmentarily revealed a figure sitting on the passenger's side. Had the sedan been parked there when they'd walked to the park, he and Max, on the opposite side of the street? The silhouette was a man. A lookout for a robbery in progress? At night, in this affluent neighborhood, it was possible. Always there were robberies. Ergo: every house had an alarm system, most wired directly into police communications, the upscale choice.

Fifteen feet separated him from the rear of the sedan. Ten feet now. He hesitated, decided to stop, decided to call to the dog—decided to wait until the dog had come to him. At night, in the city, danger waited. Savages abounded, the veldt was creeping closer.

But now they were a team, he and Max. A dog, police statistics revealed, especially a big dog with a deep bark, was the best protection. Because, like it or not, most criminals were black. Their ancestors had been slaves. And, when slaves ran away, the master called the dog.

Moving forward again, Max at his side now, he was even with the sedan's trunk. The dog walked to his left, between him and the car with the man inside. The man was sitting motionless, eyes front. The light from the nearest street lamp was dim. But was the profile familiar? Could it be . . . ?

Now, slowly, deliberately, the man turned toward him. On

the sill of the car's open window, a metal cylinder came to rest.

"Bruce . . ." The voice was soft and low, hardly more than a whisper. Should he respond? Should he . . . ?

From the cylinder, flame erupted. Something struck him in the chest. Again, the orange flame, a snake's tongue of fire, another blow to the chest. But this crash was muted, a reverberation—distant thunder, disappearing. He lay on the sidewalk. Dimly, distantly, he heard the sound of a metallic squeak, heard the rustle of purposeful movement. It was the man, swinging the car door open, getting out of the car. Now a shape hovered above him, blotting out the sky. It was Max. In this last moment Max was standing over him, looking down. Whining. Max, his only hope, the final presence.

As, visible now close beside the dog's head, the round cylinder was seeking him—

—finding him—

Erupting again, that snake's tongue of fire, so close to his eyes.

Max . . .

16

"Jeez, Lieutenant—" Bemused, Canelli shook his head as he gestured in a semicircle that swept the murder scene. "Here we go again—a rich guy gets killed with two shots to the chest and one to the head. And what've we got for a witness but a dog, for God's sake." Now Canelli's broad face broke into a wide grin. "I can hardly wait to see what Lieutenant Friedman'll do with that one. Can you imagine a poodle called as a witness in a murder trial?"

"It happened, though," Hastings said. "Up in Napa, there's a bloodhound that's famous. His name is Sherlock. When the DA wanted to introduce the dog's performance as evidence,

Sherlock had to appear in court and do his stuff. He was a sensation."

"Was the evidence admitted?"

"No problem. The judge was dazzled."

"I'll be damned. I never heard about that." Canelli frowned. "How come we don't use bloodhounds?"

"Well," Hastings admitted, "Sherlock's evidence didn't hold up on appeal."

"Huh."

"Where's the poodle now?"

"He's home with the victim's wife. His name is Max." Canelli pointed in the direction of the adjoining block.

"Has the wife seen the body?"

"Yessir. The way I get it, one of the neighbors heard Max howling, so he investigated. And there was Max, standing over his master's body, howling his head off." Once more Canelli shook his head in wonderment. "It's like one of those movies for kids, or something. You know—Lassie. Jeez—" Reflectively, nostalgically, he smiled. "Jeez, I used to love Lassie."

"So what happened next?"

"Well, the neighbor was apparently pretty cool. In fact, he had a goddam portable telephone with him. You know—like he was all set to take command." As he spoke, Canelli consulted his small spiral-bound notebook. "His name is Fink. Albert Fink. And he's a doctor, which maybe accounts for his take-charge attitude. I mean, the first thing he did was determine that Carr was dead, which he was. Then Fink called nine-one-one on the telephone. And then he called Mrs. Carr—" Another glance at the notebook. "Her name is Julia, and she lives at seven fifty-two Cherry Street."

"Is that a single-family dwelling?"

"Yessir."

"Okay. So then what?"

"So then she came here—" Canelli gestured to the murdered man lying across the sidewalk. "She got here about sixty seconds before the first black-and-white arrived, as I understand it. So there was just her and Dr. Fink here, initially. Plus Max, of course."

"How'd she act?"

"According to Gallagher—" Canelli pointed to a uniformed officer standing beside his squad car. "According to Gallagher, she was—you know—pretty cool. She asked Fink whether Carr was dead, and then she asked whether he'd been shot. By that time, like I said, there were two units on the scene, plus some neighbors, or rubberneckers, or whatever. You know how it goes, Lieutenant, even in a quiet neighborhood like this. I mean, there's always the goddam rubberneckers. You know?"

"So what happened then?"

"Well, Mrs. Carr told Gallagher she had to go home to be with her kid. Which, of course, figures. So Gallagher said she should take the dog, too. But Max, he didn't want to leave. So, the way I understand it, Dr. Fink took off his belt, so he could get Max home. I mean, the coroner and the lab guys sure as hell won't work on the body with a dog right there. So that's where she is now. Home. Mrs. Carr. Max, too."

"And there're no witnesses?"

Canelli shook his head dolefully. "It doesn't look like it, Lieutenant. Not if you don't count Dr. Fink."

"No sound of shots . . ." As he said it, Hastings surveyed the quiet, affluent neighborhood where every house was worth at least a half million and many were worth a million or more. Here there was no city traffic that would overlay the sound of shots. Here wayward noises were closely noted by householders who knew they were prime targets for criminals.

"What about shell casings?"

Canelli spread his hands ruefully. "So far, nothing." As he

spoke, the coroner's van arrived, closely followed by the lab van. The technicians were about to take over. Hastings checked the time: almost one o'clock.

"I'm going to see what the wife has to say. If everything's finished here and I'm still talking to her, you sign the body off. Okay?"

"Well—" Canelli drew himself up, came to attention. "Well, sure, Lieutenant, if you say so. Thanks."

"You're welcome. Except that you've got to take the sergeant's exam one of these days, if we keep doing this. You understand?"

Still at attention, Canelli nodded. "Yessir."

"Study a couple of nights a week, that's all it takes. You belong to—what—two bowling leagues?"

Canelli shifted uncomfortably. "It's—ah—three now." Then, earnestly: "I'm getting pretty good."

"There simply isn't anything else I can tell you." Julia Carr's voice was brittle; her eyes were hardening, turning hostile. Even though she was dressed in jeans and a baggy sweater, wearing no makeup, with her ash-blond hair tied in a scarf, she nevertheless fit perfectly into the richly furnished living room: a high-styled lady in her natural habitat. The elaborately trimmed poodle, lying at her feet, also fit.

"I was expecting to hear Bruce and the dog downstairs after their walk," she went on. "It was a ritual. If Bruce doesn't take him out for a walk, Max raises hell." She shrugged, then shook her head. "It was one of those family jokes. But instead—" As if she were puzzled, she frowned. At the sound of his name, the poodle had raised his head from his forepaws, whined once, then subsided. "Instead," she continued, "the phone rang. And Al Fink—" Suddenly she choked, then began to blink. But, as if she were angry with herself at the show of emotion, she raised her chin and squared her shoulders, determined not to surrender to tears.

"All your husband had in his pockets was a ring of keys," Hastings said. "Is that right?"

"I suppose so." She spoke indifferently, diffidently. Her eyes, clear blue, moved in the direction of the hallway door. "He usually left his wallet and watch and money on top of his desk, in the study. When he came back from walking the dog, he'd lock up and set the alarms, and everything. Then he'd go upstairs—" She hesitated; her eyes shifted slightly as she added, "To bed."

Hastings decided not to speak, decided to let silence work for him as he watched her face for some clue to her real thoughts and emotions. So far, less than two hours after the death of her husband, she'd registered shock but not grief, anger but not pain. *He'd go upstairs*, she'd said. Adding: *to bed.*

Whose bed?

Was it necessary to ask? Here? Now? As if to answer his own question, Hastings realized that he was covertly shaking his head. Later he would ask. Not now.

Now there was a more important question.

"Do you have any idea why your husband was murdered, Mrs. Carr?"

As if the question annoyed her, she frowned. "Wasn't it robbery? Someone looking for money or jewelry?"

Hastings gestured to the big dog lying at her feet. "Robbers— muggers—go after targets of opportunity. And if a robber saw a man walking a dog that size, he'd just keep on going. Besides—" Hastings hesitated, then decided to say, "Besides, it doesn't *feel* like a street robbery."

"Oh? What's it feel like, Lieutenant?" It was a supercilious question. At another time, in another place, the question would be shaded with irony, even amusement. That was certainly Julia

83

Carr's style. Even without makeup, dressed in old clothes, having just seen her husband dead, she was doing what came naturally: maneuvering to control their encounter.

Hastings waited until they were in full eye contact. Then he spoke quietly. "It feels like premeditated murder, Mrs. Carr."

"Pre—?" Incredulous, she broke off, staring at him. "Are you trying to tell me that someone *planned* to kill him?" She spoke as if she were accusing him of some gross indiscretion. Her body language was indignant, bordering on outrage. "Is that what you're saying?"

"That's exactly what I'm saying."

"But why, for God's sake?" The question ended on a plaintive note: "*Why?*"

"During the last month," he answered, "two other men were killed in almost exactly the same way as your husband was killed. They were approached on a city street in the dark, and they were shot three times—twice in the chest and once in the head, at close range." As he said it, he saw her shudder. But he also saw the sharpness in her eye, the calculation.

Calculation?

"The first two victims," he continued, "were shot by the same gun. It was an automatic, and we could identify it by marks the gun's ejector makes on the shell casings. The actual bullets couldn't be identified by rifling marks, because they were hollow points, which mushroom when they hit. But we could tell that they were twenty-two caliber, the same caliber as the ejected casings. And I'm willing to bet—" He let a long, solemn beat pass. Repeating: "I'm willing to bet that your husband was killed by a twenty-two-caliber hollow-point bullet."

"Are you—" She swallowed, a painful, spasmodic gulp. "Are you saying that Bruce was killed as—as some kind of a plot? A vendetta? Is that what you're saying?"

As she'd been speaking, Hastings's gaze had fallen to the

poodle, still lying on the floor close beside the woman's feet, his head between his paws as he watched every movement Hastings made. What had the dog seen two hours ago, on Cherry Street? Had Max attacked the killer? Or had the dog cowered at the sound of the shots? Was it possible that, somewhere in San Francisco, a killer was nursing dog bites?

"These two men . . ." Julia Carr spoke tentatively. "Do you mean Tony Frazer and—" She broke off, searching her memory.

"Gerald Manley." Hastings's attention was sharp-focused on her face now, searching for the slightest reaction. "Did you know them? Did your husband know them?"

"Yes . . ." It was a subdued response. Her eyes had wandered away; her expression was awed. "Yes . . . Bruce knew them both."

Hastings felt excitement rising—the hunter's rush at the first glimpse of his prey. "In what connection did he know them?"

"They belonged to Rabelais. All three of them."

"Ah . . ." It was a soft, grateful exhalation. Yes, the prey could be in view. Not within grasp, but for the first time in view. "Ah—Rabelais."

"You don't think . . ." As if she dreaded the response that the question would bring, she broke off. Her eyes were wide now. Her body had visibly tightened.

"Is there any other connection between your husband and Frazer and Manley? Did they ever do business together?"

"Not that I know of. But—but you don't think Rabelais had anything to do with this, do you?"

Ignoring the question, he asked, "Did you know either Frazer or Manley?"

"I'd met Tony, seen him at a few parties. And we went to his restaurant a few times. But that was it. I didn't care much for him. And neither did Bruce."

"What about Manley? Did you know him?"

"No. But Bruce knew him. They'd played cards together, at Rabelais. When Bruce heard about Gerald Manley's death, he was shocked."

"Abnormally shocked, would you say?"

She considered, then shook her head. "No, I wouldn't say so."

"Could your husband have been worried that he'd be next? Could that have been why he was shocked?"

"No, I don't think so. It was just that someone he knew had been killed—died violently. That's always a shock."

"Nothing more?"

"Not that I could see."

"What was your husband's business, Mrs. Carr?"

"He's—" She broke off, bit her lip. But, quickly recovering: "He was a stockbroker, mostly."

"Mostly?"

As she shrugged, her expression hardened. "He invested in real estate, and he had an interest in a retail storage company. There were other investments, too."

Watching her, he saw in her face something that could be distaste. Or was it contempt?

"I gather," he said, "that his investments weren't too profitable."

The contempt turned bitter as she said cryptically: "There's a recession. A lot of investors are getting burned."

"Including Bruce."

"Yes. Including Bruce."

"You've heard of loan-sharking, haven't you, Mrs. Carr?"

She frowned. Was it apprehension? Puzzlement? Something else?

"Loan-sharking?"

"A businessman gets in over his head. It happens, especially in a recession as bad as this one. He can't get any credit. At least, not from banks or other legitimate sources. He's about to

86

go bankrupt. So he goes to a loan shark—an underworld banker. He borrows money at exorbitant interest rates. And if he can't make the payments . . ." He broke off, compelled her to meet his gaze squarely. "If they can't pay, they could die."

"But—" As if he'd committed another indiscretion, she stared at him incredulously. "But the underworld. Criminals." She shook her head. "Bruce would never get involved with people like that." As if to confirm it, she swept the expensively decorated living room with a proprietary gaze. This world, she was certainly thinking, was insulated by many layers of affluence and gentility from the underworld.

"The reason I asked the question," Hastings said, "is because, as I said earlier, it looks like these three men were killed by the same gun. It's a particular kind of a gun that's often used by underworld hit men. It fires a small-caliber bullet, but it's a high-speed load, and the bullet is hollow point, which means that it can't be traced to a—"

"*Hit* man?" she suddenly flared. Repeating indignantly: "*Hit* man?"

Hastings sighed. A few minutes more and he could lose control of the interrogation—an interrogation that, so far, had been a productive one. It was time to get out, quit winners. He looked at his watch. "It's late, Mrs. Carr. I won't keep you any longer. If there's anything I can do for you—" He handed over his card. "Call me. Any time, day or night."

"Yes . . ." As she spoke, Hastings saw her running her finger over the surface of the card. To himself, he smiled. *No, Mrs. Carr, the card isn't embossed.*

17

Rituals, he'd learned, were integral. Without rituals, however simple, disorder followed. The center flew apart, leaving the void. Therefore, just as he'd done the first time, and then the second time, he'd left the oil-stained towel lying on the library table. So that now he had only to unload the pistol, and clean it, and rewrap it in the towel, and return the towel with its burden to the bottom of the clothes hamper, its hiding place. Thus did he free himself to do now what he'd done twice before: sit here in this darkened room, staring into a cold, empty fireplace.

Memories—associations—ritual—they were all of a piece, a pact, a plan.

A piece, a pact, a plan. Yes, it scanned.

Signifying that finally the plan was plain. It was as if he could see its shape emerging like ectoplasm from the dead embers of past fires once set in this fireplace: death begot death, a continuum.

Or was it the dog?

Max. Yes, he would remember that name: Max, just the single word. Bruce Carr's last word, before he died.

Max and Fouchette, one dog standing across his dying master's body, the other dog lying on its blood-drenched cushion in its own wicker basket, tongue lolling, dead eyes staring.

And, in the bathroom, the body of his father, sprawled on the white tile floor. His father's tongue, too, had bulged out between his purple lips. And his dead eyes, too, had stared at nothing.

When the police came, they said that his father had hanged himself from the light fixture. He'd probably stood on the marble ledge surrounding the bathtub and fastened the clothesline rope to the fixture. After he'd strangled to death, the fixture had broken, and he'd fallen to the floor.

The bathroom, he'd always remembered, had reeked with his father's urine and feces.

The dog's throat had been slashed; his father had left the butcher knife on the carpet beside the dog's basket.

Explaining, certainly, why he'd chosen the pistol—would never have chosen a knife.

18

"Now," Friedman pronounced, "we're getting somewhere." He nodded judiciously. "We've got these guys connected. And that's the first law of investigation, as you well know."

Hastings shook his head dubiously. "I'm not so sure. When you think about it, most of the real rich guys in town probably belong to Rabelais."

"I don't think that's necessarily true. I think it takes more than money. I think you need clout to get into Rabelais. You need to *be* someone. Presidents, for God's sake, and cabinet officers, a lot of them belong. A *lot*. Christ, a few years ago I happened to be up in Glendora, which is only a few miles from the retreat, so called, that Rabelais has up there on the coast.

It was during the week that they all get together to drink and raise hell. Which resulted, as you'll recall, in the death of a hooker. You remember that—one of the all-time great, transparent cover-ups in the annals of criminology. The sheriff who had jurisdiction, he got rich instantly. At least by his standards."

"So I heard."

"What fascinated me," Friedman said, "was the pains these guys take for their privacy. I don't mean the hooker thing—I mean in general. See, during the Second World War Glendora was used as a staging area for flying bombers across the Pacific. So there's this huge concrete runway out in the middle of nowhere. Except, as I said, that it's close to the Rabelais retreat. Thirty, forty miles, something like that."

"Seascape."

"What?"

"Seascape," Hastings repeated. "That's the name of their place up there."

"Yeah. Well, anyhow, once a year, for a week, these goddam corporate jets start landing at Glendora. I just happened to see them up there. Clara and I were staying in Shelter Cove for the weekend and we took the long way home, through the redwoods north of Mendocino. So there it was: this enormous runway in the middle of nowhere, with corporate jets parked wing tip to wing tip . . ." At the memory, Friedman smiled, nodding reflectively. "I've never forgotten it. I made some inquiries. For most of the year, the field's unattended—no gas, no repairs, nothing. But when the Rabelais guys have their party, there's a whole maintenance base moved up from Santa Rosa—fuel, mechanics, the whole works. Plus guards, of course, 'round the clock."

"Getting back to how much clout these guys have, though," Hastings said. "Maybe Gerald Manley had that kind of clout. But I don't think either Tony Frazer or Bruce Carr were in the same class with cabinet officers, much less presidents."

Friedman shrugged. "Maybe Frazer and Carr had connections. Frazer's wife, I happen to know, has a family tree that won't quit. Her great-grandfather was one of the Big Five that plundered the whole state of California to build the railroads. He probably started Rabelais, he and a few drinking buddies. So I doubt that Frazer would have a problem getting into Rabelais, if his wife made a few calls."

"Ah—" Hastings nodded.

"What about shell casings?" Friedman asked. "Anything?"

Hastings shook his head. "No luck."

"So what's that tell you?"

"Is this a quiz? Twenty questions?"

Unruffled, Friedman said, "It tells me that this time the guy used a car. Same gun, same basic MO. But he used a car. And that's where the ejected casings went. Inside the car."

"I've already thought of that. The lab guys took pictures for tire tracks. Lots of pictures."

"But there're no witnesses."

"Not unless you count the poodle."

"Well," Friedman said, "who knows? Did you ever hear of Sherlock, up in Napa?"

"Sherlock got shot down on appeal."

Friedman shrugged. "Who cares? Without Sherlock, there might never have *been* a trial. He led the way straight to the bad guy."

"I don't think Max is going to lead us anywhere."

"What's the matter? Don't you like dogs?"

"Of course I like dogs," Hastings answered irritably.

"Speaking of dogs—domesticity—how're you and Ann and her two kids making out?"

"*We're* doing fine. But her goddam husband won't leave Ann alone. I swear to God, someday I'm going to pop that guy."

"Which would be very, very stupid. 'Burly police lieutenant assaults namby-pamby society psychiatrist.' " Friedman shook his head despairingly. Then, in recollection: "Don't I remember that you assaulted his Porsche a couple of weeks ago?"

"I hit the door with my hand and the thing that keeps the door from hitting the fender broke. It was a design defect."

"Don't I remember that your insurance company paid more than a thousand dollars?"

"No comment."

Across from Hastings's desk, Friedman rose and haphazardly brushed cigar ashes from his vest—succeeding only in smudging the ash into a uniform gray. "I've got to be in court at ten. By the time I get out, we'll know what caliber bullet killed Carr. I'm assuming, of course, that it's a twenty-two hollow point."

"What if it isn't?"

"If it isn't," Friedman said, "I'd be amazed. Like, two-to-one amazed. Interested, for a dollar?"

Hastings considered, then shook his head.

"What's your next move?" Friedman asked.

"I guess I'll go over to Rabelais. There's a guy over there—Paul Butler, the assistant manager—who doesn't much care for the class of men who've joined the club. I'll see what he says about Carr."

19

"I hope," Butler said, "that we're talking off the record. As you've doubtless figured out, Lieutenant, I don't give a shit about Rabelais. I can hardly wait to see the last of these reactionary, self-serving, overprivileged phonies. But I don't fancy job hunting in this goddam recession." As he spoke, Butler dropped his voice, glanced reflexively at the closed door of his office.

"There's nothing to worry about," Hastings said. "Nobody around here will talk to me. Except maybe the waiters."

"The waiters can probably tell you as much as I can."

"I'll stick with you."

Butler smiled, but made no reply.

"So what about Carr?" Hastings asked.

"In my opinion," Butler answered promptly, "Carr was a lightweight who went for the flash and not the substance. I'd deny I ever said it—I'd lose my job if it came out that I told you—but the fact is that Carr was thirty days behind on his bar bills here. And I can tell you, when one of these so-called gentlemen falls into arrears on his bar bill, the next thing is bankruptcy."

"You're exaggerating, of course."

"Not much."

"So you'd say Carr was having financial problems."

Butler nodded silently.

"What about Tony Frazer? Did he pay his bar bills on time?"

Now Butler's nod was an emphatic affirmation. "Always."

"And how would you rate Frazer? Lightweight? Middleweight?"

"I'd rate him a lightweight, too—a pretty boy. But he was always cheerful. Nobody took him very seriously because he lived off his wife. Still, he never gave himself airs, and he smiled a lot. He was generally well liked, I'd say."

"What about Gerald Manley? Was he well liked?"

"Not really. But he was respected, at least for his power. He was one of the richest, most successful men in San Francisco."

"Did Manley make enemies?"

"I imagine he did. He could be abrasive."

"And what about Carr? Well liked?"

"I'd say so. But in recent weeks, especially, he got very tense, very jumpy. Plainly, he was a man with problems. The rumor was that his father-in-law wasn't going to carry him anymore. That's J.D. Farrell. The tycoon."

"Is J.D. Farrell a member of Rabelais?"

"Of course," Butler answered. "They were made for each other, J.D. Farrell and Rabelais. It would be unthinkable that he wouldn't be a member."

"That wouldn't be true of Frazer or Carr, though."

"No. Definitely not."

"How about Manley?"

Butler considered, then nodded. "He was almost an inevitability. Unless, of course—" Butler's handsome, urbane face relaxed into a subtle smile. "Unless there was some scandal. Like voting Democratic during his youth, something like that."

"You're kidding, of course."

"Am I? Since 1920, when the club was founded, every Republican president was a member. But not a single Democrat."

"Jesus . . ." Incredulous, Hastings shook his head. Adding: "I don't suppose they let cops in, either."

"I suppose not. And almost no actors, either. Too flashy."

"How about lawyers?"

"Of course. Lots of lawyers. Rabelais is about power. And lawyers have the power. Lawyers and bankers."

Hastings nodded, took time to reflect, finally decided to ask, "Have any of your members ever been connected with organized crime?"

"God, no. I think I know why you ask. Organized crime is a big factor in business, no question. But as far as I know, there's never been a hint that any of our guys are tainted. *That* would be a scandal—grounds for dismissal."

"Are members ever dismissed, asked to leave?"

"Not really. Once in a while pressure is exerted, though, and members simply quit showing up. Eventually they let their dues lapse. It's all very low key, no fuss no muss. Mostly it's drinking—sloppy drunks. Rabelais is very finicky about sloppy drunks."

"I suppose there's a president and a governing committee."

"Oh, sure. The president holds office for two years, and then it's the vice president's turn. Then the committee members get their turns, in order of seniority. It's all very cut and dried."

"Still," Hastings pressed, "considering how old the club is, there must've been some problems more serious than sloppy drunks."

Butler shrugged. "I'm sure that's true. A few years ago, I understand, there was a high-stakes poker game that got out of hand. You know, big bucks lost by a couple of compulsive gamblers. That can be a problem in these private clubs—compulsive gamblers, bad losers. And, in that case, the committee *did* step in. They adopted a resolution banning big-stakes gambling."

"Were you working here when Sally Dietz died?"

Plainly puzzled, Butler frowned. "Sally Dietz?"

"She's the hooker who died about three years ago, at the retreat up on the coast. Apparently your guys chipped in and had a planeload of hookers flown up from Las Vegas for the weekend. One of them—Sally Dietz—died. The Kent County coroner called it a drug overdose, and I suppose it was. The point is, though, that the whole thing was hushed up. Instantly."

"Sure it was hushed up. You've got to realize that these guys go to a lot of trouble and expense to keep Rabelais out of the papers. That's because they come to the club to play. They drink a lot and they bullshit a lot—and they make deals, too, over the drinks. A *lot* of deals. None of which they want publicized. As you probably know, no women are allowed on the premises here. But the retreat weekend, that's different. That's when these guys *really* play. Retreat week is to them what spring break is to fraternity boys. The only difference is, our guys have more money to indulge their fantasies. Of which, believe me, there're plenty. You talk about hookers. My God, remember Kennedy, our beloved president? The story is that one of his aides spent most of his time keeping JFK supplied with girls. Which, in fact, confirms my theory that, in general, the more successful these politicians and big-business types are, the stronger their sex drives. Which could explain—" A genial, rueful smile. "—Why I'm monogamous."

Caught by surprise, Hastings spontaneously smiled in return. Saying: "Likewise." Then, after a glance at his watch: "The first time we talked, did you say you'd worked here for two years?"

Butler nodded.

"And you can't think of any connection between these three victims? Any reason why the same person should want to kill them?"

"No," Butler answered, "I can't. I honestly can't." His gaze sharpened. "Are you sure the same person killed them?"

"We're not sure of anything. But it's odds-on that the same gun was used in all three crimes."

"When you think about it," Butler said somberly, "that's a pretty grim statistic. Especially if one should happen to be a member of—" On his desk, the phone warbled. "Excuse me." He picked up the phone and listened. Then, as his eyes went to Hastings, Butler nodded. Saying: "Yes, he's here now. Yes— right. I'll tell him. Yes. Right." Smiling inscrutably, he cradled the phone and spoke to Hastings. "That was Floyd Castle, the manager here. He'd like to speak to you. He's in his office."

"Fine." Hastings rose, thanked the other man, promised to keep in touch.

"Remember," Butler said, "mum's the word. My future is in your hands."

"I know."

Floyd Castle was a small, fastidiously dressed man. His pinched smile was humorless, his speech was dry and precise. His eyes were fixed and unfriendly. In his fifties, he wore a dark brown toupee, precisely parted. His complexion was sallow, a heart patient's pallor. A large diamond sparkled on the little finger of his right hand. Sitting behind a richly carved library table that served as a desk, he motioned Hastings to a chair on the opposite side.

"I don't have much time," Castle said. "So I'll come right to the point."

Hastings decided to nod, decided to say simply "Good." Plainly, the next several minutes would be nonproductive at best, obstructive at the worst.

"The members," Castle said, "are, of course, very, ah, distressed to learn that three of their, ah, number have been murdered. It—it's a terrible thing." He spoke primly, accusingly, as if, had the police been more efficient, this unpleasantness could have been avoided.

"We didn't realize until last night that the three victims belonged to Rabelais," Hastings answered. Adding: "I'd appreciate any information you could give me—any connection between the three."

As if he were displeased, Castle frowned. His eyebrows, Hastings decided, were tinted to match the toupee. Could it be eyebrow pencil?

"Connection?" Castle asked.

"The three men knew each other. And we believe the same gun killed all three." Hastings shrugged. "To us, that sounds like more than coincidence. It sounds like a pattern, like someone had a reason for killing them."

As if he were a parent who was compelled to discipline a wayward child, Castle drew a deep, reluctant breath. Leaning forward, he spoke gravely. "Lieutenant, I understand that twice you've spoken with Paul Butler. Meaning, I'm sure, that you have some idea of the, ah, nature of Rabelais."

"If you're asking whether I know this is a rich man's club, the answer is 'yes.' "

"It's more than a rich man's club, Lieutenant. It's a *lot* more."

Hastings nodded. "I'm aware of that, Mr. Castle." For a

long, deliberate moment he locked eyes with the other man. Then, quietly: "So?"

Castle's reaction was a brief facial spasm that registered both pain and exasperation. But his reply was carefully measured. "As I understand it, you haven't interrogated any of the other members of the club. Is that right?"

"We don't usually answer questions about an ongoing investigation, Mr. Castle. I'm sure you can understand why."

Visibly, the other man's exasperation gave way to distaste. "For as long as your investigation takes, Lieutenant, I'd like you to deal with me. Not Paul Butler. Is that clear?"

Hastings rose, stood silently for a moment as he stared down at the impeccably tailored club manager with his toupee and his three-piece suit and his diamond on the pinkie finger. Finally, slowly, Hastings took a card from his pocket, placed the card squarely in the middle of Castle's desk. "I'll question whoever I want, Mr. Castle," he said softly. "Whenever I want. For as long as I want. Is *that* clear?"

Seated at her desk in the small glass-walled reception room of the Inspectors' Bureau, Millie Ralston crooked her finger to Hastings as he left the elevator, bound for the coffee machine in a side corridor. Hastings pivoted, reversed direction, opened the reception room door. Holding it delicately between thumb and forefinger, Millie waved a slip of message paper.

"Chief Dwyer wants to see you."

"Oh?" Hastings was aware of a slight sinking feeling, a conditioned response. Like Friedman—because of Friedman—Hastings distrusted politicians. And Dwyer came from a long line of Irish policemen, most of them adroit departmental politicians. For Dwyer, survival was the first virtue. Followed by backslapping good fellowship. Followed at a distance by conviction and integrity.

"When?"

"As soon as you come in." Millie's smile was friendly but noncommittal. A good-looking woman in her middle thirties and a single mother struggling to raise a rebellious teen-age daughter, Millie was an amiable object of lust. Her skill in refusing dates— all dates—was a staple of squadroom banter.

"I'll go right up," Hastings said. "After I relieve myself, that is. Anything else?"

"Lieutenant Friedman said to tell you that, yes, Bruce Carr was killed with a twenty-two."

Hastings nodded. "Good." Then, a second thought: "I guess."

"Ah, Frank." Dwyer's ruddy face was glowing with pleasure at this meeting; his handshake was locker-room robust, his stocky body handball-fit. His face was handsomely squared off, his gray hair was thick and curly, the perfect complement to the robust hue of his face. His blue eyes sparkled as he held the handshake, guiding Hastings to one end of a leather sofa. "Sit down, Frank."

As he obeyed, Hastings reflected that, during a dozen-odd visits to this office, he had never before been invited to sit with Dwyer on the sofa. Always before, they'd been separated by the chief's formidable desk.

"I spoke to Pete an hour or two ago," Dwyer said. He smiled: the smile that, over the years, had graced countless newspapers and TV screens. "I wanted to give you the word I got from Mark Hauser this morning."

Mark Hauser, San Francisco's District Attorney, an adroit operator whose media smile was almost a match for Dwyer's.

The smile that now began to fade, giving way smoothly to an expression of gravity that was perhaps touched with regret.

"Hauser was calling about the Carr murder."

"Oh?" The question registered surprise. Where was Dwyer going with the soft-sell conversation? What was the angle—the inevitable angle?

"Or," Dwyer said, "as the papers are already billing it, the Rabelais Murders. Plural."

"Ah . . ." To himself, Hastings nodded. Here it was: the angle. Of course, the DA would be a member of Rabelais, along with the governor, the mayor, and certain selected minor department heads and politicians, most of them lawyers.

"I can see," Dwyer said, "that you're ahead of me."

Hastings made no reply.

"The request I got from Hauser," Dwyer said, "was that we keep a very low profile on this one. Hauser wants to minimize any sensationalism. And, of course, I agree. We've got a job to do, and we'll do it. But we aren't in the business of selling papers or boosting TV ratings. Right?"

Hastings smiled covertly: a small, secretly resigned smile. But there was no way out. Requiring, therefore, that he nod. Dutifully responding: "You don't want us to work the Rabelais connection too hard. Is that it?"

Dwyer's reply was brief and brittle: "I want you to put the cuffs on whoever's killing these guys. No more, no less. Now—" With the air of a man getting down to business, Dwyer dropped his voice as, yes, the genial sparkle in his blue eyes faded. "Now, I don't have to tell you that Pete Friedman has a hard-on for the privileged classes, or whatever you want to call them. Well, we all have our hang-ups. That's Pete's hang-up, and Pete's welcome to it, as long as it doesn't make my job tougher. I've warned Pete, though, to be careful what he says to reporters when he talks about Rabelais. And I'm warning you, too, Frank." All the geniality was gone from Dwyer's face now; it was bare-knuckle time.

Holding the other man's eyes, Hastings spoke quietly, measuring each word. "I think these murders have something to do with Rabelais. Maybe a lot to do with Rabelais. And I know of at least one reporter who's probably thinking the same way."

"Dan Kanter, you mean."

"He's the one I was thinking about, yes. There're probably others, though."

"Yeah. Well—" Dwyer spoke heavily, meaningfully. "Well, to be perfectly blunt, Frank, I'm sure that Kanter and his boss will be having a little talk. Soon."

"So much for the First Amendment." Saying it, Hastings decided not to smile.

"Kanter knows how things work. Don't worry about him."

"What about Pete and me?"

"Pete's the inside man. He can duck reporters, no problem. So far as you're concerned—" Dwyer let a hard-eyed moment of silence pass. Then, smiling, he amiably spread his hands. "So far as you're concerned, it's really very simple."

"Oh?" Hastings let his voice flatten as he said it. "Good."

"Just stay away from the Rabelais members," Dwyer said. "Don't bug them about this. In fact, don't bug them about anything. If you need information, which I'm sure you will, contact the manager. Castle. You know him, don't you?"

"I talked to him this morning."

"Ah—" Dwyer nodded. The genial smile returned, a transformation. Good actors, Hastings had once read, acted with their whole body, their whole being, from the inside out.

"Ah," Dwyer repeated, "then everything's on track, so far as you're concerned. Right?"

"Not really."

"Oh?" Once more the smile began to fade. "What's the problem?"

"The problem," Hastings said, "is that Castle hardly gave me the time of day. There's an assistant manager—Paul Butler—who's cooperating. But Castle—"

"Frank. Wait." As Dwyer raised a remonstrating hand, his fingernails caught the light. Did Dwyer use a manicurist?

"I was about to mention Butler," Dwyer said, "about to warn you about him. He's—well—he's a troublemaker, Hauser says."

"You mean like Pete? That kind of a troublemaker? And Kanter, maybe? Because if—"

"Listen, Frank—" The words cut like the crack of a whip. Now Dwyer's eyes were icy, his body tight. Against the expensive fabric of his gray flannel suit, a calculated match to his silvery hair, Dwyer's fists were clenching. "We don't have to dance around this, you and me. We don't have to bullshit each other. So I'll lay it out for you. I'll tell you, right out, that I want to go along with Hauser on this. Hauser is plugged in. That's what it means, to belong to a club like Rabelais. It means you're in the loop. And—yes—I want to be in the loop. I'm fifty-four, and I'm holding a bunch of markers like you wouldn't believe. That's to say that—yes—I've got my eye on higher office, as the saying goes. And someone like Hauser—*especially* someone like Hauser—is exactly the connection I need. So when he says 'Jump,' I say 'How high?' Now, I'm sure you've figured all this out already. So the question is—" Sitting on the leather sofa, Dwyer squared his body with Hastings's as he said, "The question is, Frank, what you'd say, when I say 'Jump'?"

During this moment, Hastings realized—this moment, and the next moment—he must not speak. Instead, he must focus on the primary test: those ice-blue eyes, boring in. Not sparkling blue, not now. Ice blue.

"That's not a question I'd ask Friedman." Dwyer spoke as softly as a lover might. "But it's a question I'm asking you."

"I guess," Hastings said, "that if you said 'Jump,' then I'd ask 'Why?' "

Dwyer's smile was rueful now; his sigh was regretful. "Yes," he said, nodding. "Yes, I guess you would. I guess I should've known."

. . .

"I have to say," Friedman said, "that I'm amazed. What if you'd been wearing a wire, for God's sake?"

"More?" Hastings pointed to Friedman's empty coffee cup. In the basement cafeteria of the Hall of Justice, they sat across from each other at a long Formica table that had been stacked at one end with the dirty dishes left over from the lunch-hour rush. Except for three motorcycle policemen sitting at a companion table, the cafeteria was deserted, the normal midafternoon slump. The motorcycle policemen wore black leather jackets; their white crash helmets were on the table, three in a row. Their conversation concerned the upcoming baseball season, handicapping the preseason trades.

"No, thanks," Friedman said. He waited for Hastings to refill his own cup from the cafeteria's coffee urn. Then, grudgingly, Friedman said, "I've got to give Dwyer credit for chutzpa, though. It sounds like a straight proposition."

Hastings frowned. "Proposition?"

"Sure." Friedman shrugged. "He's always wanted to be mayor. Every police chief wants to be mayor, it's built in. So if you go along with him on this one, he'll put you in line for a deputy chief's job. That's the basic proposition."

"Except that I'm not interested."

"Now you're not interested. But Dwyer's smart. He realizes that ambition—power—is a very infectious disease. You haven't got the disease—yet. But Dwyer hopes to infect you, once you've signed on to his game plan."

Sipping his coffee, Hastings looked at the other man over the rim of his cup. Finally, setting his cup aside, Hastings spoke quietly, ominously. "This conversation is beginning to piss me off."

"Oh?"

"The last I heard, neither one of us was interested in all the shit captains and above have to swallow. And, especially, we weren't interested in playing ball on Dwyer's team." Watching for the words to register, he paused. Then, very seriously: "Right?"

"Hey—" Suddenly Friedman smiled: a big, amiable, uncharacteristic smile, the spontaneous Friedman, a rare sight to see. "Hey, you know who you sound like, don't you, when you say 'Right' like that?"

Hastings allowed himself another moment of virtuous indignation before a smile broke through. "I guess you mean Dwyer."

"I guess I do."

"I guess you—"

"*Hey.*" A third voice chortled. "*Look.* I've got 'em both, my two targets of opportunity." Coming away from the coffee urn, carrying a cup of coffee and a bran muffin, Dan Kanter strode gingerly toward them as he eyed his coffee, which had already spilled. "Join you?"

"Sure." Friedman moved a chair away from the table, making room. "What's doing? Or is that what you're supposed to ask us?"

"What's doing," Kanter said, "is this Rabelais connection." He bit into the muffin, sipped the steaming-hot coffee. "Pure gold, mark my words, guys. Pure gold. Remember that you heard it here first." Then, grimacing: "God, this coffee doesn't get any better, does it?"

"Pure gold circulationwise, you mean," Friedman said.

"Naturally. The great unwashed populace loves it when fat cats get murdered. The more we give them on this one, the more they want."

"Did you say 'we'?" Hastings asked. Repeating: " 'We'?"

Kanter's answering smile was smug. "A slip of the tongue." Then, all business: "So how're you doing at Rabelais?" He addressed the question to Hastings. "They still stiffing you? If they are, I can help. No sweat."

Hastings and Friedman exchanged a brief, speculative glance. Then, experimentally, Friedman said, "If I were you, Dan, I wouldn't bet the farm on the Rabelais connection."

"Oh?" It was a quick, acute question, tracked by Kanter's eyes, sharp focused behind his thick, heavily rimmed glasses. "How's that?"

"Because," Friedman said as he raised three fingers, "there's an odds-on chance, in my opinion, that, one, these guys were killed because they belonged to Rabelais, or, two, they were killed because they're rich, and just happened to belong to Rabelais, which a lot of rich guys do, or, three—" The third finger folded down. "Three, the whole thing is a coincidence, with nothing really to do with Rabelais."

"I'm told," Kanter said, "that a hollow-point twenty-two was used in all three killings." A brief, definitive pause. Then: "Are you willing to confirm that? Because if you are, then you've got to forget about coincidence. You've got to figure that these guys are connected. Am I right?"

"Before we answer that one," Friedman said, "I've got one for you."

"Fine." Kanter spread his hands expansively. "So ask."

"Do you have a line to the coroner? Is that where you're getting this stuff?"

"Hey—" Kanter's manner changed to wounded innocence. "Hey, this is my business. I gather news. People talk, and I listen. You'd be surprised how easy it is, if you bother to listen. Most people don't. Listen, I mean."

"Hmmm."

"So what about the bullets? I don't mean to press you. But I'm teeing off in a little less than an hour."

Another calculating look passed between the two detectives before, in unison, they rose from the table and walked to a far corner of the cafeteria.

"What'd you think?" Friedman asked, sotto voce. "Do we go

along with him, tell him about the bullets? It could help smoke the bad guy out."

Hastings dropped his eyes to the white tile floor. "Dwyer'll be pissed if he thinks we've talked to Kanter. Really pissed."

"What Kanter's actually doing," Friedman said, "is extending us a courtesy. He already knows about the gun and the bullets. He's just touching base."

"Why doesn't he say so?"

"That's not his style. He's a fencer."

"Like you."

"Like me."

Finally, sighing with something that was either relief or resignation, Hastings shrugged. "What the hell."

"Exactly."

21

Dressed in a blue plaid sport shirt, dark-blue polyester slacks, and white leather boating shoes, Dwyer strode to the window of his office and stood with his back to the two lieutenants. His legs were braced, his back was truculently bowed. In his hand he held a rolled-up copy of the *Sentinel*. With the newspaper, he tapped his thigh ominously, rhythmically—as a field marshal might wield his baton. Today Hastings sat in a straight-backed chair. Friedman sat in a companion chair, both of them facing Dwyer's desk. The day was Saturday, the time was ten-thirty. Like Dwyer, Hastings and Friedman were dressed casually, off duty.

Finally, with the air of a grand inquisitor confronting his victims, Dwyer turned away from the window, returned to his desk, sat in his upholstered leather chair. He opened the newspaper, spread it on the desk. For a moment he sat silently, staring down at the paper. Finally he raised his eyes, looked first at Hastings, then at Friedman. Dwyer spoke very deliberately, measuring the words as precisely as a chemist might measure poison.

"The reason I called both of you at seven o'clock on a Saturday morning is that District Attorney Hauser called me at six-thirty. He was calling, as you might imagine, about this—" He pointed a rigid forefinger at the newspaper, then looked at each of the two detectives in turn. "You have, I suppose, read Kanter's piece."

As Hastings nodded, his peripheral vision registered Friedman's hand moving to the pocket of his belly-bulged sport shirt. It was a familiar mannerism; incredibly, Friedman was reaching for the first cigar of the day.

Eyeing the gesture, Dwyer said, "You probably don't realize it, Pete, but I quit smoking about six months ago. Actually, it's been almost seven months ago now."

"Ah . . ." As if the statement confirmed a long-suspected deficit in Dwyer's personality, Friedman nodded sympathetically. "Yes, I see. Good for you." But, yes, he returned the cigar to the pocket of his shirt.

Boring in, Dwyer's ice-blue eyes locked with Friedman's soft, inscrutably bland brown-eyed stare, Dwyer demanded, "*Did* you see Kanter's piece?"

As if the question required thought, Friedman frowned. Then, nodding, he said, "Oh, yeah, I read it."

"The two of you," Dwyer said, "talked to Kanter yesterday, shortly after we talked." He swept both men with a single embittered glance. "Isn't that so?"

111

In unison, they nodded silently.

"About two hours," Dwyer pressed, "before Kanter's deadline. Right?"

Friedman nodded again, casually said, "Yeah, I suppose so."

"Which means," Dwyer said, "that he wrote this story—" Once more he pointed to the paper. "He wrote this story between the time he talked to the two of you in the cafeteria and the time they locked up the *Sentinel* for this morning's edition."

Friedman shrugged. "I guess so, yeah. The timing sounds about right. Of course, Kanter said he was playing golf yesterday afternoon."

"Golf, eh?"

Friedman nodded, his eyes round and innocent.

"And you believed he was going to play golf?"

Friedman frowned, looked at Hastings for confirmation. Saying: "I didn't think much about it one way or the other. Did you, Frank?"

On cue, Hastings shook his head.

"Okay—" Making an obvious effort to control himself, the bad cop with the ruddy, blue-eyed, white-haired Irish good looks, Dwyer nodded. Repeating: "Okay. So I guess you can call the next question."

As he turned to look at Hastings, Friedman's full lips upcurved in a gentle smile. It was Hastings's turn.

"You're wondering what we said to Kanter," Hastings said.

Dwyer nodded grimly. "That's exactly what I'm wondering."

"Well," Hastings said, "mostly we just listened. By that time—yesterday—he pretty much had everything figured out."

"He told you that—told you what we had on the murders?"

Hastings nodded.

"He told you he knew about the ballistics match on all three murders?"

"Well, that's not strictly true, of course. They're all twenty-twos, but that's all we've—"

"You know what I mean, Frank. Don't play word games with me."

Concentrating on holding his eyes steady, locked with Dwyer's, Hastings made no reply.

"So what'd you do?" Dwyer demanded. "He's got the Rabelais connection, we already know that. And now he's got the ballistics connection. So what'd you do?" The question was directed at both men.

"For the most part," Friedman answered, his voice steady, "we just listened, like Frank said."

"Oh." Dwyer nodded furiously. "Oh. You just listened. I see. You both knew what I wanted you to do. I wanted you to cool Kanter off. But instead you just listened." Across the desk, Dwyer was beginning to breathe hard. His ruddy face was reddening. The muscles of his face were tightening, bunching up. His eyes began to protrude. Finally, speaking in a low, clotted voice, Dwyer said, "Yesterday morning I told both of you— separately—to put a muzzle on Kanter. And I told you why. Exactly why. I—I leveled with you, for God's sake. And for that—trusting the two of you—I get this." Once more, one last time, he pointed to the newspaper and the page-one story under Kanter's byline. "Christ, Kanter's got as much on this case as *I've* got."

"That's the whole point," Friedman said. "We don't have anything. We *need* something. Sometimes, when you need something, publicity helps."

"What you need," Dwyer said, "is to listen to me when I tell you to do something. Is that clear, goddammit?" Furious now, he again looked from one man to the other. "What you need, goddammit, is to learn two little words—'no comment.' You don't nod. You don't smile. You say 'No comment.' Have you *got* that?"

Instead of replying, Friedman turned to Hastings. "What we should've done, Frank, is tell Kanter to talk to the chief." As if he were reflecting, Friedman nodded mock-somberly. "Yeah, that's what we should've done."

Behind his large, uncluttered desk, struggling for control, Dwyer sat as still and as silent as a judge, deliberating. Finally, as if he were about to pass sentence, he said, "Both of you have the same problem. You've got no feel for politics. You want to get along, you've got to go along. It's the way the world works."

In bogus agreement, Friedman nodded, sighed. "The world, yeah. There's the world. But then—" A delicately timed pause. "But then there's us."

"No . . ." Icily controlled now, Dwyer shook his head. "You've got that wrong, Pete. There's the world, all right. And there's you, that's true. But then—" Dwyer's pause was diabolically precise. "But then there's me. And I'm the one who's going to make sure neither one of you ever makes captain, if this thing blows up for me."

In unison, Friedman and Hastings nodded, exchanged sidelong glances—suppressed small-boy smiles.

22

Naked, Phillips sat up in bed, turned to his right to switch on a bedside lamp, then twisted to look at her. She lay on her back, her face exquisitely profiled against the sheen of the white pillow. The sheets and pillow cases were silk, one of his indulgences. She'd pulled the sheet up to cover her breasts; her hands were folded serenely across her stomach, just above the pubis. She wore only one ring: the emerald he'd presented over dinner, his birthday gift to her. Until now, tonight, she'd preferred not to wear rings. Thus, on her thirtieth birthday, he'd forced a choice on her, imposed his will.

Until now, imposed his will.

"I don't think I'm getting this," Phillips said. He smiled: a slow, complacent smile. "I suppose coitus dulls the mind. Would you run that by me again?"

"I said," she answered, "that I've decided this is-the time for me to make some changes. Call them midcourse corrections. After all, in thirty more years, I'll be sixty. Or, more to the point, I'll be forty ten years from now." She smiled: that small, private smile, always Penny's little secret. "My assets will be sagging by that time. And I don't intend to be caught by surprise." She spoke as she always spoke: in her upper-class English accent, coolly and calmly and archly matter-of-fact. And, yes, enchanting. He'd never known anyone like her—never had anyone like her.

"So? What's the bottom line?"

"Ah. Yes. The bottom line." Gently she mocked him, ever so British.

Matching the mockery, he spoke ironically. "Sorry. I didn't mean to speak businesseze. I know how it offends your sensibilities."

"Since it isn't your native tongue," she answered, "I assume you were putting me on. Am I right?"

"Tell me about your birthday blues. Then we can play word games. And by then . . ." He touched her stomach just above her navel. It was one of her preerogenous zones, she'd once told him. One of several.

Still looking up at the ceiling, her face still perfectly profiled, her long, dark hair overspreading the silken pillow, all of it perfection, she said, "It's not the birthday blues, Brandon. So don't patronize me. That's what you do, you know. You with your fame and your fortune, on your many and varied power trips—you patronize me. You don't realize it. But you do."

"I only patronize inferiors. Of which, I'll admit, there are legions. But not you, Penny." He smiled. "Even if you sagged, I'd never patronize you. In fact, somewhere in the secret recesses of my soul, I sometimes hear a small voice saying 'She's

116

smarter than you are.' Admittedly, the voice is only a whisper. But still—" Leaning closer, he let his finger wander. Beneath the silk of the sheet, her flesh offered a special excitement. Word games or sex games—with Penny, the excitement was always there, always heightened by the unexpected, the unpredictable, the inventive, sometimes the utterly abandoned and ribald.

But, even as he felt himself quickening, he also felt the endless tug of expediency beginning. Soon, within the hour, he must be in his car, driving to his home. It would be after midnight on a Friday night before he got home. In her bedroom, beautiful in a lace nightgown, Jeannie would be watching TV.

Beautiful, but drunk.

"Are we still talking about me?" Penny asked. "Or are we on you now?"

"We're still on you. But quickly, please. Be concise. And then—" He touched her breast, a delicate tracery of fingertips on silk.

As if she were disconnected from the sensation he knew she was feeling, she said, "I think I need to be alone for a while."

"Alone?" He frowned. "In what sense? For how long?" As he said it, he touched the silken rose of her nipple. It was as if he were stimulating his own genitalia, his coupled with hers. Could she guess, even remotely guess, at the power she held over him?

"For as long as it takes to find a suitable man and marry him and get on with the business of having children. Two, I think."

As if the movement were independent of his will, he realized that his hand was no longer touching her. His genitals were no longer tumescent. At the center of himself, there was suddenly a void. He realized that his eyes were fixated on the emerald. Only hours ago, when she'd slipped on the ring, he'd felt that, yes, she was finally his. Had she known when she'd accepted the ring that she would say this to him—do this to him? When

117

she'd smiled at him so intimately across the table, when she'd touched his hand, almost a maiden's gesture, had she known she intended to say this?

"You're the most exciting man I've ever known, Brandon. You're rich and you're powerful and you're very, very smart. You're a complex, imaginative, surprising man. And, for the reasons noted above, you're a world-class lay." As she said it she smiled: that subtle, complex smile he'd always known he would never forget.

"But—" Now, genuinely regretful, she smiled. "But you aren't the man I'm going to marry, Brandon. I don't know who he is, not now. But he's not you, that's all I know."

"Now, listen, Penny, this isn't something we can settle now. Not in ten minutes, here's your hat and thanks for everything. You know it, and I know it. We're—Christ—we *belong* to each other. We're a fit. We—"

On the floor below, a buzzer abruptly sounded. It was the front door. At eleven-thirty on a Friday night, someone was ringing her front doorbell.

"Jesus." Startled, he reflexively drew away from her, sat up straight in bed, faced the open bedroom door. "Who the hell is that?"

"I can't imagine." Also facing the open doorway, also sitting up in bed, her breasts exposed, she was frowning.

"If this was New York twenty-five years ago," he said, "I'd think Jeannie had hired a private eye, a photographer, for a divorce action." At the thought, he smiled. Adding: "Anything's possible, I suppose."

As, once more, the buzzer sounded: a longer, more insistent peal. Listening, Phillips visualized the first floor, and the entryway, and the front door. The downstairs was in darkness. The entryway was generously proportioned. And, yes, there was a peephole in the good, solid oaken door.

"Is the door double locked?" he asked. "Bolted?"

"I imagine so. It's habit, you know. Rote. Who can ever tell these things for sure?"

Another peal, this one also insistent.

"Can you see someone at the door from the front bedroom window?"

"No."

Now the sound of knocking began, a measured succession of meaningful knuckle raps.

"Whoever it is," he said, "he's not going away."

"I wonder if it could be an emergency. You know—the police, telling everyone we've got to turn off the gas, something like that."

"It's not the police," he answered, his voice low and tight. "If it was the police, they'd be banging at the door. Not—"

Once more the door buzzer.

"*Shit!*" He threw back the covers, went to the chair on his side of the bed, slipped into his shorts. His jacket hung neatly on the back of the chair; his shirt and tie and underwear were draped on the seat. Two years ago, when they'd first met, in love's abandon, they'd thrown their clothes on the floor.

His attaché case stood on the floor beside the chair. On the dresser—his side of the dresser—he'd put his keys, his loose change, his billfold. Debating, he decided to take the keys, unlock the attaché case, which he opened flat on the floor. A revolver nestled in its own inletted recess.

"Jesus," she breathed, "what's that?"

"It's a three fifty-seven Magnum."

"D-do you—have you always carried it? In that attaché case?"

"That's right." With the revolver in his right hand, he used his left hand to unlatch the cylinder, let it swing out. Yes, the pistol was loaded. All six chambers.

"Jesus, Brandon. Let's think about this."

"I don't intend to shoot anyone. But I don't intend to take any chances, either. Turn off the light."

119

"I want to get dressed."

"Get dressed in the dark, then."

Obediently arching her smooth, supple body, she leaned across the bed, switched off the bedside lamp. In the last moment of light, he saw her eyes. She was both apprehensive and excited. In her upper-class, ladylike way, Penny could be turned on by danger. On a dare, she'd once learned to parachute. She'd made four jumps; she'd never felt more alive, she'd said.

"You stay here, in the bedroom. I'll see what it's all about."

"Be careful, for God's sake. Don't do anything foolish."

"Don't worry." He went out into the hallway, walked into the front bedroom, cautiously drew back the curtains.

As, again, the buzzer sounded.

Someone, then, at that moment, was standing on the tiny front stoop, pressing the doorbell.

In his bare feet, with the .357 in his right hand, he went to the head of the stairway. The stairs led directly down to the front entryway. Slowly, soundlessly, with his left hand gripping the carved balustrade, he began descending the staircase. The front door opened from the right, outside. Was the bell button also on the right? The front stoop was no more than a single large step, perhaps a foot above ground level. Did shrubbery grow close to the door? He couldn't remember. He'd bought the house soon after they met—an "investment," he'd told Penny. "A love nest, more like it," she'd retorted mischievously. Adding quickly: "But I love it. I really do."

At the floor level now, less than ten feet from the front door, he was standing motionless, listening. His mouth, he realized, was slightly open. One could hear better, he'd once read, if the mouth was slightly open, a miscellaneous bit of meaningless information.

Silence.

Except for the sound of a car passing in front of the house, nothing stirred.

One slow, soundless barefooted step at a time, he was advancing toward the front door. On the walnut grip of the revolver, his palm was sweating; the grip was slick. He shifted the pistol to his left hand, rubbed his right palm on the seat of his shorts, returned the revolver to his right hand. Within arm's length of the front door now, he rested the fingertips of his left hand on the oak paneling. Then, holding his breath, he raised his eye to the magnifying optical peephole. In the wide-angle lens, he saw the small front garden and the sidewalk and the street beyond the garden—and nothing else. He could even see the shrubbery beside the door. Unless the intruder was crouched on his hands and knees beneath the peephole, close to the door, there was no one out there, and therefore no danger.

Should he ease open the door, look for a crouching figure on the stoop? He pressed his ear to the door. Nothing. Aware of a sudden warm rush of relief, the flip side of fear, he stepped away from the door, straightened, drew a long, slow breath, surprisingly tremulous.

Had he ever been afraid? How could he know? How could he confess fear to himself?

One cautious step at a time, he was backing toward the stairs. From behind, up the stairs, he sensed movement. Penny, in jeans and a shirt at the top of the stairs. Of course she hadn't obeyed him, hadn't stayed in the bedroom.

With the revolver lowered, muzzle down, he turned his back on the front door, began climbing the stairs. Soon it would be midnight, his witching hour. The successful philanderer kept faith with the one who waited. Therefore, he would take a quick shower. Then he would dress. Then he would—

The sound of the buzzer split the silence, seemed to shatter the darkness.

"Ah—" It was a stifled, inarticulate monosyllable, the sudden rush of fury, blind to caution, to consequences. A half-dozen steps took him to the peephole. Nothing had changed. Could it be a child, too short to be seen—a pint-sized prankster? He drew back the security bolt, turned the door knob, let the door come open.

But how could—why would—?

An explosion. An orange ball of fire.

He was staggering back, struggling to keep his balance, struggling to stay on his feet. It was a primal urge. To fall was to die; the pack would attack. He was struggling to bring the revolver up. Another explosion, another blossom of orange fire. But now there was no sound. And the pain had gone, a numbness now.

The revolver—where was the revolver?

Penny. Had Penny . . . ?

23

"According to the lady," Canelli said, "he was a big-shot criminal lawyer. Brandon Phillips." Canelli frowned, shook his head. "I never heard of him, I don't think."

"I have." Hastings yawned, blinked, glanced at his watch. One-thirty, and counting. "And she's right. He was a big shot. He operated all over the country."

"But does he live here? In San Francisco?"

"As far as I know, he does."

"Jeez . . ." It was an awestruck rejoinder, one of Canelli's revelations. "What'll you bet he belonged to Rabelais?"

Hastings looked down at the victim, sprawled faceup on the parquet floor of the entryway. Automatically he visualized the preliminary scene-of-the-crime report: White male, middle aged. A hundred eighty pounds, perhaps twenty pounds overweight for his height and frame. Regular features, full head of medium gray hair, medium long. Clothing: a pair of white boxer shorts, bloodstained. Jewelry, one ring with a large blue stone, possibly a star sapphire, no wristwatch. Torso completely bloodstained, beginning to coagulate. Head bloody on right side. Blood pooled beneath the body, also coagulating. Significant objects and physical findings: one large-caliber stainless-steel revolver with four-inch barrel, possibly a Ruger. Preliminary on-scene conclusion: victim opened the front door in response to a burglar's ring, threatened burglar with revolver. No indication that victim's revolver was fired, no sign of a struggle. Time of homicide: 11:30 P.M.

"What about the coroner?" Hastings asked. "What's the delay?"

"Jeez, Lieutenant, I guess you didn't hear about that goddam explosion and fire at a gay bar south of Market. They figure it was gas. Three dead, I heard. Marsten and Lieutenant Friedman are over there. Then there's the usual Friday night action—a knifing, a shooting out at Hunter's Point. So—" Canelli interrupted himself, looked up. *"Ah."* He smiled, pointed to the coroner's van turning the corner of Alvarado and Diamond, coming toward them. "Speak of the devil."

"What about shell casings?" Hastings pointed to two lab technicians working with hand-held floodlights and cameras. "Anything?"

"Nothing," Canelli answered. "But, jeez, all this goddam shrubbery, it could take days to find anything."

Hastings looked through the open front door of the small two-story Edwardian town house and up the central staircase. It was down these stairs that Brandon Phillips had come, nearly naked, revolver in his hand, to open the door to his murderer.

"Where's the woman?" Hastings asked.

Canelli gestured to the stairway. "She's upstairs in the bedroom, Lieutenant. First door on the right at the head of the stairs. The way he's laying—" Canelli pointed to the body. "—We can't close the door without moving his leg there. Breaking the rules, in other words. So, jeez, the house is cold, with the front door open. And if you run the goddam furnace, you heat the whole outdoors. It's only forty degrees, you know. So I told her to stay in the bedroom with the door closed, get into bed, whatever. She's real nice, you know. British. A looker."

"What's her name?"

"It's Penelope Weston, how about that? I mean—" Canelli grinned. "I mean, how many women have you ever known named Penelope?"

Hastings gestured to the lab technicians. "If they don't find any shell casings, I want you to post an all-night guard. I want this fully secured, until the techs can come back tomorrow, in daylight."

"Yessir."

"And see that the coroner's guys pay attention to what they're doing. If this guy *did* belong to Rabelais the media is going to be all over this one. So I want lots of documentation. *Lots* of it."

"Yessir."

Hastings moved his head in the direction of the stairway. "I'm going to talk to Penelope Weston. Come tell me when you're ready to move the body."

"Yessir."

Hastings knocked twice. "Miss Weston?"

A moment passed, followed by a blurred voice: "Yes? Who is it?"

"It's Lieutenant Frank Hastings. I'm co-commander of Homicide. Can I come in?"

"Yes . . . come in."

He pushed open the door, entered the bedroom. The room was imaginatively furnished, a mix of antiques and modern. One wall was covered by paintings. The bed was queen size; the bedclothing was quilted and ruffled and fluffed, complementing the antiques. Wearing an incongruous Giants sweatshirt, Penelope Weston was sitting up in bed with two huge ruffled pillows at her back. She was in her late twenties or early thirties; her oval face was framed by loose shoulder-length brown hair. Against the pallor of her face, her eyes were large and dark and stricken. She gripped the silken counterpane with both hands, as if she were afraid to let go. Her voice was low and husky, also stricken.

"It's so cold," she said. "I can't seem to get warm." She tried to smile, a brave effort that failed. "I don't usually receive men whilst I'm in bed." She spoke with a cultivated English accent; her eyes were fixed on his as if she were a small, vulnerable child desperately seeking reassurance.

"We've got to leave the front door open for a while," Hastings said, "so it doesn't make sense to have the furnace on." As he spoke, he went to a small, delicately carved chair. Was the chair intended to support his two hundred pounds?

"Please—" She released the counterpane with one hand, gestured to the chair. "Sit down, Lieutenant." The gesture was graceful, an evocation of good schools and lessons in etiquette.

"Thanks."

"It's shock, I suppose," she said. "The cold, I mean, the reason I'm so cold. It's shock. I—God—" Once more she was gripping the counterpane with both hands, a desperate grip. "I saw it, you know. I was standing at the top of the stairs, and I saw him get shot. I saw—" Suddenly she broke off, shuddered, began shaking her head. "I was paralyzed, I remember. Absolutely paralyzed. All I could think of was what would happen if he came up the stairs after me, and I couldn't run. That's

126

all I could think about. I—Christ—Brandon was lying there, dying. And all I could think about was why I couldn't run."

"People do unpredictable things when they're in danger," Hastings said. "Everyone does. Without exception."

"I've never been in danger." She said it softly, musingly. "I was in an automobile when it rolled over up in the Sierras during a snowstorm. But—" She let it die, then began shaking her head. Now she seemed dazed, confused by her own thoughts.

"Did you actually see the assailant?" Trying to bring her back, focus her attention, Hastings put an edge on the question.

She shook her head. "No. He—first he started ringing the doorbell and knocking. I thought it was a prankster, maybe a teenager, from the neighborhood. Then I thought maybe Brandon's wife had hired a private detective to harass us, maybe even get pictures. Brandon said the same thing, except that he was joking. But then Brandon began to get angry. He got his gun—he kept it in his attaché case—and we turned off all the lights, and he went down the stairs to investigate. But then it stopped, just when he got to the front door. The doorbell ringing and the knocking, I mean. It stopped. So he started to come back here, upstairs. But, God, it started again, when he'd just gotten on the stairs. So then he got mad. He had a temper, and I could tell he'd had enough. He was by God going to kick someone's ass. So he went back down the stairs, and unbolted the door, and jerked it open. And then—" Suddenly she sobbed: a single wracking sob, torn from the depths of her. To this woman, Hastings realized, crying didn't come naturally. When she cried, it wasn't meant for the effect.

"And then . . . ?" Hastings prompted.

"And then there were the shots."

"How many shots?"

"Two, I think." She frowned. "Or maybe three. I can't remember."

"Phillips didn't fire a shot from his gun."

"I—I don't know. All I heard was the noise—the explosions."

"Did Phillips say anything?"

"I think he just—just sighed. He didn't scream, didn't yell, nothing like that. He—it seemed as if he were disappointed at something. Like he was—you know—dismayed, at what happened. And tired, too. Very tired. Because suddenly he sat down on the floor, as if his legs were weak. Then he—he just sighed again, and lay down."

"You say the murderer was a man. Why do you say that?"

"It—" As if the question baffled her, required more energy than she possessed to frame an answer, she shook her head. "I don't know. It's—I suppose it's usage. Anyone that's anonymous is called 'him.' It's—" She released the counterpane, made a small, fretful gesture. "It's grammar, that's all."

"You mentioned Mr. Phillips's wife, said she might've hired a detective." Watching for a reaction, Hastings paused. There was no reaction. Only her dark, tragic eyes, staring at him. "So I'm assuming that the two of you—you and Mr. Phillips—were lovers."

Now, for the first time, her face registered something beyond the numbness of shock. She drew a deep, resigned breath. "We were lovers, yes. But—God—tonight I told him that it was over. I said I wanted a husband, children. Had I but known—" An ironic sigh, a bitter twisting of the mouth, a gesture of the hand that protested the ruthlessness of fate. "Had I but known that all I had to do was give it an hour or two . . ." For a moment she lay silently, seemingly passive. Then, explosively: *"Shit!"* Still sitting up in bed, her body suddenly tightened, then twisted, as if she were fighting off an enemy.

Penelope Weston was herself again, coming out of shock. Fair game.

"Back to his wife," Hastings said. "Were they living together?"

She nodded. "They live—lived—in Seacliff."

"Is she aware that you and her husband were lovers?"

Defiant now, she raised her chin, hardened her gaze. "I've no idea, Lieutenant. None at all. I'm afraid you'll have to ask her that question yourself." Her English accent had broadened, deepened, developed a cutting edge. It was encouraging, something to push against.

"I intend to ask her."

"Why?"

He frowned. " 'Why'?"

"Someone comes to my door and makes a nuisance of himself. A burglar, I'd think—high on drugs, out of his skull. When he saw Brandon's gun, he panicked. He shot Brandon, and then ran away before anyone saw him, saw his face."

Hastings decided to smile. "That's certainly a possibility."

"So why poke about in his marriage, his private life?"

"Because," Hastings answered, "it's *only* a possibility. One possibility. There're others. And, according to the statistics, when a husband's been cheating on his wife and he gets killed, the chances are better than fifty-fifty that his wife did it. Or, if she's wealthy, maybe she hired someone to do it. That happens, by the way. More often than you might think."

"Jesus . . ." As if she pitied him, she shook her head. Then, speaking thoughtfully, speculatively, her dark eyes attentive now, no longer large with shock, she said, "Is this what you do—poke around in the muck?"

He hardened his gaze, hardened his voice. "Murder's a messy business, Miss Weston."

"A dirty job, but someone's got to do it. Is that it?" Her smile was wry, ironic.

"That's it exactly." He sat silently for a moment, watching her. "A looker," Canelli had said. Yes, now he could see it: a patrician face, and the manners to match. All of it made more intriguing by a quick, agile mind and a quicksilver irreverence that added the spice of unpredictability. If the body and the moves matched the face and the intellect, Penelope Weston would be irresistible.

"Tell me about Brandon Phillips." It was an order, not a request. At two o'clock in the morning, it was time for hardball, get in and get out—get home, get back to bed.

"He was a brilliant lawyer," she answered promptly. Then, a test: "Didn't you know that?"

He sighed. "Miss Weston. Let me ask the questions, okay? It's late. Both of us need sleep."

"I don't expect to get much sleep tonight." She spoke ruefully. Then, when he made no reply, she began again. "He was a famous criminal lawyer. That's why I thought you'd know of him—because he's conducted the defense in some famous criminal trials."

"I imagine," Hastings said, "that he had enemies."

As if she were indifferent to the question, she shrugged. "I suppose so."

"He was a criminal lawyer," Hastings pressed. "His business was dealing with criminals—murderers, a lot of them. In a business like his, people get killed."

"To be perfectly honest, Lieutenant, Brandon and I almost never talked about business. Or, at least, not his business."

"What business, then? Yours?"

"As a matter of fact, yes. I have an art gallery on Sutter Street. It's quite successful, actually. We were partners in the business, Brandon and I." As if she were reconsidering, she broke off. Then she decided to admit "When I say we're partners, what I really mean is that Brandon put up the money. The silent partner, in other words. Just like—" She gestured to include the room, the house. The gesture was accompanied by a rueful twist of her lips. "Just like he bought this house when we began seeing each other. An investment, he said."

"I don't think you much liked the arrangement." He ventured a person-to-person smile. "Am I right?"

As she looked at him, her expression turned speculative, then man-to-woman candid. "Brandon Phillips was the most exciting man I've ever known. He introduced me to a life that I'd never have seen otherwise. He was rich, and he was generous, and he was a first-class lover." Measuring his reaction to what she'd said, she calmly, coolly let a moment pass as she watched him. Finally: "I'll miss him. Even when I told him we had to break up, I knew I'd miss him. And now—" She sighed, shifted her body beneath the covers. "And now there'll be the guilt, the regret." As she spoke, she turned her head away from him. Was she going to cry, really cry? To forestall the possibility, break up the rhythm, Hastings rose. Saying: "There's just one more question, Miss Weston. Then I'll leave you in peace."

"Oh?" With obvious effort, she turned to look at him. "What's that?" Suddenly exhausted, she spoke softly, without inflection.

"Did Brandon Phillips belong to Rabelais?"

"As a matter of fact, he did. Why?"

"Just checking. Good night, Miss Weston. I hope you can sleep. You'll be guarded, the front of the house and the back, too."

"Thank you."

24

Trick or treat, the children called it. *All Hallows Eve*, a night for pranksters. Ring the doorbell, wait until the door opens, shout something silly, scamper off into the darkness.

He'd never done it as a child.

Even if he'd had the chance, been willing, his mother would never have allowed it. Unthinkable, she would have pronounced, that he would join the rabble, do what other children did, shout and shriek and run and romp. "Remember," she would say. "You must always remember. Special people do special things."

Vividly he could recall her voice as she said it: that soft, melodious cadence. And the caress. And then the two sensations fusing, forever a unity. Sound and touch. And, yes, sight: her face, forever etched in his consciousness, that face in the likeness of her cameo, the one she left for him so long ago. It was an eternal likeness, therefore an icon. Sometimes, fearing robbery, or a fire, he kept it with him.

But not tonight. And not the other nights, either. Because it was essential, he knew, to compartmentalize, keep perspective, keep the power separated from the objective, keep the essence pure.

All Hallows Eve . . .

Children, playing their games.

Children in a pack: vicious, remorseless. Animals, bloody at tooth and claw, falling on their prey. Small boys, transformed into monsters. Banshee screams, eyes wide and wild. Dragons' eyes blazing.

Only behind the fence had he been safe. Only behind those thick iron bars. But then the girls had come in their starched dresses, simpering, their voices so sharp, their eyes so malevolent.

Running. Endlessly running. If the others were animals, then so was he: a small, desperate animal, scampering away, burrowing, always bleating, terrified.

All his life, all those lengthening years, terrified. So alone. So afraid.

But only until now. Only until he saw the blood bright on their flesh. Only until he heard the blood gurgling in their throats. Only until he saw them fall, saw their eyes turn to stone. Only now was he free. Because boys became men. And men must pay.

So that now, sitting here in this darkened room in front of this empty fireplace, he could once more allow his eyes to close as he let his thoughts return to the instant the pistol came alive in his hand and the blood blossomed on Brandon Phillips's naked chest.

25

"Don't tell me," Friedman's voice said on the other end of the telephone line. "The guy was rich and famous and belonged to Rabelais."

"I know you had a late night, too," Hastings said. "But I thought we should talk before one of us calls Dwyer."

"Or, more to the point—" Friedman broke off, yawned noisily. "More to the point, before Dwyer calls us."

"Hmmm."

"What're the details?"

"It's Brandon Phillips. Ring a bell?"

"Huh?" It was as close as Friedman ever came to registering surprise, losing his cool. "That's a big fish. Same MO?"

"Yes and no. The locale was inside, not on the street. Phillips was shacked up with his girlfriend in Noe Valley. It's a house, a small two-story Victorian. Someone rang the doorbell repeatedly. Brandon had a gun. He went downstairs to investigate. He opened the door and got shot."

"The murder weapon, of course, was a twenty-two automatic firing hollow points."

"Probably."

"And silenced, doubtless."

"I'm not sure."

"Shell casings?"

"So far, no. But there's a lot of shrubbery around the porch. I left a black-and-white unit there last night—two units, in fact. And the techs'll be back this morning."

"It's odds-on," Friedman said, "that this guy isn't just killing rich guys. He's killing Rabelais members."

"Looks like it."

"This guy's got a plan. An agenda. And he doesn't make mistakes. He's four for four, for God's sake."

Hastings agreed morosely.

"So what orders do we get from our beloved Chief Dwyer? Lay off, he says."

"He doesn't really say lay off," Hastings answered. "He just wants to call the shots. Which, after all, is his privilege. He's the chief."

"If this thing blows up," Friedman pronounced, "Dwyer's going to hand us the shitty end of the stick. You know that, don't you?"

"Blows up?"

"Right now," Friedman said, "Dwyer's actually running a cover-up, because he doesn't want to antagonize the fat cats at Rabelais. And, obviously, that's what the fat cats want—their precious privacy. But that could change. Fast. They're going to figure out that their buddies are systematically being murdered.

135

Who knows, maybe this guy intends to run right down the Rabelais membership roster. And when that sinks in, these guys are going to demand action."

"Quiet action."

"Okay," Friedman said. "Quiet action. But action. My God, four of these guys have gotten killed. Put yourself in their position. Wouldn't you start to worry? A lot?"

"So what's the plan?" Hastings asked. As he spoke, down the hallway, he saw Ann wave as she went from their bedroom to the bathroom. On a gray, cold Saturday morning in March, she'd been sleeping in. Later, after he'd had a nap, they hoped to go out for brunch.

"I think," Friedman said, speaking slowly and deliberately, "that one of us should call Dwyer and ask him to meet with both of us. Repeat, *both* of us. That way, if he tells us to lay off, we've got our asses covered, at least partially. We're each other's witnesses."

"What if he tells us he's taking personal charge of the investigation?"

Still speaking slowly, following where the logic of his own thinking led, Friedman said, "I doubt that he'd do that. Dwyer's slippery, but he's not dumb. He could be caught short. The guys at Rabelais don't want any spotlights shining on them, but they're sure as hell going to want the murderer caught. And Dwyer doesn't know shit about conducting a murder investigation."

"Okay—so who's going to call him?"

"You," Friedman answered promptly. "He likes you better than he likes me. A lot better."

"Hmmm."

"Bye."

Glowering at the hallway wall over the phone stand, Hastings broke the connection, consulted the Rolodex, reluctantly punched out Dwyer's home phone number. It was an unlisted number usually given out to captains and above. But both Hastings and Friedman had declined a captaincy, preferring instead to co-command Homicide.

"Yes?" Unmistakably Dwyer. Unmistakably short-tempered.

"It's Frank Hastings, Chief."

"I've heard about it," Dwyer snapped. "I just got off the phone with D.A. Hauser."

"I thought I should call you before I took any further action."

"What about Friedman? Does he know Phillips was murdered?"

"Yes. I just called him. He was in the field last night, too. So this is the first chance we've had to talk."

"All Hauser knows is that Phillips is dead. What're the particulars?"

"Phillips was shacked up with his girlfriend. He went to the door to confront someone who was ringing the doorbell. Phillips had a gun, a three fifty-seven, I think. But he got shot, apparently when he opened the door." Hastings was aware of the pleasure he felt describing the murder of Brandon Phillips, another fat cat, dead. When had he ever heard Dwyer sound so cautious, so harassed?

"I guess you know," Hastings said, still savoring the moment, "that Phillips belonged to Rabelais."

Ignoring the remark, Dwyer said, "Besides Rabelais, is there anything linking this one to the other three? Any physical evidence?"

"Not yet. They can't do the autopsy until this afternoon, and we weren't able to conduct a real search for the shell casings. There're just too many bushes. But if the bullets are twenty-two-caliber high-speed hollow points, I'd say that was pretty conclusive. And, to me, the entrance wounds look like they could be twenty-twos."

"What about the media? Kanter? Are they turning up the heat?"

"I don't know, Chief. I got back home about three o'clock this morning, and I just got out of bed. I've talked to Pete, and that's it."

"Yeah . . ." It was a dubious-sounding response, as if Dwyer suspected something suspicious.

"Assuming there's a match on the shell casings and the bullets," Hastings said, "how do you want us to proceed at Rabelais? Should I still stay away from everyone but the manager? Castle? Or—" A deliberate, hard-edged pause. Then, gently: "Or should I back off entirely, let you handle it?"

"Christ, Frank, I've got a whole police department to run. Can't you and Friedman handle Homicide?"

"What I want—what we need, Pete and I—are guidelines. Instructions."

"I know what you're doing, Frank. You're taking out insurance. You know that, don't you? You're aware of what you're doing."

Hastings felt the quick flush of rising anger. "Insurance?" He spoke quietly, ominously. Ann was coming out of the bathroom, the sound of a flushing toilet behind her. Seeing his face, she frowned, an anxious, unspoken question. He shrugged, grimaced, shook his head. The message: yes, it was yet another departmental hassle, politics as usual. Her expression softened sympathetically as she pantomimed a drinking gesture, offering coffee. He nodded gratefully.

"If this thing blows up, makes us look bad," Dwyer said, "you want someone to blame. Right?"

"I've already told you what I want. I want to know when I'll get a free hand. Otherwise . . ." He drew a long, grim breath. "Otherwise, I'd like to be taken off the case."

"I'm sure you and Friedman have talked about this. I'm sure I'll get the same song from Friedman."

"You'll have to ask him."

"Friedman has a problem. You know that, don't you? He

138

can't take direction, can't stand supervision. And anything he doesn't like, he calls politics. Which, in his book, is another word for shit. You're aware of that, aren't you?"

Hastings made no reply.

In the silence that followed, Hastings sensed that the other man was carefully calculating his next move. Finally: "You're limiting yourself, Frank. I want you to think about that. Friedman's going to stay right where he is. He's happy. His wife, I understand, inherited a bundle. So he can afford to play his little games. Well, that's obviously no concern of mine. What *is* a concern of mine, however, is Friedman's job performance. He's got enough money that he doesn't give a shit. So that's how he does his job—he doesn't give a shit. Well, as I say, that's his decision. But—" Another tactical pause. Then, paternally: "But I hate to see you make that mistake, Frank. I hate to see you trotting along behind Friedman. Do you understand what I'm saying?"

"Yeah," Hastings said, his voice heavy with unspoken contempt. "Yeah, I think I do see what you're saying."

"Politics is just another name for survival, Frank. They're the same side of the coin. You understand that, don't you?"

No reply.

"*Don't* you?" The two words crackled with authority.

"Why don't you talk to Pete and then get back to me? Or, better yet, why don't the three of us get together, get this straightened out?"

"Get what straightened out?"

"This investigation—guidelines."

"Is that Friedman's idea, having a meeting? Insurance?"

"I—"

"It sounds like Friedman's idea."

"Well, he—"

"I'll call Friedman. Where is he?"

"He's at home. Last night he had to—"

"Never mind the excuse, Frank. I'm sure Friedman doesn't need help with an excuse." Abruptly, the line clicked, went dead.

"By God," Friedman chortled, "you did it, Frank. You slipped it to Dwyer. Right between the second and the third ribs."

Holding the phone in his left hand and a cup of coffee in the other hand, Hastings asked, "What'd he tell you?"

"Nothing, really. He just told me what he told you—that he was trying to make a team player out of you. He used that expression twice, at least. 'Team player.' But he didn't talk like he'd had much luck."

"You're right. He didn't."

"So now," Friedman said, "odds-on, he's going to call you up and tell you to go to work, question whoever you want at Rabelais."

"I don't believe it."

"Wait and see. Check your watch. In an hour he'll call."

Sipping the coffee, Hastings made no reply.

"What you apparently did," Friedman said, "was convince Dwyer that either both of us worked on the case, no strings attached, or neither of us do. Right?"

"I *tried* to convince him."

"Yeah, well, you succeeded, old buddy. He got the message. But, naturally, he's got to save face, have the last word."

"The last word?"

"He told me," Friedman said, "that you would be allowed to work the case in the field as you see fit, no strings. But I had to keep my head down, stay away from Rabelais."

"*What?*" The spontaneous movement that accompanied the exclamation tipped the coffee cup, spilled coffee on the floor beside the phone stand. "*What?*"

"When I was in grammar school," Friedman said cheerfully,

"I spent a lot of time standing in the corner. As I look back, I figure it was time well spent."

Hastings gulped the coffee, then said, "Okay, you had to stand in the corner when you were a kid. But you're no kid, for Christ's sake. There's a *principle* involved, here."

"I understand what you're saying. But think about it. What Dwyer's telling us we've got to do is, in fact, what we usually do. You work outside, and I work inside. We—"

"But you're the *senior lieutenant*."

"Okay. So I've got seniority. So then I'll give you a direct order. Go along with the dumb son of a bitch. And don't worry about me. The last time I had to stand in the corner, I let the air out of the teacher's tires. *All* her tires."

"You're kidding."

"You know I'm not."

"How old were you?"

"Eight, I think. Maybe nine."

"Jesus."

26

"Ah, Lieutenant." Castle rose from behind his desk and gestured to a visitor's chair. The gesture was smooth and practiced, the understated flourish of a headwaiter who had made good. The smile was undertaker-solemn. "You've come about the death of Brandon Phillips." The manager of Rabelais shook his head dolefully. "It's a terrible business. Ghastly. And, I must tell you, the membership is concerned. Very concerned, as you might imagine."

Dressed in a seldom-worn three-piece suit, his best one, Hastings sat down, crossed his legs, adjusted his trouser creases. Would Dwyer be reassured, to see him dressed like this?

"I'm curious . . ." Hastings glanced at his watch. "It's only

142

been twelve hours since Mr. Phillips was killed. How'd you hear so quickly?"

"Mr.—" Castle broke off, cleared his throat. Then, cautiously: "One of our members called this morning to tell me."

"Which member was that, Mr. Castle?" As he spoke, Hastings took out his notebook and ballpoint pen, looked expectantly at the other man.

"I—ah—" Castle coughed apologetically. "I don't really think that's relevant, Lieutenant."

"Mr. Castle—" Hastings gathered himself, hardened his voice, stared at the manager until, sooner than he would have thought, Castle dropped his eyes and shifted uncomfortably in his upscale leather swivel chair. Once more the combination of silence and a long, hard, official stare had done the job, the interrogator's most effective tactic.

"Mr. Castle," he repeated, "let's get a few things straight here." Once more he waited, this time until Castle managed to lift his eyes, meet Hastings's gaze. Then, speaking very deliberately, as if he were a coach explaining the elementary rules of the game, Hastings said, "The first thing is that I decide what's relevant. Not you. Me. And the second thing is, when I ask a question, you answer. Have you got that?"

"But—" Castle moistened his pale lips, cleared his throat. "But I told you the other day, I tried to explain that—"

"This is today, Mr. Castle. And last night the fourth member of Rabelais was killed in a little more than five weeks. We've definitely got physical evidence connecting the first three murders, and by this afternoon we'll probably have the same evidence on the Brandon Phillips murder. So I'm going to ask you again, one last time. Who called you this morning?"

"Well, it—" As if he were surrendering, submitting to a disgrace, Castle spoke with deep reluctance. "It was Charles Schrader. He's—ah—president of Rabelais. This is his second term."

"And what did Mr. Schrader say? Did he tell you to do anything special?"

Castle frowned. "I don't understand."

"The last time I was here, you told me not to talk to any Rabelais member, not to question them. I suppose those orders came from Mr. Schrader."

"Well—there's an executive committee, of course. And it was one of those, Mr. Harrington, who actually told me."

"How long've you been manager here, Mr. Castle?"

"Twelve years." The answer came promptly, reflexively proud. It was, Hastings knew, the same kind of association Saks Fifth Avenue salesclerks felt, identifying with their rich and powerful customers, snobbery with a twist.

"So you were a manager when Sally Dietz was killed at your yearly retreat."

The question registered on Castle's face, revealing a sudden calculation, an instantaneous caution. And—yes—the first flicker of something that could be fear.

"Weren't you?" Hastings pressed.

"Yes," Castle answered, "I was. Except that she wasn't killed. She took drugs. Too many drugs." But his voice was low: a guilty man's voice, or the voice of an accomplice. Once more his eyes had fallen away.

"That death was covered up," Hastings said. "Swept under the rug. Just like now, these murders. You're trying to—"

"No!" This time Castle spoke sharply, his eyes bright with outraged virtue. Repeating indignantly: "No, this isn't a cover-up. It's nothing like—" Suddenly he broke off, momentarily confused.

"Nothing like the Sally Dietz cover-up." Hastings spoke gently—smugly, he knew. "Is that what you were going to say, Mr. Castle?"

"I—I don't know anything about that. *Nothing.*"

"You mean you don't know about Sally Dietz—about her death?"

"Well, certainly." Transparent, Castle sought to summon an indignation that could cover his confusion. "Certainly I knew Sally Dietz died. But it was a drug overdose. I've already told you that."

"You don't think she was killed—that a member of Rabelais killed her? You don't think—"

"*What?*" It was an explosive burst of stiff-necked, bug-eyed indignation. Repeating: "*What?*"

As Hastings watched his victim squirm, an incredible thought suddenly surfaced. Was it possible that Rabelais sheltered a murderer, a homicidal maniac, a madman who'd killed a hooker and was now killing whoever might have witnessed the crime? Or was it more complicated—more titillating? Could it have been an orgy that went too far: a half-dozen middle-age millionaires off for a drunken weekend, suddenly to discover that, slips, they had a dead hooker on their hands? Were snuff games popular among the Rabelais membership? Or, a reverse twist, could a handful of them have killed Sally Dietz, and now someone was avenging her? Or could it be blackmail with a difference: "Pay to keep me quiet, or else die"?

"Lieutenant Hastings . . ." Castle cleared his throat discreetly, looked meaningfully at his desk. The message: work was waiting, and time was fleeting.

Deliberately ignoring the hint, Hastings said, "Forget about Sally Dietz. Let's talk about Tony Frazer and Gerald Manley and Bruce Carr and Brandon Phillips." He waited until, once more, Castle signified that, yes, Hastings had his grudging attention. Then: "Aside from the fact that all four belonged to Rabelais, do you know of any other connection between those four men?"

In the small, tastefully furnished office, a silence began—

and lengthened. Letting the silence work for him, Hastings watched as Castle struggled to control his expression. But, slowly, the mask began to slip. Until, finally, Castle gave up. His eyes fell, his head came down. Slowly he began to shake his head. In moments, mutely, he'd admitted defeat, surrendered.

When he finally began to speak, his voice was low, the pattern of his speech hesitant, without certainty, perhaps without hope.

"I—I began to wonder, when Bruce Carr was killed. But I—I didn't know he'd been killed, not until you came to the club and told us. So it—it took a while, for it to sink in, for me to think about it. And then, when it finally dawned on me, after you left, I thought, God, I—I couldn't call you. I—I just couldn't. Besides, it was only speculation, it wasn't anything really definitive." He raised his eyes anxiously. "You understand that, don't you?"

"Frankly, Mr. Castle, I don't understand *any* of that. Go back. Start at the beginning." As he said it, Hastings drew his chair closer to Castle's desk, opened his notebook expectantly on the desk, ballpoint pen ready.

"I—" Harried now, Castle raised an apologetic hand. "Wait just a second, Lieutenant. It's—" He reached for his telephone. "It's almost noon. The lunch hour, you know. I've got to find Paul—Mr. Butler. You remember him. He's got to cover for me, on the door."

Struggling to conceal his excitement, Hastings nodded impassively, gesturing for Castle to make his call. Waiting for Castle to communicate briefly with Butler, he watched the manager's face. What did it register? Guilt? Simple anxiety? Something else?

What else?

Castle hung up the phone, drew a long, shaky breath. "This—this is sure to have occurred to a lot of our members by now. It's—there'll be no question about it, once word gets

146

around that Mr. Phillips got killed. I mean—" He took a handkerchief from an inside pocket, carefully blotted sweat from his forehead. He refolded the handkerchief, returned it to his pocket. Then, resigned, he began again to speak, this time in a low, leaden monotone. His eyes were haunted.

"I—I don't imagine you know much about the operation of the club, about its schedule."

Hastings shook his head. No, he didn't know.

"Well," Castle said, "we're open every day except Sunday for lunch and dinner. But except for Wednesdays, there usually aren't many diners. Maybe forty for lunch. And sixty, I'd estimate, for dinner. The dining room, just to give you some idea, can accommodate almost three hundred.

"But on Wednesdays, that's different. Wednesdays is the big day at Rabelais. That's when everyone congregates, you see. There'll be perhaps a hundred for lunch, at least. And at least two hundred for dinner. After dinner, there's often entertainment. So that some Wednesdays, if there's an especially good after-dinner program, the dining room might actually be up to capacity. Of course—" He frowned anxiously, as if to correct a significant omission. "Of course, there's the grill, you understand. And also—" Now he winced, as if he were about to make a shameful admission. "There's also the gaming room. That's—ah—that's on the second floor, with the dining room. The game room, I mean."

Puzzled, Hastings nevertheless nodded encouragement. He'd finally gotten Castle talking. This wasn't the time to interrupt.

"They—the members—they play cards, in the game room. And backgammon, too. And dominoes. They—" Castle bit his lip. "They play bridge, too. Bridge is very popular. And then—of course—" He cleared his throat, with a visible effort making full eye contact. "And then, of course, there's poker." Now, as if the worst were over, he drew another deep breath, this one easier, more self-controlled.

Hastings frowned. "Poker?" As he said it, he remembered Paul Butler's reference to a high-stakes poker game, a scandal. Was this the connection between the four victims? Was it possible? As he looked at the man across the desk he realized that, yes, it was possible.

Castle nodded, a single harassed inclination of his impeccably barbered head. "Yes. That's—you see—that's what I've been trying to tell you. The four of them, they all played in the same game."

Hastings's first thought was a wayward wish that Friedman were there. This, undeniably, was a situation made for Friedman's sense of soak-the-rich irony, pinpricking the pompous, watching them deflate. Murder at Rabelais, the club that banned cops and actors and Democratic presidents. Incredible. B-movie incredible.

"The game that was outlawed, you mean. The high-stakes game."

Castle's expression was pained. "I wouldn't say 'outlawed,' exactly."

Unable to stop himself, Hastings grinned, saying: "There was a poor loser. Is that what you're saying? A sore loser, who kills people when he loses to them?"

"Lieutenant . . ." Deeply reproachful, Castle shook his head.

"Sorry." He mastered the grin, then said, "Go ahead, tell me about the game—who the players were, how long the game lasted."

"It's hard to say when it started. I'd say, rather, that it evolved. After all, this is a private club, and there's always been gambling. There still is. Poker, bridge, backgammon—whatever. It's always played for money. A penny-a-point for bridge, to give you an idea. That's not small change, of course. A bad night, and you can easily lose fifty, sixty dollars at penny-a-point bridge. And poker's the same. A dollar a chip, and you'll drop fifty or a hundred, if the cards go against you. But, to these people, the members, a hundred dollars is nothing."

"But this poker game was different."

"This game was definitely different. Not in the beginning. But it became more—" Searching for the word, frowning, Castle broke off. Then: "It became more malignant, I guess you'd say. More dangerous. It's only to be expected, I suppose. Nationwide, there're more than eight hundred members, most of them rich. All it would take are a couple of compulsive gamblers, and there's a problem. And that's what developed. Problems. Until, finally, the executive committee took action."

"When was the game—" Hastings hesitated, searching for a more acceptable word than "outlawed." "When was it disbanded?"

"About two and a half years ago. It only lasted for about a year, maybe a little more."

"How many men were involved in the game?"

"It varied. Five or six, usually. Four, sometimes—or sometimes seven, depending on who was in town that week."

"So there were seven regulars, it sounds like."

"I'd say so, yes."

"Who else, besides the four we already know about?"

"One was Dominick Abel, the theatrical impresario."

"Impresario?"

"He staged concerts, mostly. A wonderful, exuberant man, very cultivated. He died just a few months ago. A heart attack."

"Who else?"

"Louis Fields." Expectantly—unsuccessfully—Castle waited for the name to register. Then: "Fields is famous, actually. Or, at least, very well known in sporting circles, especially aviation circles. He flew fighters in World War Two. He was an ace, in fact. He comes from Stockton, originally, from a pioneer family. I understand that, literally, the family owns a significant portion of downtown Stockton. And Fields himself owns the airplane that holds the record for the fastest propeller-driven airplane. It also won the unlimited class at Reno the past three years. It's a Bearcat, if you know anything about airplanes."

Hastings shook his head. "Afraid not."

"He also races those oceangoing speedboats. Himself. He cracked up a few years ago, almost died. But a year later he was back racing. All that, plus he had rheumatic fever when he was a child. So he started out very sickly. A fascinating guy."

"Does he live in San Francisco?"

"For the most part, yes."

"Okay, that's six players. Who's the seventh?"

As if he were admitting to something shameful, pronouncing an obscenity, Castle said, "That's Gordon Johnson. Actually, it was because of him that the game was, ah, asked to disband. In addition to being a compulsive gambler, Johnson was also a sloppy drunk. A *very* sloppy drunk. Also, he had a vicious temper. When he drank, which was most of the time, he became very unpredictable. Sometimes he was maudlin, and sometimes he was insulting—or worse. As you can imagine, playing poker, he was a bad loser. And that's all he did—lose."

"Is he dead?"

Castle shook his head. "I don't know. But he no longer belongs to Rabelais."

"Was he asked to leave?"

"No. He couldn't pay his dues, I gather. Or, at least, he *didn't* pay his dues. So—" Castle shrugged. "So he just quit coming around. Thank God. It only takes a few like him to ruin things, you know."

"It sounds like your membership committee screwed up on Johnson."

"His father was a respected surgeon. A civic leader. He was a wonderful man, Dr. Johnson. He was a widower for most of his life and raised two children by himself. He died four or five years ago. That's when Gordon started to go wrong."

150

"Is it a tradition, that sons belong to Rabelais if their fathers belong?"

Castle considered, then said, "I'd say it's *almost* a tradition. Or, to put it another way, Gordon would never have gotten in if his father hadn't been a member. A respected member, as I said."

"Does Gordon Johnson live in San Francisco?"

"I have no idea."

"Who would have an idea?"

"Sorry, Lieutenant. I can't—"

On the desk, Castle's phone warbled. "Excuse me." Then, into the phone: "Floyd Castle speaking." As he listened, Castle's manner changed from muted impatience at the interruption to deference. "Yessir," he said finally. "He's right here, in fact. His name is Hastings. Lieutenant Hastings. He's commander of the Homicide Department, I gather." As he said it, Castle looked at Hastings for confirmation.

Hastings shrugged, whispered, "Co-commander."

Nodding, Castle listened attentively for a moment. Then: "Yessir. Just a moment, please." He covered the mouthpiece, spoke to Hastings. "It's Louis Fields. The man we were just talking about. He'll be here in about twenty minutes for a late lunch. He wants to know whether you're free to have a drink with him in the bar."

Pleasantly surprised, Hastings nodded. "Fine."

Castle made the arrangements and hung up the phone. "If you like," he said, "I'll show you around. You haven't seen more than the lobby and the offices, I don't think." He said it perfunctorily. Signifying that, of course, someone of Hastings's status would never have been permitted beyond the lobby.

They left the office, went through the lobby, where Paul Butler had taken up his station, greeting the lunchtime arrivals. The lounge was beyond the lobby. With its soaring ceiling, richly inlaid parquet floor, elaborately carved woodwork and leather-

151

and-oak furniture, the lounge was a stereotype of the affluent men's club. And, yes, a handful of well-dressed, gray-haired men sat in their brass-studded leather wing chairs, reading the *Wall Street Journal*.

Two generously proportioned archways opened on the bar from the lounge. Unlike the lounge, the bar was crowded, ringing with boisterous good fellowship. The barroom was smaller than the lounge; its walls were walnut-paneled, decorated with hunting prints and framed sporting posters from an earlier era.

"You'll meet Mr. Fields in here," Castle said. "Tell the bartender who you are, and he'll get you two together. There's never any cash at Rabelais, all the food and drink go on the member's account." He hesitated, then said, "If you'd like a drink, though, while you're waiting . . ." He left the offer in limbo.

"No, thanks. Can we see the rest of the building?"

"Certainly." Castle led the way to a bank of two elevators, and they rode up to the second floor. Like the lounge, the dining room was large and luxurious, with lofty ceilings and high, narrow windows draped in aged green velvet. At noon, half the tables were occupied; red-jacketed waiters worked efficiently, discreetly. Without exception, the diners wore conservative three-piece suits, even on a Saturday. And, yes, most of them were gray-haired. And, yes, they looked the part: the men who held the power, made the country run—and pocketed the proceeds.

"I imagine—" Castle cleared his throat discreetly. Repeating: "I imagine that Mr. Fields has an engagement for lunch. So . . ." He let it go delicately unfinished.

Amused, Hastings nodded. "I understand. Mr. Fields doesn't eat with the help."

Looking slightly pained, Castle turned away from the entrance to the dining room and led the way to another room that was smaller and more conventionally decorated, less ostenta-

152

tiously. The room was filled with tables, many of them topped in green felt, with built-in racks for drinks. Only a few of the tables were occupied with players, some of them playing cards, some playing dominoes or backgammon. None of the players acknowledged their presence. Like all the other Rabelais members that Hastings had seen, the players were dressed for the world of finance, or law, or power politics.

"The gaming room," Hastings said.

"Yes . . ." Castle's voice was hushed, as if Hastings had evoked something sacred, therefore forbidden. Then, discreetly, Castle nodded to the large round green baize poker tables. All the tables were empty, one having obviously been only temporarily abandoned, a lunchtime break.

"That's where they played," Hastings said.

Instead of replying, Castle turned, went to the archway that opened onto the corridor, then turned back to face the gaming room. Even though they were out of earshot of the players, Castle spoke discreetly, sotto voce: "Actually, that's not where they played. The game we're talking about—the high-stakes game—started out at one of those regular poker tables. They're pretty much in the center of the room, as you see. But then, as the stakes rose, and the players became serious, they used another smaller table, over in the far corner of the room." Once more he nodded, directing Hastings's attention. "It was as if they were doing something clandestine, you see." As he spoke, Castle drew back a gleaming white cuff, consulted his watch. "We'd better get you to the barroom. Mr. Fields'll be here any minute. He's very prompt. Most successful men, I've found, are usually very punctual. It's interesting."

As they walked out into the foyer and waited for an elevator, Castle said, "There're four stories to the building, plus a basement. The top two floors are rooms for the members. For those who live out of town it's convenient to have a place in San Francisco."

"Ah—" Hastings nodded. "Yes. I see."

"Then," Castle continued, "there's the basement. Most of which is actually a theater."

Hastings blinked. "A theater?"

Castle nodded. "It's not generally realized, but many of the members love to perform. Some of the things they do are spoofs, but some are serious plays. And then, of course, they import talent and put on special programs. Just last week it was Astronauts' Night. It was marvelous. You've never seen more gold braid. And there was film footage from NASA, things you'd ordinarily never see. Fascinating." As he said it, an elevator arrived, and they descended to the ground floor. Hastings waited until they'd gotten to the lobby before he said, "The third and fourth floors—do members actually live there? Permanently?"

"There're three suites, and they're permanently occupied by older members who're alone. Then there're six single rooms, with baths, of course. Those are—" Castle broke off, his attention fixed on the outside door and the man just entering the building. "Ah—" Pivoting to fully face the newcomer, Castle spoke to Hastings aside. "Ah, here's Mr. Fields now."

Fields was a small, wiry man who projected energy, decisiveness, and a quick-moving impatience. Perfunctorily returning Castle's professional nod of formal greeting, Fields turned to Hastings, his hand extended.

"You're Lieutenant Hastings." Predictably, Fields's handclasp was as hard as an oak knot. His face was tan and seamed; behind stylish aviator glasses, his bright blue eyes were clear and shrewd, constantly in motion. His graying hair was sparse and cut close; his beard was also graying, also close-cropped. Unlike most of the Rabelais membership, Fields wore a checked sports jacket and a red wool tie, as if he were dressed for an English hunting weekend. Dismissing Castle with a brief nod of thanks, Fields asked, "Like a drink?"

"Just coffee, thanks."

"Or would you really like nothing?" Asking the question, Fields looked directly into the other man's eyes, probing.

Hastings smiled. "Nothing is fine."

"Good. We'd probably be interrupted in the bar. Generally, at Rabelais, the members don't butt into conversations unless they're invited. In the bar, though, it's a different game. Here—" He beckoned to the lounge, then briskly led the way to a far corner of the spacious room. They sat at opposite ends of a leather couch, turned to face each other.

"I don't mind telling you," Fields said, "that I'm scared shit-less. I've been traveling in Japan and Formosa for almost two weeks on business, just got back yesterday. I left the day Carr was murdered, and I didn't hear about it until I got back. Actually, it wasn't until last night that I heard about it, from my wife. Maybe, after two weeks, it wasn't news anymore. I suppose that happens. And, of course, my wife didn't know who played in the poker game. She didn't know that Carr and Manley and Frazer all belonged to Rabelais, either. Maybe she blocked it out." Fields smiled: a quick, engaging smile, just as quickly gone. "My wife, you see, is a feminist, for which I applaud her. And Rabelais drives liberated women crazy, for obvious reasons."

"Your wife didn't go with you on your trip."

"No. Her aunt is very ill. Dying, in fact."

"Sorry."

"Well—" Fields paused briefly, considering. "Well, she's a wonderful woman, and she's almost ninety. She's had a good life. I only wish her passing could be easier." When Hastings made no response, Fields continued. "In any case, I was here the night Gerald Manley died. I mean—" He circled the room with a brisk gesture. "I mean, I was *right* here, at the club. Manley was here, too, as you doubtless know. He was playing cards. We were in the same game, in fact. Poker." As he said it, he smiled again: a quick, bright, rueful smile. "Low-stakes poker, as you may also know."

Answering the smile, Hastings nodded. "I know."

"I remember thinking," Fields said, "when I heard of Manley's death, that it was a coincidence, both he and Tony Frazer belonging to the club, and both playing in the poker game."

"The big-stakes game, you mean."

Fields nodded grimly. "Right." Then, continuing: "And then, last night, when I got home and my wife told me that Bruce Carr died two weeks ago, I realized that, Christ, I could be on the murderer's list. And then, this morning—Jesus—I heard that Brandon Phillips was shot last night."

"It gets worse," Hastings said.

"How can it get worse?"

"It's almost certain that all four men were killed with the same gun."

"Well—" Fields frowned, then shrugged. "Well, I don't consider that very big news. It's what I assumed—that some nut is killing us off, one by one."

For a moment Hastings sat silently, covertly studying the other man, deciding, assessing. Was Fields scared? Really scared? If he *was* scared, was it a plus, or a minus? Fields was a talker—a smart, irrepressible, don't-give-a-damn talker, a natural-born individualist. But could he be trusted with privileged information? Talkers could help—and also hinder.

"I've decided," Fields was saying, "that in a day or two, as soon as I get a few things straightened out, I'm going to take my wife and the dog and I'm going to get out of town. I don't intend to tell anyone where I'm going, and I don't intend to come back until you guys catch this creep. Meanwhile, I don't plan to go walking at night, or answer the door, or otherwise do anything dumb. And, yes, I own a handgun, which I know how to shoot."

Hastings considered, then decided to say "In your place I guess I'd do the same."

"There's this saying among pilots," Fields said, quoting the doggerel: " 'There're old pilots and bold pilots, but no old, bold pilots.' Well, I'm old, all right. I'm almost sixty-eight. But I intend to get a lot older. Believe it."

"Smart. Very smart." As he said it, Hastings made his decision. Yes, he would trust Fields, bet the farm. "Until this morning," he said, speaking deliberately, carefully weighing the words, "my co-lieutenant and I were getting a lot of pressure to lay off this investigation. Or, rather, stay away from Rabelais members. I was told I could talk to Castle. Period. Not to Paul Butler, not to anyone here."

Behind his sparkling gold-rimmed aviator glasses, Fields's clear blue eyes blinked. "You're joking."

"No."

"But *why?*"

"As I understand it, for Rabelais members, the only thing worse than a breath of scandal is not paying your bar bill. I guess getting murdered is considered a scandal."

Fields guffawed, a sharp, spontaneous acknowledgment of the awful truth. "I guess," he admitted, "that pretty well sums it up." Now he shook his head. "This outfit—Rabelais—they're a bunch of kids, that's what they are. Rich, smart, powerful, essentially good-hearted kids. Rabelais is their playpen, and God help anyone who spoils the fun."

Hastings smiled, studied the other man for a moment, then said, "You aren't exactly a Rabelais booster."

Fields snorted. "I'm third generation. It was *expected* that I'd join. And, let's face it, I love to play poker. Plus the food here is great. But I don't have more than three real friends in Rabelais. I've always thought it was because they suspect I'm a Democrat. Which, in fact, I am."

"I'm assuming," Hastings said, "that someone in the club

could be the murderer. Someone who might be connected to that poker game."

"I know . . ." For the first time, Fields's voice was hushed, his eyes round and awed. Repeating softly, incredulously: "I know."

"Who do you think it could be?"

Fields's reply came promptly but reluctantly. "It's gotta be Gordon Johnson." A pause. Then, ironically: "But what else could I say? I mean, who's left? There's Dominick Abel, but he died. Then there's me. I have an alibi for one murder, at least. So—" Still ironically: "So that leaves Gordon. Also known as Crazy Gordon." He looked at Hastings attentively. "You know about him, I gather."

"I don't know enough. What's his story?"

"Johnson was a drunk and a compulsive gambler. As far as I know, he's failed at everything. Marriage, business, human relationships—you name it. In fact, he precipitated the incident that led to the demise of 'the game,' as we used to call it."

"What happened?"

"It was a mess," Fields said ruefully. "A real mess. There was this waiter—Anton was his first name, I remember that. He was a strange little guy. A Czech, or a Hungarian, something like that. He was a little deformed, a little hump-backed. But he was the perfect waiter, one of those guys who're born to serve their so-called betters. Well, anyhow—" Fields drew a long, deep breath. "Anyhow, we were playing poker. The game was almost over. We always quit around eleven o'clock. The game was always on Wednesdays, which is the big day at Rabelais. We always had lunch, and then we'd start playing poker. We'd play to dinnertime, and eat in the gaming room, at the poker table. Then we'd start playing again after dinner."

"So—" Hastings calculated. "That was about eight hours of poker."

Fields nodded. "That's about it. And I must tell you, Lieutenant—" He spoke somberly, as if he were admitting to something shameful. "I must tell you, those Wednesday games were the highlight of my week. I lived for those games."

"So you're a gambler."

"Oh, yes—" It was another somber admission, seriously spoken. "Oh, yes, I'm a gambler, all right. I love it. But just poker, nothing else, except for baccarat, at the casinos. But the difference between me and Gordon Johnson is that I'm a winner. He's a loser."

"So what happened, with Johnson and the waiter?"

"Well—" Another sigh, weighed down with reluctance and regret. "Well, it didn't involve Anton, except indirectly. As I said, it was almost eleven, and we'd just agreed to play one last round. Gordon, of course, was sloshed. And, of course, he was losing. So then he caught three kings, I think it was, on the draw. Anyhow, it was three of a kind. And then, surprise, when he drew two cards, he caught the fourth king, or whatever. But, of course, he was too drunk to pay attention to who was drawing what—and there's Dominick Abel, sitting across the table, drawing only one card." Fields refocused his gaze to meet Hastings's. "Are you a poker player?"

"Some. I know how it goes."

"Well, then, you know—I *hope* you know—that you've got to be careful betting into a guy who's only drawn one card, even though he hasn't been betting heavily before the draw. Typically, he's either drawn a four-card flush, and he's looking for a fifth card in the suit, or else he's got a four-card straight. Or he might've drawn two pair, and now he's got a full house. Well—" Plainly awed at the memory, marveling even in retrospect, Fields shook his head. "Well, it turns out that Dominick caught, all right. He started out with four hearts in sequence— and he drew one card and had a straight flush. Which, as you doubtless know, is the only hand that beats four of a kind." Once more he broke off, remembering. Then: "Well, they started to bet, Gordon and Dominick. As I'm sure you know, they're playing no-limit poker. *Gentleman's* no-limit poker, or so we thought. Meaning that, yes, out came the checkbooks and the IOUs. By that time, those two guys were raising each other thousands of dollars a pop. It was awesome, I've never seen anything like it, before or since. One round, I remember, was for five thousand. Just imagine!"

"Who decided to call?"

"Dominick, of course. Christ, Gordon'd be there yet, betting those four kings with IOUs."

"Were Johnson's IOUs good?"

"No," Fields answered, "it turned out they weren't good. But that's not the story.

"What's the story?"

"The story is that, when they laid down their cards, Gordon went berserk. Absolutely berserk. No one there—the old-timers—ever remembers a scene like that."

"What'd he do?"

"He accused Dominick of cheating, that's what he did. He was raving. Standing up at that goddam poker table, his eyes wild, waving his arms like a goddam madman—I can still see it. He claimed that Dominick and the waiter—Anton—were in cahoots."

"Ah—" Hastings nodded. "Yes, I see."

"Anton was supposed to have looked at Gordon's hand when he was serving a drink and then passed on the information to Dominick. All it would take, of course, would be a nod or a shake of the head, providing Anton had seen both hands. Which is why you're supposed to keep your hand protected. It's the first rule of poker."

"So what happened then?"

"By that time," Fields said, "there was a real crowd gathered. Everyone was—well—awestruck, that's the only word for it. I know I was. I—Christ—I just sat there with my mouth open, gaping. So then Gordon turned to Castle and demanded that Anton be fired. Right there. Right on the spot."

"Did Castle do it?"

"Of course he did. What else could he do? And, for shame, none of us stuck up for Anton. After all, he was just a funny little guy with an accent and a crooked body."

"So what happened then?"

"What happened was that everyone in the gaming room left. They settled their accounts, and they left. If they spoke, it was in whispers. And no one looked at Gordon. I especially remember that. I was the last one through the door. I looked back and there was Gordon, still standing at the poker table. He was blinking, I remember—blinking very hard. And his mouth was trembling, like he was going to cry. And, of course, he could hardly stand up because he was so drunk. It was a pitiful sight. I felt bad about leaving him there. But the feeling didn't come over me until I'd gotten home, no credit to me."

"Did you ever see Johnson again?"

"I saw him once, on the street. It was probably two years ago. He looked terrible. He looked like a goddam bum. A drunken bum. I just looked the other way."

"So you think," Hastings said, "that he could be killing you guys off, one at a time. For revenge."

Fields shrugged. It was an impatient gesture, as if he were growing restless. "Theorizing is your department, Lieutenant. Me, I'm leaving town. Maybe I'll even leave the country until you catch this guy."

"Do you have any idea where I could find Gordon Johnson?"

Fields shook his head. "None. None at all."

"Friends? Family? A business, even if it's folded?"

"The only thing I know about him is that his forebears got very, very rich farming rice in the Central Valley. They also got rich in real estate, mostly in Fresno. I remember Gordon saying once that, when his father was alive, they had four airplanes—two Stearmans for crop dusting and a Beechcraft and a Centurion. That's a lot of airplanes."

"I have to say," Hastings said, "that I find it pretty improbable that Johnson's killed four men because he lost at poker. I've heard of some sore losers, but . . ." He shook his head, let it go unfinished.

"Well, Lieutenant, I'm not here to sell you anything. You wanted an opinion, and I gave it to you." Now there was an edge to Fields's voice, a hardness of the eye that matched the voice. Time, Hastings knew, was running out.

"Why *are* you here, Mr. Fields?"

A puzzled frown, a narrowing of the vivid blue eyes. "I beg your pardon?"

"You wanted to see me. Why?"

"That should be obvious, Lieutenant. I wanted to know whether you're making any progress on these murders. Also, I wanted to check in, before I go out of town. Otherwise, you might suspect me."

"I appreciate that, Mr. Fields." As he spoke, Hastings produced a business card. "So far, except for Butler and Castle, you're the only source of information we've got. I can understand why you want to get out of town. However—" He handed over the card. "However, I'm going to ask you to keep in touch. *Really* keep in touch. Every place you go, either here or abroad, I want to know about it. I want hotel names, phone numbers, everything. I've got a voice recorder, so phone me any time of the day or night. Will you do that?"

"Certainly." Fields took the card, carefully tucked it into his wallet. The wallet, Hastings noticed, was alligator.

"Thank you." Certain that Fields would soon break off the interview, Hastings nodded, smiled, tentatively waited for the other man to rise from the couch.

But instead of rising, Fields remained seated. As he looked at Hastings, his expression changed from thoughtful to speculative. Finally he said, "There's, ah, something else that maybe I should mention. It's, ah, gossip, really. Scuttlebutt. I'm afraid—" He smiled mischievously. "I'm afraid it violates Rabelais's first unwritten law, which is that you're not supposed to air the club's dirty linen, as you so correctly perceived. But the, ah, fact is that, reputedly, there's another connection between those four guys that got killed—between them, and Gordon Johnson, too."

"Oh?" Expectantly, Hastings settled back in the leather sofa. "And what's that?"

"You've, ah, heard about our yearly retreat, up on the north coast."

Hastings nodded. "Yes, I have. Everyone but the President shows up, I understand." Hastings smiled, decided to say "You lay in lots of food, and lots of booze—and lots of girls, too."

Fields's face was mobile and expressive, everything up front, and as Hastings spoke of the girls, Fields's reaction was instantaneous, both surprised and expectant. Signifying what? Had Hastings stumbled on something, a lucky shot?

Probing now, delicately feeling his way, he ventured, "Sally Dietz, for one. Remember her?"

"Ah . . ." It was a soft rejoinder. "You know, then."

Hearing the words, listening to the inflections, Hastings felt excitement suddenly rising, felt expectation quicken.

"I don't know as much as I'd like to know. The Sally Dietz thing was a cover-up, that's obvious. And the cover-up came from the top. Right from the top."

"But—" Now Fields frowned, transparently puzzled. "But that's all you know? That it was a cover-up?"

This time Hastings decided not to answer. Instead, impassive, he watched—and waited. Fields was committed now. Behind him, a gate had closed.

"The retreat, so called," Fields said, "runs for eight days, Monday to Monday. Most of the action, obviously, goes on from

Friday night to Sunday night, with most of the guys coming in Thursday or Friday. Well—" He drew a deep, reluctant breath. "Well, Tony and Gerald and Bruce and Brandon and Gordon drove up Thursday, during the day. The plan was to have dinner and then start playing poker on Thursday night. They intended to play all night—or most of the night, anyhow. The retreat is actually a collection of cottages scattered along the cliffs overlooking the ocean, with two large central buildings, the lodge and the restaurant cum social hall. It's all very rustic, very— very elemental. And very, very beautiful. Aside from retreat week, it's a wonderful place to go for a weekend, even though it's a long drive. I go up there a lot. But not during retreat week. To be perfectly honest, the sight of the rich and powerful at play doesn't amuse me, never did.

"A few of the cottages, so called, are really quite large, some of them two stories. The guys—the five guys—they rented one of the large cottages, so they were all going to live together until Monday."

"What about you and Dominick Abel?"

"Dominick's mother was dying, so he couldn't make it." Fields smiled. "A death in the family, that's the only excuse that's acceptable for not showing up for retreat week."

"What was your excuse?"

Fields's half laugh was rueful. "There's no way I'd spend three or four days under the same roof with that crew. Gordon Johnson was a drunk, and Tony Frazer was a twit. The others—" He shrugged. "They were just poker-playing buddies. No more."

"So what about Sally Dietz?"

"Yeah—well—" With the air of regretfully getting down to business, Fields settled himself. Saying: "Well, Friday afternoon, along with all the CEOs in their corporate jets, Sally Dietz and about twenty party girls from Las Vegas flew in. Their jet belonged to—" Second thinking, he interrupted himself. Amending: "They made the trip courtesy of one of the members, let's say."

"And Sally Dietz ODed and died. And it was hushed up."

For a moment Fields studied the other man carefully before he repeated: "And that's all you know?"

"It wasn't my jurisdiction. I just know what I heard through the grapevine. Obviously—" Hastings gestured, a signal for the other man to continue. "Obviously, there's more."

"Yeah . . ." Fields nodded heavily. "There's more, all right."

"She was screwing around with your poker buddies," Hastings guessed. "The four that are dead, plus Gordon Johnson. They were screwing around, and she ODed. Is that it?"

Once more, heavily, Fields nodded. Then he smiled. It was the first suggestion of spontaneous good humor that Fields had revealed since the ghost of Sally Dietz had materialized. "Good guess, Lieutenant."

"Do you know any of the particulars?"

"Not really. I've just heard the same whispers that everyone else has heard."

"And how'd they go, these whispers?"

"Maybe a kind of a half-ass orgy. Maybe Sally Dietz and another girl, that's one rumor. In any case, Sally Dietz died in that cottage. It was quite a damage-control problem, as you might imagine."

"So you're thinking that the death of Sally Dietz could be connected to these murders."

"I have no idea, Lieutenant." It was a brisk, no-nonsense rejoinder. Plainly, having said what he'd intended to say, Fields's thoughts were turning away. "I'm just trying to help out." Now his smile twisted mischievously. "Without, of course, inconveniencing myself unduly."

"If there's a connection between Sally Dietz and your poker-

165

playing buddies, the ones who were there when she died, then you wouldn't be involved. You weren't there when she died. So you might not be in danger."

"True. However, I don't choose to gamble." Fields rose, extended his hand. "Gotta go, Lieutenant. Will you keep me posted?"

Hastings nodded. "And *you* keep me posted."

"That sounds like an order."

"It is."

27

"What d'you say . . ." Friedman took two quarters from his pocket, held them extended in his open palm. "Feeling lucky?"

Hastings took one of the quarters, flipped it, banged it down on the black Formica tabletop. "You call."

"Odds." Friedman flipped his own quarter, banged it down. Simultaneously uncovering the two quarters, they discovered two heads. Friedman sighed, took out his wallet, dropped a twenty-dollar bill on the table.

"I can remember," Friedman said, "when I ate lunches for a whole week on twenty dollars."

Not replying, Hastings signaled Florence, their waitress, for more coffee. Using both hands, she deftly poured refills while she picked up the check and the twenty-dollar bill. "You guys look like you're real deep in thought," she commented. "It's Saturday, you know. Time to relax, work in the garden."

"There's a sex murderer out there somewhere," Friedman said. "We've got to apprehend him before he strikes again. How'd you like to be bait, Florence? When d'you get off work?"

"God," she said, "nothing changes. Always the bait." She smiled, turned away, walked to the cashier.

"Is she married?" Hastings asked.

"Not currently, I don't think. But she's got a son in medical school."

"*Florence* has a son in *medical* school?"

Friedman regarded the other man as a scientist might regard a strange insect. "You're a snob, you know that?"

"A snob?"

"Waitresses have kids in medical school."

"Yeah. But *Florence*?"

Friedman glanced at his watch. "Three o'clock. Why don't we go home, give it a rest until Monday? I've got Marsten running down Gordon Johnson."

"Has Marsten got anything?"

"Jesus, Frank. You called in—what—two hours ago, from Rabelais? We've been sitting here eating for an hour, give or take. I already told Marsten to take Sunday off, and he's only going to work until five o'clock today. So let's go home. The NBA championships are on, after all. Besides, according to your theory, Fields is the last one on the hit list. And he's leaving town. So what's the hurry? According to your theory—"

"*My* theory? Did I say it was my theory?"

"Okay. *Our* theory." Once more Friedman consulted his watch. "They're just about tipping off now."

Ignoring the remark, Hastings said, "Is anyone working on Sally Dietz?"

"I put Sigler on that. But he's got to start up in Kent County.

I doubt whether he'll be able to do anything on it until Monday, either."

"What about the waiter that was fired? Anton."

"That one was easy. He lives on Sacramento near Larkin. He's lived there for fifteen years. His last name is Rivak."

"Sacramento's right on my way home."

"Good." It was an elaborately long-suffering response. Then: "I figure the Celtics have got maybe twenty points on the board by now."

"Jesus, Pete, come *on*. You're acting like we aren't taking any heat on this one. I've got to call Dwyer by six o'clock tonight. Without fail."

Friedman shrugged. "Me, too. But, what the hell, the game'll be over by then."

"We have to decide what we're going to tell him."

"I plan to tell him what I told Kanter, a couple of hours ago. 'It's all coming together,' I plan to say. 'We'll probably have a statement any time.' "

Hastings hardened his gaze deliberately, dropped his voice a meaningful half-octave. "Will you be serious? Please?"

"Ah—" Mock sadly, Friedman shook his head. "I was afraid of this. All these rich guys dying, you're losing your sense of humor."

"I'm *not* losing my sense of humor, dammit. I'm just—"

"See? Profanity."

"Christ, Pete. Come *on*."

Friedman sighed elaborately, sipped the last of his coffee, wiped his mouth with a napkin while he regarded Hastings quizzically. Finally: "Okay—what to say? Well—" He furrowed his brow, considering. "Well, truthfully, none of this makes sense to me. I mean, what've we got? A guy loses at poker, and three years later, or whatever, he decides he's going to kill off his erstwhile fellow card players? Is that a credible motive? Or a Las Vegas hooker ODs while she's doing business up on the

169

coast, and her pimp decides he's entitled to deferred compensation? Or how about a strange-looking waiter who holds grudges?" Friedman shook his head morosely. "I just don't see a motive in any of it. None. Zero."

"Except that we haven't talked to any of them. Take Johnson. It sounds like he was right on the brink. It sounds like he lost ten, twenty thousand on that one hand. And he was already screwing up his life. When Fields saw him two years later, he looked like a bum, Fields said. A drunken bum."

"Okay," Friedman said, "let's stipulate that he's a drunken bum. Is a drunken bum capable of pulling off four very well executed murders? Think about it."

"Hmmm . . ."

"In my opinion," Friedman said, "just theorizing, you understand, the Sally Dietz angle might be something. Except—" Exasperated, Friedman shook his head. "Except it's hard to figure a motive. If she was blackmailing those guys, and they decided to kill her and then cover it up, that'd make sense. But this is exactly the reverse. She's dead, all right. But so are they."

"All except Johnson."

"Yeah . . ." Distracted, Friedman tapped lightly on the tabletop with his spoon. "Yeah, Johnson . . ."

Hastings began to speak randomly, as thoughts shifted, refocused, shifted again. "If I'm not mistaken, these two things— the poker game thing and Sally Dietz—they came within a few months of each other. Maybe that's some kind of a connection."

"If there's a connection," Friedman said, "it's sure not visible to the naked eye."

Still speaking at random, Hastings said, "I wonder if we're thinking too small."

Amused, Friedman looked up. His broad, swarthy Buddha's face settled into a tolerant smile. "Too small?"

"Maybe these guys were doing a pseudosnuff thing in that

cabin. Who knows—they could've been taking pictures, something like that. Then it all went wrong, and the girl died. So . . ." As the thoughts began to skew, he broke off, exasperated with himself.

"So," Friedman said, picking up the beat, "let's say Johnson, as usual, is in a drunken stupor when the girl is killed. His four buddies decide, hey, they'll wait for Johnson to wake up, and then they'll tell him that, slips, he killed the girl. 'But don't worry,' they say, 'we'll cover for you.' So then he discovers what's happened, discovers that he's been set up for a murder that's been preying on his mind for three years, ruining his life. Naturally, he's pissed off. So—bang, bang, bang, bang. All perfectly logical."

"You're kidding, of course."

"I'm doing what homicide detectives are paid to do. I'm theorizing."

"Hmmm."

"Listen," Friedman said, looking at his watch, then picking up his change and leaving a tip, "we're just wasting our time until we get something from Marsten and Sigler. So you go home, watch Ann's kids play little league, whatever. I'll watch the basketball game. Monday morning, we'll be able to confront this thing with clear heads." He pushed his chair away from the table and stood up.

"Have you got Rivak's address? I may as well see him. It's right on my way home."

"You won't make me feel guilty, working while I watch the game. You realize that."

"I realize that. Yes."

171

28

As Hastings waited for traffic to clear, he matched the address written on the slip of paper with the address of the apartment building across the street. Like the neighborhood, the building was old and grimy and in need of renovation. It was the gap-tooth windows that told the story, with their mismatched curtains, some of them tattered, some hanging askew. Sacramento near Larkin was the western edge of Chinatown. Most of the buildings were four or five stories, each one attached to its neighbor. Almost all the buildings were walk-ups, Hastings knew. The rents were low, the maintenance was minimal and the plumbing unreliable. As Hastings crossed Sacramento, a carefree group of Chinese children gamboled past him on the sidewalk, trailing shouts of laughter. At least three of the children carried plastic small arms: MACs, or Uzis or miniature AK-7s.

The outside lobby of Anton Rivak's apartment building was grimy marble; the mailboxes were rusted, with some of the doors hanging open. Like the lobby walls, the floor was marble, badly chipped and cracked.

A. Rivak, 307: it was a hand-printed card inserted in a slot above a bell button. Without much hope, Hastings pressed the button. But, a half minute later, the door latch buzzed and Hastings was inside. Except for a narrow table littered with circulars and a straight-back chair with a torn seat, the lobby was unfurnished. There was no elevator, and the stairs to the upper floors were narrow and smelled strongly of disinfectant. The carpeting on the stairs was threadbare; the hand railing was chipped so badly that several colors of paint showed through in layers. The corridors opening off the staircase smelled strongly of ethnic cooking. A few steps short of the third floor, climbing at a steady rate, a test, Hastings realized that, yes, he was breathing hard. Twenty years ago, wearing pads and a helmet and cleats, he'd run the length of a football field in twenty-one seconds, fourth best time on the Lions.

Apartment 307 was in the rear of the building. Out of habit, on the chance that Anton Rivak could be a killer, Hastings pressed the button beside the door, stepped back, unbuttoned his jacket, loosened his revolver in its spring holster, moved his right hand to belt height, close to the concealed revolver. From a nearby apartment came the sound of voices raised in anger. From a different direction, rock music blared.

The door opened promptly. Fields's description had been accurate; the man standing in the open doorway was small, less than a hundred and fifty pounds. His chest was hollow; his back bore a small hump. In a sallow face the color of parchment, his eyes were unnaturally dark, improbably large. His dark-brown hair was lank, his head narrow, his neck scrawny. On a Saturday in the late afternoon, he wore a wrinkled white shirt and a somber tie, neatly knotted. Incongruously, he clutched a knitted shawl close around his shoulders.

Showing his shield in its leather case with his left hand, Hastings smiled, let his right hand drop to his side. Here, now, there was plainly no danger.

"Mr. Rivak? Anton Rivak?"

With his eyes on the shield, the normal response, Rivak nodded. "Yessir, I am."

"I'm Lieutenant Frank Hastings, San Francisco Homicide Squad. We're looking for background information relating to an open case. Could I talk with you for a few minutes?" Hastings looked expectantly over Rivak's shoulder, down a short, narrow hallway.

"Oh. Yes. Certainly. Please . . ." Rivak stepped back, gestured for Hastings to enter. Rivak's accent and his manners suggested a good European education.

"Thank you." As Hastings walked slowly down the hallway to the living room, he took the inventory as he went: everything was clean, but the apartment needed paint. The well-worn rug in the hallway was Oriental, and looked as if it could once have been valuable. The hallway walls were hung with a dozen prints and pictures, all modestly framed. Many of the prints were ink drawings of European settings: castles, town houses, street scenes. Many of the pictures were botanical: stylized renderings of plants and flowers.

The living room was large, with a single window facing north. Through the window, the distant top spires of the Golden Gate Bridge were visible above the city's rooftops.

"If I was on the next floor up," Rivak said, "the view would be better. Much better."

Nodding, Hastings turned away from the window and reflexively made his quick policeman's survey of the living room.

The furniture was old and worn and dark in color. But, years ago, the chairs and tables and lamps had doubtless been expensive. Like the rug in the hallway, the living-room rug was Oriental, worn but serviceable. The leather of the couch was cracked across one arm, but the couch's original quality was apparent. What were the odds, Hastings wondered, that the apartment was furnished with Rabelais castoffs?

When Hastings was seated in an armchair, Rivak chose a straight-back chair, facing him. Rivak's expression was attentive, his manner solicitous, as if he were awaiting a command, some chance to serve.

"The reason I'm here," Hastings said, "is that I'm investigating the murders of the Rabelais members."

"Ah—" Rivak nodded. It was a knowing nod, suggesting that, yes, he'd already guessed why Hastings had come. "The murders. Amazing. Truly amazing."

"Did you make the connection between them—that high-stakes poker game at Rabelais?"

"Of course. Yes." Rivak nodded gravely, but said no more. He sat as before: expectantly, attentively. Watchfully yet passively. Fields had said that Rivak was born to be a servant. To himself, Hastings nodded. Score another insightful point for Fields.

"At what point did you make the connection?"

Rivak's dark brows drew together, as if the question distressed him. Holding the shawl that covered his shoulders, his hand tightened almost imperceptibly. Then, suddenly, he coughed: a deep, wracking cough that tore at his narrow, hollow chest. "Sorry—" He shook his head apologetically. "I've got a cold. A bad cold. It's this building. There's no heat, except at night. It's steam heat. The landlord expects everyone to be at work during the day, so he doesn't provide heat. He claims—" Once more he coughed, noisily raised phlegm. With his free hand he plucked a tissue from a box on the small table beside his chair. Mutely shaking his head, another helpless expression of apology, he spit into the tissue, dropped it onto the floor beneath the table, where there were already several used tissues.

"Maybe you should go to bed," Hastings said. "Keep warm."

Rivak nodded. "I will, as soon as you leave." As he said it, his large, dark eyes registered another twinge of anxiety. The message: by expressing a desire to be in bed, had he inadvertently been impolite, made Hastings feel unwelcome?

"Okay, I'll be brief."

Rivak nodded: another gravely measured inclination of his narrow, bony head.

"Tony Frazer, Gerald Manley, Bruce Carr, and, now, Brandon Phillips—they were all players in that high-stakes game. All murdered. All murdered by the same person, there's no doubt of that. And they were all carefully planned murders. They could've even—" Hastings broke off, considering. Should he go on, finish the sentence? How much did he want this ex-waiter to know—and not know? Finally: "They could've even have been done by a professional killer. We're looking into that possibility."

As Hastings had been speaking, Rivak's pale face had tightened anxiously; his gaze had fixated on Hastings's face. "I—" He blinked, faltered. Then: "I'm sorry, but I—I didn't know about Mr. Phillips. When . . .?" Rivak broke off. Awed, he began to shake his head, unable to finish the fateful question.

"Last night. Late. It'll be in the afternoon papers, probably."

As if the knowledge of Phillips's murder had immobilized him, Rivak remained motionless, simply staring, clutching his shawl closer to his slight, misshapen body.

"I understand," Hastings said, "that you always made it a point to serve the men playing in the poker game. Is that true?"

Hesitantly Rivak nodded. "Yes. It—it was understood that I'd be their waiter. It was a custom."

"And I also understand that one of the players—Gordon

Johnson—got you fired from your job. He accused you of helping Dominick Abel win a very big hand. In other words, he accused you of cheating."

Rivak began to slowly, sadly, doggedly shake his head. It was a gesture expressing both sadness and denial. There was resignation, too—and the pall of an empty life. "I didn't do it. I never would have done that. Never."

"None of the players thought you did. If they thought that, then they would have thought that Dominick Abel cheated. And they didn't think that."

"Did you—" Rivak moistened pale lips with a small pink tongue. "Did you talk to Mr. Fields?"

"That's right," Hastings answered promptly. "I did."

Rivak nodded gently. "Yes, I thought so. Mr. Fields is a very unusual man. Very friendly. Very fair. He's—" Rivak broke off, plainly deciding whether to go on. Finally he ventured, "He's not like most of them at Rabelais." Rivak shook his head, an affirmation. "He's better. Much better."

"That was—what—three years ago, that you were fired?"

"Almost three years. Not quite."

"And did you find another job?"

Rivak shook his head. "I could have found a job. I had offers. But I decided not to do it. I'm sixty-three, and for the past several years my health hasn't been good. I've always saved my money. So . . ." As if he were reminiscing, he broke off, then shrugged his bony shoulders.

"Were you working at Rabelais when Sally Dietz died?"

The reaction was instantaneous, as if an electric shock had jerked Rivak's body upright in the chair, then just as suddenly released him, left him limp, drained. Only the eyes were alive, searching Hastings's face with fierce, burning concentration.

"Wh—" Once more the pink tongue circled the pale lips. "Why are you asking me that?"

"Mr. Rivak—" Hastings let one long moment of silence pass, then another moment. "I'm here to ask the questions. Not answer them."

"Oh . . ." He blinked, frowned, finally nodded. "Oh. I see. Yes."

"So? *Were* you working at Rabelais when she died?"

Recovering, Rivak managed to nod, managed to say "Yes, I was. She died in the summer, almost three years ago. I—" A brief, pained pause. Then: "I left the following December." As he said it, he seemed to smile at his own hesitation. It was a haunted smile that left the eyes still empty and stricken, unnaturally large, sunk deep in their dark sockets. "That's the way I think of it—that I left Rabelais. Even though, of course, it isn't true. I suppose everyone does that, tells himself the same harmless lies until finally they seem like the truth."

"Were you at the retreat when she died?"

Hesitantly—cautiously—he nodded. "Yes, I was. We—most of the staff—we were up there for the retreat week."

"The five men—the four dead men and Gordon Johnson— they shared a cabin. Is that right?"

"It wasn't exactly a cabin. There were two floors, and several bedrooms upstairs."

"Sally Dietz—" Hastings let a beat pass, let the significance sink in. "She died in that cottage." His voice was flat, tactically noncommittal: merely verifying. Not asking. Not searching.

"Ah . . ." It was a low, wounded monosyllable. The message: whatever the provocation, a good servant instinctively protects his master from the rabble's scrutiny.

"She died there," Hastings repeated, his voice hard, his eyes uncompromising. "*Didn't* she?"

Finally, in surrender, Rivak nodded. Almost whispering: "Yes. She was there."

"And you were there, too."

"I—" As if his throat had suddenly closed, Rivak broke off.

Then, almost inaudibly: "No, I wasn't. I—I was there earlier, serving dinner to them. Or, rather, snacks. Late-night snacks from the dining hall. It's all very rustic at the retreat, you see. Everyone—all the men—they take their meals at the lodge. But after dinner, they can have snacks delivered to the cottages. They—"

"Wait. Let's go back. I want the sequence. I want to know what happened. Hour by hour, minute by minute. Do you understand?"

With his eyes fixed on Hastings's, Rivak nodded gravely. "Yes, I understand."

"The retreat was the third week of August," Hastings said, reciting from memory. "Eight days, Monday through the following Monday. Sally Dietz arrived from Las Vegas on Thursday, along with several other party girls. They arrived on a private executive jet. Is that right so far?"

"Yessir." Now Rivak's voice was subdued, without inflection. Without hope.

"What time did the girls arrive, would you say?"

"It was about two o'clock in the afternoon."

"All right—" Satisfied, Hastings nodded. "Now, I want you to tell me everything you know about Sally Dietz and the party girls and the five poker players, from the time the girls arrived at the retreat until the time Sally Dietz died. *Everything*."

As Rivak began to speak, his body seemed to lose strength as he sank back into his chair, exhausted. As he clutched the shawl closer to his narrow chest, his voice was almost a whisper. "The girls always stayed in Glendora. That's a small town just up the coast. There's a motel in town, and several Rabelais members always share in renting the whole motel for the weekend. So there's always a lot of driving back and forth, Fridays and Saturdays."

"I gather," Hastings said, "that the officials of Rabelais don't sanction any of that."

"Oh, no." As if he were shocked, Rivak roused himself, primly shook his head. "Oh, no. Not at all. It's all—ah—unofficial."

"Okay—" Hastings gestured encouragement. "Go ahead. It's Thursday, at two o'clock. The girls have just arrived at the motel in Glendora."

"Yes. Well, I have no idea what they did Thursday. Or, rather, Thursday night. It wasn't until the next night—Friday—that Sally Dietz went to the gentlemen's cottage."

"The poker players, you mean."

"Yessir."

"Okay." Hastings gestured encouragement. "Go on."

"Well, as for myself, I spent Friday afternoon at the lodge. That's the center of everything, all the activities, as I said. There's a bar, of course, and lots going on. Friday afternoon, I remember, the coast was sunny. Which, during August, it isn't always. So there was a great deal of activity on the beach. There was an air show, too. On Friday afternoon."

"An air show?"

Rivak nodded. "There were three or four old airplanes—biplanes. They did stunts, right over the water. It was very exciting. But, of course, there was a lot to do in the dining room and kitchen, so I was really too busy to watch it. Friday nights and Saturdays were the big nights, you know."

"Where were the girls, during the afternoon on Friday?"

"I suppose they were in the motel. As I've said, I was very busy. And the girls would never come in the lodge. Even if they went to the cottages, it was always at night. They had to be careful not to be noticed. At least—" He frowned, searching for the phrase. "At least, not officially noticed."

"Were there any private cottages? With only one Rabelais member?"

"No, sir. Most of the cottages sleep four, at least. Some of them sleep six or eight."

"Did most of the action—the sex—happen at the motel?"

Rivak nodded gravely. "Yessir."

"What about the five poker players?"

"Well, again, I have no idea what they did Friday afternoon, because I was so busy. But after dinner Mr. Phillips told me that they'd be playing poker at the cottage that evening. Which, as I think I told you, they'd done the evening before, on Thursday. And he asked me to come to the cottage when I finished clearing the dinner dishes and setting up for breakfast. He said they'd want snacks, and ice, while they played."

"Was this a normal thing to do, at the retreats?"

Rivak frowned. "I'm not sure I follow you, sir."

"A group played poker, or had a private party in their own cottage. Did they usually get their own waiter?"

Rivak nodded. "Yessir, that was normal. Of course, Fridays and Saturdays were the big nights at the lodge, so most of the gentlemen were there, at the lodge. There was always a program. Very good programs, too. Especially on Saturdays. That's when they have the roast. That year it was Mr. Cross."

When Hastings frowned at the name, puzzled, Rivak offered discreetly: "The secretary of defense."

"Ah . . ." Impressed, Hastings nodded. "Yes." Then, back to work: "So what happened next, Friday night?"

"I got to the cottage about ten o'clock," Rivak said, "with the ice and snacks. A woman was there, one of the party girls. She was serving drinks. She was—" He broke off, searching for the words. Then, fastidiously: "She was in her bra and panties. And she—she was teasing them."

"Teasing them? In what sense?"

"She would brush up against them, when she served them drinks. Things like that."

"It was Sally Dietz."

"Yes."

"All right. Go ahead—" Hastings waved encouragement, a command.

"Well, except for Mr. Johnson, the gentlemen weren't drinking much. So she and Mr. Johnson, they were—ah—playing around with each other. And a couple of the men—Mr. Frazer and Mr. Manley, who'd only had two or three drinks—they began touching the woman, too. It was—I really—" Plainly confused, actually ill at ease, he broke off, began primly shaking his head. "It was amazing, to see what was happening. Those three gentlemen, how they—they encouraged each other, dared each other, actually pushed each other at the woman, like little boys, playing games."

"By this time, I gather, they'd forgotten about poker."

"They were *forgetting* about poker, I'd say."

"What happened next?"

"I don't know."

Hastings frowned. "What?"

"Mr. Carr told me I could leave. He said I should leave immediately, and then come back the next morning, and clean up. I reminded him that, the next morning, I'd be serving breakfast, so that I wouldn't be able to clean up until later. He said that would be fine, that I should just leave. And that's what I did. I just left."

"They wanted to get rid of you before the real party started."

Rivak nodded: a judicious inclination of his bony head. "I'm afraid so. Yes."

"What happened then?"

"One of the cottages is reserved for the help. I went there and went to bed."

"You weren't tempted to peek—look in a window, to see what the poker players were doing?" Hastings asked the question as if it was an accusation.

"Oh, no, sir. I'd never do that."

"All right." Hastings spoke shortly, skeptically, a calculated projection of the hard-edged interrogator at work. "Go ahead. What happened next?"

"All I know, sir, is that the following day, just before lunch, the police arrived. Apparently Sally Dietz was found dead that morning in one of the motel rooms."

"Was it the state police, do you remember? Or local authorities?"

Rivak shook his head. "I couldn't say. There were two cars, I remember that. And three or four men."

"In uniform?"

Rivak frowned. "One or two of them were in uniform, if I recall correctly. And one man, at least, was in street clothes. I believe he was the sheriff of Glendora, the town where the motel was located. I remember him especially because he wore a wide-brimmed hat."

Amused, Hastings said, "A cowboy hat? Like that?"

"No, not that big. But western."

"Who did the police question, at Rabelais?"

"They talked to Mr. Castle, I believe."

"Anyone else? Any Rabelais members?"

"I'm sure they did, but I don't know who. You see, the police arrived just before lunch, as I said. I was very busy, as you can imagine. But there was a great deal of—" Rivak broke off, searching for the word. "—Of tension, certainly. People coming and going, a lot of anxiety, that everyone was trying to conceal. At least, that was my impression."

"Did the police talk to you?"

"No, sir, they didn't."

"Did you volunteer the information you had?"

As if the suggestion was in poor taste, Rivak primly shook his head. "Oh, no, sir."

"Why not?"

A pause, a search for the right words. Then: "It would have been . . . presumptuous. Inappropriate. Very inappropriate."

183

Hastings fixed the other man with a stern, disapproving stare. "You thought it would be inappropriate to help the police with a homicide investigation?"

Unabashed, Rivak's retort was prompt and direct. "If they had questioned me, I would have answered their questions. But I didn't think it was my place to volunteer, put myself forward."

Hastings decided not to reply, decided instead to harden his stare. But, still unabashed, Rivak insisted: "It wasn't until dinnertime, when the police had gone, that I learned about it, found out what really happened, that one of the girls from Las Vegas was dead. And, even then, it wasn't until the next day—Sunday—that I learned the dead girl was the one who'd been at the poker game. After all—" He broke off, searching once more for the words. "After all, it wasn't my club. I was an employee. Among the members, the story spread instantly, I'm sure. But the staff, the help . . ." He shrugged expressively, shook his head.

"Did you know the girl's name by then?"

"No, sir, I didn't." Rivak's voice was firm, his eyes were steady. Until, suddenly, another spasm of coughing wracked his frail body. He excused himself, spit into another tissue, dropped it on the floor with the other tissues, excused himself again. His eyes, Hastings saw, were wet from the coughing. But, stubbornly, Rivak insisted: "It wasn't until the last day of the retreat—Monday—that I knew her name."

"Were the police still on the premises Monday?"

"Not that I was aware of, no, sir."

"What about Sunday? Were they there on Sunday?"

"Not that I saw, sir."

Hastings nodded thoughtfully, shifted his gaze to a far corner of the room. So far, the strange little man's story had the ring of truth, gaps and inconsistencies included. The local sheriff had gotten the call from the motel owner, both of them small-town lodge buddies, probably. Both of them knew what the girls

184

from Las Vegas had been doing—and with whom they'd been doing it. Covering his ass, the sheriff would have called the state police. Together, showing the flag, they would have put in an official appearance at Rabelais, short and sweet, very low profile. The state police would make the right entries in the right logs. Then, straight arrows, they would have gone back to catching speeders on the freeways. While the sheriff had gone back to his swivel chair, where he'd waited for a lawyer from Rabelais to come and talk. At the end of the talk, the lawyer would have left an envelope stuffed with money on the sheriff's desk. Rest in peace, Sally Dietz.

He returned his gaze to the little man sitting wrapped in a shawl, his dark, tragic eyes steady on Hastings. Watching. Waiting.

Watching for what?

Waiting for what?

If he was ever to know, he must try another combination, twirl the dials again.

"Since you left Rabelais," he began, "have you ever seen any of the men who—"

At his belt, his beeper chirped. Hastings pressed the beeper's recall button, craned his neck, read Friedman's home number on the tiny screen. During the last few hours, despite the basketball game, Friedman had discovered something.

"May I use your telephone?" Hastings asked.

"Yes—please." Anxious to be of assistance, Rivak rose, went to the hallway, opened a door to the apartment's single bedroom. "It's on the dresser." With a servant's practiced wave, he gestured for Hastings to enter the room, then discreetly withdrew. Leaving the door open, Hastings dialed Friedman's number. As he waited for the connection, Hastings looked around the bedroom. It was a small room with one window that overlooked the city to the north. The single bed was neatly made, with no bedspread, only a blanket. Except for the dresser that was set against the east wall, the only other furniture was a straight-back chair. Like the entryway to the apartment, the east wall above the dresser was covered with photographs and pictures, half of them unframed.

The entire west wall, floor to ceiling, was covered by a framed collection of insects. The collection was uniformly displayed in shallow shadow boxes framed in narrow black and backed with white cotton.

"Hello."

Still scanning the insect collection, Hastings spoke into the phone: "It's Frank, Clara. Pete just called me."

"Oh, yes. Wait." Muffled, Hastings heard her shout. Then, to him: "How are you, Frank?"

He smiled. "You mean since yesterday, how am I?"

"God. Cops. You guys always—"

"Frank?" It was Friedman's voice on the extension.

"See you, Frank. Great talking to you." In good humor, Clara Friedman clicked off.

"Are you at Rivak's?" Friedman asked.

"Yes."

"Anything?"

"Yes and no. Did the Celtics win?"

"Unhappily, no. However, since it was a lopsided game, I didn't mind taking the time to talk to Marsten and Sigler."

From long experience, Hastings could pick up an air of excitement that, despite Friedman's best, most blasé efforts, lay just beneath the surface of Friedman's banter.

"So what's happening?" Hastings asked. Mindful of Rivak within easy earshot, he spoke brusquely. As he spoke, he withdrew his notebook and ballpoint pen from an inside pocket and opened the notebook, ready.

Taking the cue, Friedman said, "In a nutshell, Marsten discovered that Gordon Johnson lives at the Tides Motel, which is on Lombard near Gough. Or, more accurately, he *manages*

186

the place. How about that for a comedown in status: from card playing at Rabelais to coping with deadbeats and dirty linen?"

"Huh . . ." Surprised, Hastings wrote *Tides* on the pad. Then: "What else?"

"I saved the best for the last, you'll be glad to learn." Despite Hastings's eagerness, Friedman let a beat pass, building the suspense, Friedman's favorite sport. "That being that, surprise, Sigler located Sally Dietz's father. He lives in San Francisco."

"Ah . . ."

Could Friedman hear in his voice the quick rush of excitement he felt? Did Friedman sense that, suddenly, hope of a solution to the Rabelais murders had appeared: the prey, suddenly flushed.

"Ready?" Friedman asked.

"Ready." Once more, the ballpoint pen was poised.

"You're going to love this," Friedman promised, his voice involuntarily pitched to a note of playful anticipation. "The guy lives in a halfway house for loonies."

"Loonies, did you say?"

"Well, technically, it's a drug rehab program. But Dietz, apparently, isn't playing with a full deck."

Hastings considered, then decided to say "I'll call you later."

"Right." A pause. Then: "Frank?"

"Yes."

"Don't talk to Johnson or Dietz alone. Give Canelli a call. He's at home, and I've told him to wait until you call. Clear?" The last word was edged with an unmistakable note of command, the senior Homicide lieutenant, giving a direct order.

"That's clear. I'll call you in fifteen, twenty minutes, from home."

"Good."

29

"So tell me," Friedman's voice said, "how'd it go with Rivak?"

Taking the telephone on its long cord into the living room, Hastings sank into the deep armchair beside the bookcase, his favorite, and put the telephone on the floor beside the chair, with the handset propped in the hollow of his shoulder and one leg slung over the arm of the chair.

"It could be," Hastings said, "that Sally Dietz is what this whole thing is about. She and those five poker players were all together in that cottage, and Sally started out in her bra and panties. The guys were drinking and playing grab ass, even when Rivak was there. Then they sent him home to bed. Then the party really got started, probably."

"And Johnson's the only one alive who knows what happened after Rivak left."

"The obvious theory," Hastings said, "is that Johnson killed her. And now he's eliminating the witnesses."

"Except that it's so *obvious*. It's like he's drawing us a goddam map that leads right to him."

"Not as long as the Sally Dietz cover-up held, it wasn't obvious."

"Except that it never really held," Friedman answered. "Everyone knew there was a cover-up."

"*We* knew that. The question is, did Johnson know?"

"Let's not forget Dietz," Friedman said. "Sally's father. Maybe he's avenging the death of his daughter. He's loonie, so he doesn't care whether he draws a map to himself or not. A lot of these guys subconsciously want to get caught, so they can be punished."

"But suppose it isn't Sally Dietz. Suppose it's the poker game. That poker game was obviously the end of Gordon Johnson. That cheating incident, so called, was the last nail in his coffin."

"In that case," Friedman said, "he'd go after Louis Fields."

"Fields has been out of town during the past few weeks."

"Hmmm."

"Maybe Johnson is over the edge," Hastings mused. "A loonie, like Dietz. Maybe he doesn't care whether we come after him."

"If it's Johnson," Friedman said, "and it's revenge, why wouldn't he kill Rivak?"

Hastings shook his head at the phone. "If it *is* Johnson, and if that poker game really was the last straw, then maybe what he's really doing is going out in a blaze of glory. And you don't kill waiters if you're going out in a blaze of glory."

"Ah . . ." There was a hint of approval in Friedman's voice. "Yes, good point. As you mature, you're developing a certain flair. For which, if you don't mind, I'll take some credit."

Careful to conceal his pleasure, Hastings shrugged. "Be my guest."

"What about Rivak as a suspect?" Friedman asked. "What about a blackmail try that didn't work?"

Hastings blinked. "What?"

"Think about it," Friedman said, obviously warming to his theory. "Sally Dietz died in August, almost three years ago. Rivak knows it's murder but decides to keep quiet. Or maybe, like I said, he does a little blackmail. The five players oblige. What the hell, they can afford a little blackmail. But then, a few months later, Johnson goes off the deep end and gets Rivak fired. Rivak is pissed. He demands more money from his five pigeons, since he's unemployed—and since it's all their fault. Maybe they balk. And maybe, meantime, Rivak's beginning to brood about his situation. Those five guys, after all, have ruined his life. So he decides to kill them, one by one. And Johnson, naturally, is the last to go, since he's the worst."

"If he's the worst," Hastings said, "I'd think he'd be the first one killed."

"Well," Friedman answered airily, "loonies have their own logic. It's an established fact."

"There's another problem."

"Oh?"

"There's nothing to indicate that Sally Dietz was murdered. ODed, yes. Therefore an embarrassment to Rabelais, of course. But murder . . ." Hastings let a dubious silence pass. As, from the back of the flat, Ann's older son Dan was coming down the hallway, dressed for a teen-age Saturday night. Making a three-step detour into the living room, Dan smiled, doubled up his fist, feinted, cuffed Hastings on the shoulder.

"Go get 'em, Tiger. Grrr."

Smiling in return, Hastings tried to trip Dan. On the telephone, Friedman was saying "Well, fortunately, there's an easy way to get some answers. We ask these guys where they were last night, we'll have a start. What about Rivak? Is he alibied?"

"He was home working on his beetle collection. He went to bed about ten. Alone."

"Is that beetles as in bugs? Or as in the musical group?"

"Bugs. One whole wall of bugs. That's what Rivak does—collects beetles, and kills them and dries them and mounts them. He also trades specimens with other people. Worldwide. Do you know how many species of beetles there are?"

"No. But I know you're going to tell me."

"A hundred thousand. Maybe two hundred thousand."

"What's Rivak's story, apart from waiting tables and collecting beetles? According to what Louis Fields told you, he sounds kinky."

"Kinky?" Hastings frowned at the phone. "Did I say kinky?"

"No matter. What's he like?"

"He's a funny little guy. Pale face, very unhealthy looking. Deep lines around the mouth. He's slightly hunchback. He's in his early sixties. He's got all his hair, though, and it's almost black, so he looks younger. He was born in Europe—Hungary, I think he said. Came to this country after the Hungarian uprising, in the fifties. All his life he's been a waiter. He worked at Rabelais for years."

"Is he forthcoming?"

"Very. Especially after I asked him about his beetles. That was after you beeped me. I couldn't shut him up."

"Do you think he could've killed those guys?"

"Christ, who knows?" Hastings shifted irritably in his chair as Ann came into the living room and sat opposite him on the sofa. Her expression was patient and steady; in her eyes, he could plainly read a question. He knew the question and, sadly, she knew his answer. It was Saturday evening. Billy, her youngest, was with his father for the weekend. Dan wouldn't return until midnight. Hastings had promised dinner out, just the two of them. Italian, they'd decided. A new place in North Beach.

"Just a second, Pete." Hastings covered the mouthpiece, turned in his chair to face Ann squarely. "Honey, I'm sorry—" He gestured helplessly. "It's the Rabelais thing. It could all be coming together."

She nodded, half smiled, reached for the paperback book she'd put on the coffee table earlier. "I've got some red snapper," she said. "I'll cook that and make a salad. You won't be real late, will you?"

"No. Two, three hours."

As she nodded and opened her book, Hastings spoke into the phone. "Is Canelli available?"

"Yes. He's waiting for you to call him."

"What's the rundown on Dietz?"

"I talked by phone to the woman who runs the place where he's living. Her name is Florence Le June. Sigler talked to her for some time, says she's very cooperative, very conscientious. Apparently she's part of a new drug program—halfway houses, with funding from the state. I talked to her on the phone. She says Dietz's real problem is booze, not drugs. She says Dietz is very unpredictable, but in certain moods he can be fascinating. Or maybe she said mesmerizing. Anyhow, she also says that Dietz lacks self-control and flies into rages for odd reasons, at odd times. She thinks it's probably when he's sneaked something to drink, but she's not sure. What's really interesting, though, is that, surprise, Dietz is a preacher. His first name is Raymond, by the way."

"A *preacher*?" As he said it, Hastings saw Ann's head come up, saw her look at him quizzically, interested. "A real preacher?"

"He's a revivalist. He grew up down in the Central Valley. Stockton, maybe. He—"

"Are you sure? Stockton?"

"Why?"

"Because that's where Fields comes from, I think."

192

"Hmmm." Friedman let a beat pass. Then: "Well, in any case, Dietz was one of these boy evangelists. His father was an evangelist. With a tent, and everything. That's where Raymond got his start."

"So he grew up, married, and had a daughter named Sally," Hastings said. "Who, of course, became a hooker, because her parents wouldn't let her go out with boys when she was in high school. So, in time, Dietz went bonkers, because his daughter was a fallen woman."

"So naturally," Friedman said, picking up the beat, "when she ODed in the line of duty, screwing around with the Rabelais poker guys, Dietz heard God tell him to avenge his daughter's death. It figures."

"Do you know anything about his history? How long has he lived in San Francisco?"

"No idea," Friedman answered. "But Florence Le June, odds-on, can tell you."

Across the living room, Ann put her book aside, glanced at her watch, pantomimed a phantom glass raised to her lips, and questioned Hastings with her eyes. He nodded, pantomimed working a seltzer bottle. He'd take a seltzer and ice, with a wedge of lemon, his favorite. As she nodded, rose, and left the room—while, yet again, he admired the play of her blue-jeaned buttocks and thighs—Hastings spoke into the phone.

"You've done it again, Pete."

Definitely not taking the bait, his trademark gambit, Friedman said only, "Oh?"

"You've built the suspense, saved the best for the last."

"Dietz, you mean. The crazed evangelist."

"Compared to an ex-playboy who plays grab ass with hookers and loses at poker—compared to a strange little man who collects bugs and maybe resents having been fired from a nothing job a couple of years ago—there's no comparison. Dietz has got to be our boy."

"I see. So, like I said when I paged you at Rivak's, don't take any chances with this guy. *None.* You're to take Canelli in with you. Don't leave him in the car. And I want at least one unmarked unit right there, for backup. Got it?"

"Got it." As Ann came into the room, gave him his drink, and then ran a light, provocative finger down his neck beneath the ear, Hastings said, "First I'm going to have dinner. Then I'll see Dietz."

"And Johnson, too? Tonight?"

"Let's see how it goes."

"Right. But remember, safety first. I've got a feeling on this one."

"Safety first."

30

As the door swung open to reveal a large, cheerful-looking woman with brassy blond hair that could be a wig, Hastings decided "Mrs." was a better bet than either "Miss" or "Ms."

"Mrs. Le June? Florence Le June?"

She nodded readily as she looked down at the shield in Hastings's hand. It was a definitive moment, and Florence Le June passed the first test. Her eyes were steady as she looked directly at Hastings, then at Canelli.

"I'm Lieutenant Hastings and this is Inspector Canelli, Mrs. Le June." As he spoke, Hastings looked beyond the woman, into the house's interior. At that moment a tall, gaunt man with a deeply etched, hollowed-out face and haunted eyes appeared in an interior hallway that intersected the entryway. With his eyes fix focused straight ahead, the man disappeared as quickly as he'd appeared, a ghostly apparition.

"If you've got a few minutes," Hastings said, "we'd like to talk to you. First we'd like to talk to you, then to Raymond Dietz."

"Ah—" Florence Le June nodded regretfully. In the pale light of the porch lamp, her pancake makeup was so thick that it flaked. "Ah—Raymond. Please—" She led the way to a small, ill-furnished, garishly lit room that adjoined the entryway. She closed the front door, locked it, pocketed the key, and joined them, closing the hallway door as she entered the small room.

"I understand," Hastings said, "that this is a halfway house for recovering addicts."

She nodded. "It's a new program—a pilot project."

"How many—" Hastings paused, to choose the word. "How many guests do you have?"

"Four, right now. I'm expecting another gentleman next week. I only take men. I'm licensed for six men."

"Are you a nurse, Mrs. Le June?"

She nodded. "Yessir, I am." Good-humoredly resigned, she grimaced. "For more years than I care to think about."

"Are some of your patients on medication?"

"They're all on medication. The doctor comes by once a week to give them checkups and update their prescriptions."

"Tell us about Raymond Dietz."

She looked at Hastings with calm appraisal. In the room's bright overhead light, her heavily made-up face could have been a harlequin's. But, beneath the badly drawn eyebrows, surrounded by black mascara and green liner, her eyes were shrewd. Her voice was measured.

"I'd like to know," she said, "the reason that you're asking. I'm not trying to make your job harder. But I have a certain responsibility to these men. It's not good for them to be disturbed. You understand."

Hastings nodded. "I understand." He considered, then said, "We're in Homicide, Mrs. Le June. We're working on an open case, and Mr. Dietz's name came up. We've got to talk to him." In apology, he spread his hands. "That's all we can tell you right now."

"He's in trouble, then."

"No. This is an absolutely routine investigation. However, we *do* want to interrogate him." He hardened his gaze, lowered his voice. "One way or the other, either here or downtown, we're going to talk to him. You may as well understand that, Mrs. Le June. And if I were you, if I was concerned for Mr. Dietz's welfare, I think I'd want to see him questioned here, in his own home, where you can at least monitor what happens. Do you understand what I'm saying?"

Resigned, she sighed, nodded. "Yes," she said softly, "I see. I understand."

"Is Mr. Dietz here now, on the premises?"

"Yessir, he is. He's in his room."

"I noticed that you locked the front door behind you," Canelli said. "Does that mean that you control the comings and goings of your patients?"

"It's not that I *control* them," she said. "They're all free to come and go as they like. They're encouraged to come and go, in fact. Two of the gentlemen have jobs. Good jobs," she said proudly. "It's part of the program. But there are rules. And one of the rules is that I have to know when they leave and when they get back."

"Is there a curfew?" Canelli asked.

"Weekdays," she replied, "I ask them to be in by eleven o'clock at night. Weekends I tell them midnight, maybe a little after. Twelve-thirty, though, that's the cutoff. I don't make it a rule, not in the sense that they're punished for not obeying. The only rule is that, when they go out, they're not to drink or take drugs. If they do that, then they're out of the program."

"You said earlier, though," Canelli said, "that sometimes they sneak drinks."

She looked at Canelli for a moment, considered, then said, "Nobody's perfect, Inspector. I'm not, and neither are they. But we try. And, generally, we work things out. It takes understanding, though. A lot of understanding, sometimes."

"Still," Hastings said, "you monitor their movements. You know where they are nights."

"I've got the key to the door," she answered. "*That's* a rule. I lock the door, and I unlock it. That's not my idea. It comes from Sacramento. It's part of the program. I don't have anything to say about it. I'm a contractor. I do what I'm told."

"Last night," Hastings said. "Did Mr. Dietz go out last night?"

As if she sensed the make-or-break significance of the question, she looked squarely at Hastings, then said gravely, "Yessir, Mr. Dietz did go out last night."

Careful to keep excitement out of his voice, Hastings said, "At what time did he leave?"

"I'd say about nine o'clock."

"Are your patients allowed to drive?"

"Two drive, two don't." She said it defensively, plainly reluctant to reveal that two of her "men" were prohibited from driving. Mrs. Le June's instincts, Hastings decided, were generous and caring. The packaging was bizarre, but the product was first rate.

"Mr. Dietz—does he drive?"

She nodded. "Oh, yes, Mr. Dietz drives. That's no problem."

"Does he have a car?"

"Yes. It's old, but it seems to run fine."

"Where did Mr. Dietz say he was going last night?"

"He was going to a movie. That's where most of my men go. To movies. Usually on Fridays or Saturdays. I always tell them it isn't so crowded other nights. But they never pay any attention." She shook her head good-naturedly.

"Did he go alone?"

She nodded. "As far as I know, yes."

"What time did he get home?"

"It was a little after midnight."

"Twelve-fifteen, would you say?"

"Probably, yes."

Calculating, Hastings nodded silently. Phillips had died at eleven-thirty. By car, on a Friday night, the drive from the murder scene to the Le June residence would take twenty minutes, no more.

"How long have you known Raymond Dietz, Mrs. Le June?"

"Five months," she answered promptly. "I started here—began the program—six months ago. Mr. Dietz was my second gentleman."

Hastings looked at the closed door to the entry hall. Could Dietz have seen them arrive? Could Dietz be listening at the door? If he asked Mrs. Le June to check, would she be offended? Would she turn uncooperative?

Involuntarily lowering his voice, he asked, "What can you tell me about him, Mrs. Le June? What kind of a person is he? Is he violent? Is he in control? I know he used to be an evangelist. Does he still preach? Does he talk to God?"

She sat silently for a moment, studying him. Then: "Mr. Dietz doesn't talk to God, at least not as far as I know. And he doesn't rant and rave, either. He's a very soft-spoken person. He's very—" She searched for the word. "—very intense, there's no question about that. I'm no doctor, but I'd say he's manic-depressive. Sometimes he's very quiet, very withdrawn. That is, he doesn't talk at all. He—he seems to be listening, when he's like that—listening very carefully. But then some-

199

thing sets him off, and he'll become very—very excited. He has very strong opinions about certain things. But, no matter how excited he gets, he never raises his voice. And he's never been violent. Ever."

"What kinds of things set him off?"

"Oh . . ." Vaguely, she waved. "Sin, I guess you'd say. He's very concerned about morals—about pornography, things like that." She hesitated, then decided to say "One of the other gentlemen—Mr. Katz—had a copy of *Playboy*. And the truth is that Mr. Dietz got very upset about it. He didn't shout, or anything. But he *was* upset, no question."

"Upset in what way? Was he upset that Mr. Katz was reading the magazine? Or was it that—" He exchanged a quick, significant look with Canelli. "Or was he upset that women would pose like that, naked?"

Thinking about it, she frowned thoughtfully. "I guess it was both."

"Is Mr. Dietz married?"

She shook her head. "No, he's a widower. He's actually had a very tragic life. His only daughter died a few years ago. It was food poisoning, very sudden. And then his wife left him and later killed herself. It was—" She lowered her voice, sadly shook her head. "It was very hard for him. *Very* hard. When Mr. Dietz came here, Dr. Bergman warned me not to talk about his wife."

Notebook ready, Canelli asked, "What's Dr. Bergman's full name?"

"It's Herman Bergman. He's on the staff at Franklin Hospital."

"Is he a psychiatrist?"

"Yes."

"What about the daughter's death?" Hastings asked. "Did Dr. Bergman say anything about that?"

"Well, he mentioned it. Like I said."

"Did he say that it could've been something other than food poisoning?"

"You mean—" She licked her lips, shifted her eyes. Finally: "You mean like suicide?"

"I was thinking of a drug overdose."

She shook her head. "No, Dr. Bergman didn't say anything about that."

"Does Mr. Dietz ever talk about his daughter?"

"No. Never."

"What about his wife—her suicide? Does he ever talk about that?"

She shook her head. "Never."

Hastings nodded thoughtfully, then looked questioningly at Canelli, who shook his head. Hastings turned to the woman. "I guess that's about it for now, Mrs. Le June. You've been very cooperative, very helpful. Now if you'll get Mr. Dietz for us, we'll talk to him and then be on our way."

"Shall I ask him to come down here? Or would you rather see him in his room?"

"His room will be fine."

31

Dietz sat in a threadbare armchair that had been placed against the wall beside a small fireplace. He wore striped pajamas and a blanket-style bathrobe with a braided sateen tie. His pale, bony feet were thrust into run-over slippers. In his fifties, Dietz was a gaunt man of medium height. Like the man who had appeared in the downstairs hallway, a sleepwalking apparition, Dietz's face was deeply creased, a ravaged mask of psychic torment. Like Anton Rivak, his eyes were dark, and burned with some secret inner passion. His hair was white and thick and wild, an Old Testament evocation. Against the pallor of his skin, his mouth was wide and shapeless, an angry red scar gouged out in the pallid flesh of the face. His voice was low, and vibrated with suppressed passion.

"I don't understand the reason for all these questions, Lieutenant. You realize that I am an ordained minister of the gospel." As he spoke, Dietz fixed Hastings with a manic stare. Demanding: "You acknowledge that."

Exchanging an exasperated glance with Canelli, Hastings sighed, nodded, spoke patiently. "Yessir, I acknowledge that. But you've got to acknowledge that I need an account of your movements last night from ten till—"

"But you talk about Sally. First you ask what I did last night. Then you ask about Sally. Then you say you're investigating a murder." Dietz raised a long, bony forefinger. His fingernails, Hastings saw, were dirty and broken. "Plainly, you're trying to confuse me, throw me off balance. But that will never happen, Lieutenant. *Never.*"

"What we want to know—the first thing we want to know," Hastings said, "is where you were last night between—"

"Because I'm here—" Dietz raised his hand, gestured to the neatly kept room. "Confined against my will by a woman with a ring of keys, you think you can find me guilty and put me behind bars. But I'm used to persecution, Lieutenant. Our Lord Jesus was not afraid, did not bend, and neither will I bend. I will never surrender. When I see evil, I speak out. And if I must take up my cross and carry it to the place of crucifixion, then I'll do it. But it will be my choice. If I confess, then it will be of my own free will and will therefore be the truth. Do you understand that, Lieutenant?" He fixed Hastings with his dark, blazing eyes. His whole body had gone rigid, plainly possessed by a righteous indignation.

Aware of his own rising frustration, the interrogator's bane, Hastings looked away, shifted in his chair, drew a long, deep breath. They'd been at it for almost an hour. And Dietz was winning, not losing.

Discreetly clearing his throat, Canelli was looking at him. The message: Canelli was requesting a turn. Gracelessly, he knew, Hastings nodded permission.

Canelli began guilelessly, his moon-faced specialty. "From what you've said, Mr. Dietz, I gather that you're pretty famous. Especially down south, in the Central Valley. The way I get it, you started preaching when you were only a little kid, with your daddy."

With apparent reluctance, seemingly in spite of himself, Dietz shifted his attention from Hastings to Canelli, who was raising his eyes, as if he were seeing some heavenly vision. His gaze rapt, Canelli spoke fervently, in a low, hushed voice. "I'm Catholic. My whole family is Catholic. We're Italians, you see, and that's how we were raised. I was an altar boy. Father Spinelli—" Canelli shook his head reverently. "I'll never forget Father Spinelli. We used to have a basketball team, and Father Spinelli was our coach. But anyhow, what I was going to say, I remember thinking when I was about twelve, maybe thirteen, that, jeez, how wonderful it would be to preach, and look down, and see all those faces looking up at you—waiting for the word." As he said it, Canelli stole a glance at Dietz. Had it worked? Had he connected? Except for the dark, burning eyes boring in, there was no hint, no clue.

"Your father," Canelli ventured, "must've been proud. Very proud. I'm single, myself. I hope to get married, but I'm thirty-two already, so I have to wonder, will it ever happen? I mean, jeez, if you don't get married, have children, what's the point?" Once more, covertly, Canelli searched Dietz's face for a reaction. Still nothing. Except that, with his right hand, Dietz began to scratch at his left forearm beneath the blanket-style bathrobe.

"Mrs. Le June . . ." Canelli spoke the name softly, with infinite respect. "What a wonderful, caring lady. When she told us about your daughter, how she died, there were tears in her eyes."

Still, Dietz's face remained impassive. But, behind his dark, fervent eyes, a spark began to glow.

"Something like food poisoning," Canelli went on, "it's so—so terrible. So unfair. The victim isn't doing anything wrong, isn't even aware that he—or she—is taking a risk. And then . . ." Sadly Canelli gestured, shook his head. "And then it's all over. Terrible." He ventured another oblique look at Dietz, then decided to let silence settle. The Le June house was within a few miles of San Francisco International; overhead, on takeoff, an airliner was thundering into the sky.

"And then your wife," Canelli said. "Poor Mrs. Le June got all choked up talking about your wife. She and your daughter, your only child, gone. It's no wonder that—"

"All my life," Dietz said, "I've been misjudged." His voice was disembodied, dreamlike; his eyes were vague, unfocused. "You're like all the rest of them. You think it was wonderful, being a child evangelist. Appearances—the visible—it's so pitiful how easily people are fooled. They saw me, heard me—believed me. And my father, they believed him, too. But at night, at home, when the curtains were drawn and the shades pulled down, my father drank. And raved. And drank. He kept a cane hung on the coat rack in the front hallway. His shepherd's crook, he called it. If we displeased him when he drank, he would get the cane. He would chase my mother and me with the cane. If he caught me, then my mother would try to save me." Slowly, catatonically, he shook his head. "She was so pitiful, my mother. For all of her life, she was a victim. Sometimes I used to think that the only time she came alive was when she was trying to protect me. Even when he—he died, she didn't come alive."

"It must've been terrible," Canelli said, his morose expression so convincing that, for a moment, Hastings was persuaded.

"I didn't realize how terrible. Not until, when I was thirteen, I got to the shepherd's crook first."

"Ah . . ." Deeply sympathetic, Canelli nodded. "You got the shepherd's crook first, so you could protect your mother."

"I was thirteen," Dietz repeated, his voice still dull, his eyes still empty. "And a year later, he was dead."

"Ah . . ." Once more, Canelli nodded. Then, probing: "How did he die, Mr. Dietz?"

Ignoring the question, Dietz said, "I delivered the funeral oration. Afterward, I had no memory of what I said. It was the first time I was ever transported out of myself, into another dimension. I preached for more than an hour, they told me afterward. Two weeks later, on Sunday, I preached again. And then . . ." As if he were unsure of his surroundings, Dietz blinked, finally focused on Canelli. "And then I was someone. I was only fourteen, but I was someone. There were pictures of me in the newspaper."

"Fourteen . . ." Marveling, Canelli shook his head. Then: "Do you mean that, beginning when you were fourteen, you were on your own, managed your own affairs?"

"There was Clayton," Dietz said. "He was my cousin. He managed everything."

"Your wife," Canelli said. "Was she young, when you married her?"

At the question, Dietz's eyes sharpened. "Do you—know about Carolyn?"

Canelli glanced at Hastings for instructions. It was time to bluff, take a chance. But what were the stakes—and the risks? Hastings raised his shoulders a half inch. Canelli was on a roll. The decision, then, was his.

Canelli drew a deep breath, took the gamble. "We know your wife left, and we know your daughter died. So we wondered, could they be connected, those two things?"

As Canelli said it, Dietz's fingernails had been digging into his left forearm beneath the bathrobe. With every passing moment, the scratching had become more intense. Now, with eyes gone feverish, body straining as if to resist the constraints of invisible bonds, Dietz moved his right hand to the neck of his pajamas. He began scratching at his left shoulder under the pajamas. His gaze was fixed on Canelli. Watching. Waiting.

But Canelli revealed no emotion. He, too, could only watch and wait.

When he finally began to speak, his eyes still locked with Canelli's, Dietz's voice was a hoarse, harsh whisper. "I am surrounded by death. Sometimes, in the night, I know I am death. My father and my mother, Sally—they're all dead. My father was too cruel to live, and my mother was too timid. And Sally—" He began to shake his head as, slowly, his body went slack. "Sally was already dead. Before she died, she was dead."

"But you still had to avenge her," Hastings said, his voice hushed. "Tony Frazer and Gordon Johnson and all the others at Rabelais—you had to punish them, make them pay." As he spoke, Hastings searched the other man's face for a reaction, "Didn't you?"

In the lengthening silence, now sitting slack in the chair, eyes fallen, Dietz made no response, gave no sign that he'd heard. Then, as the roar of another airliner began, growing louder and louder until it passed overhead, then returned the room to silence, Dietz stirred, roused himself, finally met Hastings's eyes. As if he were bothered by some minor inconvenience, puzzled, Dietz frowned. Saying fretfully: "Rabelais?" Beneath the bathrobe, his fingernails once more began tearing at the flesh of his shoulder.

Conscious of the necessity to keep his voice noncommittal, revealing nothing, Hastings repeated the name of the club, then repeated the names of the dead men in the order they died. Finally repeating: "The poker players."

"Poker players?" As if he were annoyed now, valuable time wasting, Dietz's manner became restless, resentful. Repeating: "Poker players?"

"Aw, come on, Mr. Dietz." Canelli spoke harshly now, no longer the good cop. "You know what we're talking about. You know what Sally was. You've just told us that you knew. And you know she didn't die of food poisoning. And you—"

Suddenly Dietz sprang to his feet. Eyes blazing, he raised his right arm, pointing to the door with a trembling forefinger. Arm still raised, head held high, legs braced wide, Dietz stood motionless, limbs locked, rigid. It was a biblical pose: the prophet in a blanket bathrobe, the head crowned by a corona of wild white hair. In the silent room, his voice was thunderous. "*Leave*. You've done the damage you came to do, raked up the memories, exposed the wounds. So now—" The quivering forefinger moved to menace Hastings, then moved again to the door. "So now, *leave*."

32

"Well, Lieutenant—" Canelli shook his head heavily. "You want my opinion, I think we're screwed. I just can't see us getting a warrant on what we got. I mean, okay, the guy's balmy. And, okay, he probably could've killed those guys. But all we've got are hunches. And with that lady—Florence Le June— standing watchdog at the door, there's no way we can get some freelancer to get in there, toss the place for the gun."

They sat in their unmarked car, both men staring at the Le June house. It was a standard San Francisco row house: a stucco façade embellished by imitation Spanish tile and decorative rough-hewn timbers, with a large picture window that looked out on a block of identical houses, each one built over a narrow garage and attached to its neighbor on either side. Some of the small front gardens featured stunted palm trees, most did not. At eleven o'clock on a Saturday night, the neighborhood was peaceful. Only a mile away from the ocean, the weather was overcast, cold and foggy and damp. A ten-year-old Ford sedan was parked directly in front of the Le June house.

"That's probably his car," Hastings said. "And if he's got the gun, it'll be either in his room or else in his car."

"Unless he's got it stashed somewhere." Canelli spoke morosely.

"Someone like that, I doubt that he'd stash it. Somehow it doesn't fit."

"Except that you can't really figure loonies," Canelli said. "That's why they're loonies."

"We didn't find out where he lived before he came here."

"I know," Canelli said. "I'll check it out." He gestured to the radio. "Shall I put in the call?"

"I'll do it," Hastings said, switching on the radio. "I want to order the stakeouts." He called Communications, identified himself, asked for the duty chief, asked for a discreet channel. Moments later a familiar voice crackled in the speaker. It was Harold Peirce. Years ago, they'd graduated together from the Academy.

"Frank. What's happening?"

"Nothing's happening," Hastings answered sourly. "That's the problem."

"So what can I do for you?"

"I need two more stakeouts. Plainclothes, unmarked cars." He gave the names and addresses of Dietz and Gordon Johnson. While he discussed the details, Canelli crossed the street and copied down the Ford's license plate number. Hastings read out the number, adding: "We think it's Dietz's car, but you should check. Get his previous addresses, any priors, anything at all.

210

He's about fifty, fifty-five. Medium height, maybe a hundred sixty, no more. Wild white hair. Not real long, but bushy. Strange, piercing dark eyes. His face looks—" He hesitated. "Well, his face is wild, too, very deeply lined. Like a mask, that's the impression you get. The guy's supposed to be a revivalist."

"A what?"

"An evangelist, from down south, apparently. He started preaching in a tent, with his father. Down in the Central Valley somewhere."

"Huh . . ."

"On this stakeout—Dietz—I want someone as soon as possible, someone good. I've got the subject stirred up, and sometimes they pack a bag and take off. But, if this guy runs, he'll probably be armed and dangerous. So be sure and advise caution."

"Yessir."

"The Johnson stakeout can wait for an hour, at least. It might even be a bust. But I figure if he's managing a motel on Lombard Street, and it's Saturday night, he's probably there. After I talk to him, I'll give the information—description, and everything—to the stakeout. So our guy shouldn't make inquiries. It might spook the suspect."

"Right."

"What about the Louis Fields stakeout?"

"That's the protective one," Peirce said. "He's not a suspect. Right?"

"Right."

"Nothing to report."

"What about Rivak?"

"That's Penziner and Whaley. I just talked to Penziner. They went on at five o'clock. But at about ten o'clock—an hour ago—Whaley got the, ah, stomach flu, otherwise known as the shits. He was covering the back, and Penziner was covering the front. So now we've only got the front covered. You want me to send another man?"

Mentally Hastings calculated: four stakeouts, eight men. Ten, altogether, on the Rabelais killings. When Cost Control looked at the time sheets, they would not be pleased.

"Let me talk to Penziner. Can you patch me through?"

"Sure."

"You stay in the net."

"Right. Hold on."

Less than a minute later, on the discreet channel, Penziner's voice materialized: "Yessir?"

"Is there an alley behind Rivak's building?" Hastings asked.

"No, sir. But there's a rear exit and a small courtyard back there. If Rivak wanted to run, he'd have to hop a fence."

"Has Rivak got a car?"

"Yessir. It's a Corolla, about five years old. But I don't know where it is. It's parked on the street, probably. His building doesn't have garages, you know."

"Could you see Rivak's apartment from the back?"

"Yessir."

"But not from the front."

"Right. But I figured I had to take the front. Like I said, unless he hops fences, he's got to come to me."

"No question." He paused, calculated. Then: "Harold?"

"Yessir," the Communications supervisor answered.

"Get two men over to Rivak's, then let Penziner go home."

"Yessir."

"Right," Penziner acknowledged. "Thanks. Out." He clicked off.

"Harold?"

"Right here, Lieutenant."

"I'm leaving now to interrogate Johnson. Inspector Canelli'll

212

stay here until the stakeout arrives, then he'll need a ride to Lombard Street."

"Yessir."

"Can I have this channel for the next two hours?"

"No problem," Peirce said.

"Good. Well, I'd better get to work."

"Gottcha."

33

From outside the living room headlights flashed, moving as the
car left the reservation parking area, making its way to the guest
parking lot. The last vacancy, then, was filled; now the NO
VACANCY sign would be switched on, tonight's mission accomplished. In the half-dark living room, the headlight beam shone
briefly on the bottle that rested on the glass-topped bureau. The
previous manager, an ex-marine, had been a chain-smoker. At
his own expense he'd had glass tops made for the suite's flat
surfaces, to protect them from neglected cigarettes. Then, surprise, a vacancy in top management had opened up when the
marine, a man named Murphy, had broken up a fight on Lombard Street, a block from the motel. One of the combatants had

pulled a knife, and Murphy had died where he fell. The burial, it was said, was conducted with full military honors.

Testing himself, he rose from the chair and stood motionless, feet close together, arms extended, chin elevated. On the TV screen in the half-light, a digital clock pulsed out the seconds: five seconds—fifteen seconds—finally thirty seconds. Perfect. Rock-steady perfect. With the empty glass in hand, permission granted, he began his approach to the bottle. His progress was slow and steady, himself in command of himself. He was, after all, only fifty years old. There was time. Colonel Sanders, after all, had been sixty-five when he'd started his string of southern-fried-chicken franchises.

He poured the bourbon carefully, a precise half glass full. With the volume turned down, the TV images were a third presence in the room—himself, the backlit bottle of bourbon, and the electronic images: the eleven o'clock news, a chronicle of disasters. Already he'd seen a building burning and a body covered with green plastic, lying on the sidewalk, with blood running in rivulets from under the green plastic.

Somewhere, in some equation, there was a correlation: violent death and advertising revenue, tit for tat. TV screens and computer screens, everything could be rationalized, the culture of the bottom line: one erg of violence equaled one erg of market share. Make a profit, and the drinks were on the house. Make a mistake, slip into the red, and they all looked through you. All the drinking buddies, all the women with their sidelong glances, they all looked away.

His father—how many ergs of profit had his father generated, the way he died? Even his mother, dead of natural causes, had boosted the circulation numbers.

But Sally Dietz, poor Sally, had died in the wrong way, in the wrong place, at the wrong time.

He lifted the glass, sipped, lowered the glass. In the window, another swath of headlights swept in a circle, a disappointed

215

traveler. Or, more likely, a man and a woman, barroom lovers, looking for a room. No baggage, no pain. No gain, when the room grew light with the morning sunshine, the Sunday morning blues.

Another sip, followed by a practiced appraisal of the whiskey left in the glass. Soon the endgame would begin, that most delicate calculation: how to make the day come out even, the liquor's gift of courage captured in its fullness, then phased into the forgetfulness of sleep, that most merciful of conditions.

But first, between the next sip and the balm of sleep, his duty must be done. For fifteen thousand a year, plus room, plus food, he must now take up his duties, make his nightly rounds, offer words of encouragement to his faithful staff.

Fifteen thousand . . .

How much money did Jeffrey make? Jeffrey, who had given him so much pleasure, that chortling, bubbling, blue-eyed baby, now twenty-five years old, newly graduated from Stanford Law. When he'd gotten the embossed invitation to the graduation and realized that the letter was postmarked the day of the ceremony, he'd felt the whole world shift, then fall away.

When—if—he got an invitation to Donna's wedding, what date would be stamped on the envelope? Did Donna know—could he ever tell her—that she alone fulfilled him? When he began his climb back, that long, inevitable journey, did she know that only she could sustain him? Donna, nineteen years old now, so beautiful when last he'd seen her. So free. So graceful when she moved, so carefree when she laughed. Their mothers were different, accounting for the difference between the two of them: Jeffrey, no longer the bubbling baby, was now the sober-sided lawyer, a stranger, already middle-aged, already thickening at the waist.

But Donna would always be his. When he'd smiled, Donna had laughed. Always.

He sipped again, examined the drink again, calculated again, this calculation an examination of the inner periphery, the sphere within the sphere, himself confronting himself. First the scrutiny must focus within. Then must come the outward view, alert for the first definitive manifestations of—yes— his partnership with the contents of the magical bottle: that amorphous softening, the sadness diffused, the harsh lines softened, all of it balanced, in perfect equilibrium. How could he surrender, give it up? Even though it had betrayed him, left him hanging, sent him crashing down, yet it was all that mattered, the focus of everything: the magic that turned the glare of noon into sunset gold, the miracle that muted the screams of agony, all the cries for help. Even his own.

Carefully, noting once more the level of the amber fluid, he set the glass aside, rose, steadied himself, checked himself. Yes, all was well. Signifying that now he could compose himself, leave his manager's apartment, make the night's final inspection: the day's last changing of the guard, a check of the room tally, the desk clerk's closing report, a chronicle of problems, real and imagined. The keys would pass from the off-shift clerk to the on-shift clerk, and the ritual would be complete, another day in the life of Gordon Johnson, mercifully ended.

During the short walk from his apartment to the motel office he picked up two empty Styrofoam cups, assorted food and candy wrappers, and an advertising circular. He dropped the debris in the trash barrel in front of the office, paused, drew a deep breath, gathered himself, and pushed open the office door. "Showtime" was the with-it expression. Time for the last performance of the day.

Bill Kelley, newly hired, newly arrived in San Francisco from Akron, Ohio, looked up from the magazine he was reading, a copy of G.Q.

"Everything under control?" Johnson smiled. Kelley was a

morose, introverted youth with a bad complexion who, sure enough, chose not to return the smile. In the game of life, Kelley was an odds-on loser.

"All full." Kelley closed the magazine, glanced at the wall clock, yawned. His replacement at the desk, midnight to nine, was due to arrive in exactly ten minutes.

"Any problems?"

Kelley looked at a notebook. "The last ones—two guys—were pretty drunk. And there're two families with noisy kids. I put all of them in the east wing. Maybe they'll—"

A car bounced up from the driveway, came to a stop in one of the visitors' parking slots. Automatically, Johnson glanced at the motel sign. Yes, NO VACANCY was lit. The new arrival was an expensive Japanese muscle car, all white, low-slung and powerful looking. A man was behind the wheel, a woman sat beside him. As the headlights died the man turned to kiss the woman, a rough, fervent embrace, recklessly returned. Saturday night lovers, at least half drunk. *Hot sheeters*, in motel jargon.

"Want to go for a price?" Kelley asked. "Give 'em the reserve room?"

Johnson watched the man as, tearing himself away, he stroked the woman's breast, laughed, swung the door open wide, said something as he slammed the door, strode unsteadily toward the office. In his middle twenties, tall and well built, with styled hair, the man wore a leather bomber jacket and tight blue jeans, the barroom stud's uniform of choice.

Johnson shrugged. "If he'll pay. If—" In the tiny office behind the lobby, the phone rang.

"That's probably for me," Kelley said. "I've got my brother's car."

"All right—" Reluctantly Johnson took his place behind the counter as the newcomer came through the door. The man's manner matched his look and his car and his clothes: smooth, confident, narcissistic, all of it accented by an aura of arrogance and the raw urgency of sex. As the sordid little deal was being struck, all cash, double the normal rate, the required name and address written on the reservation card transparent fakes, no auto license number required, Johnson took the key to the reserve room from the board and handed it over. Later, he and Kelley would split the seventy-dollar overcharge.

"It's in the east wing, ground floor." Johnson pointed. "You can swing around here, go back the way you came, turn right at the end, and you're there."

"Right." As the man accepted the key, he took a ten-dollar bill from his pocket, put it on the counter. "There. That's for your piggy bank, Pops." He turned away, left the office, crossed the wide concrete apron to the expensive sports car where the woman waited. They kissed, groped each other wildly, their bodies writhing in the darkness of the car, Saturday night sex gone wild. Then, once more tearing himself away, the man started the car, switched on the lights, revved the engine as he swung the car in a wide, wild circle in front of the office. As the car passed within a few feet of the motel lobby, light from inside the plate glass shone on the woman inside the car. She turned full face to look into the lobby as, in that instant, their eyes met.

Donna.

The shock of recognition was simultaneous, momentarily motion stopped:

He behind the counter, frozen.

Donna already gone, the muscle car's taillights winking red in the darkness.

Donna, a pickup from a singles' bar, shacking up. A hot sheeter.

In the office behind the counter, Kelley was saying good-bye, cradling the phone. "A real sport," he said, looking expectantly

219

at the tens and twenties lying on the shelf behind the counter as he came into the office. "Shall I—" He moved closer to the money, gesturing expectantly. Meaning that he would put seventy dollars into the cash register and take thirty-five dollars of the seventy remaining, a tip for a pimp.

Thirty-five dollars—three bottles of medium-grade bourbon.

"Hey—" Kelley said, frowning, looking at him. "Hey, you all right? Gordon? You feeling okay?"

Moving away from the money, one hand braced on the counter, Johnson began to shake his head. As he did, the room rocked from side to side, that terrible sensation, collapse without hope, all of it sliding away, taking him with it. Meaning that he must leave, must escape.

"I—I've got to lie down. See you tomorrow." He pushed himself away from the counter. Standing unsupported, he turned to face the door.

Donna, naked, writhing in a stranger's caress, her body locked with his.

"Hey—" Rounding the counter, Kelley was placing a hand on his forearm. With his free hand, Kelley was opening the door. "Hey, take it easy, Gordon. Okay?"

"Yes . . ." With great effort, he nodded. "Yes. Okay."

"So I'll see you tomorrow. Right?" Kelley's eyes, too close, were anxious.

Safely through the door, free of Kelley's grasp, he was still nodding as he turned to his left, toward his apartment. Thank God, the apartment was on the ground floor. To climb stairs would be—

"Hey—" Once more Kelley was beside him, gripping his forearm. "Hey, you forgot the money. You—"

Blindly he pulled free, staggered, found his footing. *"No. No!"* Was he screaming? Creating a disturbance? Ahead, he could clearly see his door, number five. As a young man, weekending in San Francisco, he might have stayed in a motel like this one, might have gotten lucky in a bar, taken her to a motel, fucked until he was exhausted, then given her twenty dollars "for the cab fare."

Would Donna, in the east wing, take twenty dollars and leave afterward? Her mother had taken almost a million dollars in a lump sum, plus three thousand dollars a month.

Donna, in the east wing.

As the image seared his consciousness, as he threw open the door to number 5, his only refuge on earth, he tried to stifle the scream of pain, of endless desperation. He slammed the door, went to the bureau, and the bottle. Yes, the bottle was where he'd left it, exactly where he'd left it, an essential beginning. But now, in the darkness, he must search for the glass. It was necessary that he find the glass, which still contained perhaps an inch of bourbon, perhaps a little less. He'd carefully left the glass with liquor still in it, something to come home to, after he'd seen Kelley, done his business. It was necessary, an essential element of control, that he left the glass not empty. Because once the glass took over, not him, there was no hope. It was a question of dominance, of—

Yes, he remembered; he'd left the glass on top of the television. Conscious of an overwhelming gratitude, he turned, saw the glass. Like the bottle, the glass picked up light from outside, even though the room was dark. So, like the bottle, the glass glowed softly, a promise of hope. She was, after all, nineteen. They might, after all, be planning marriage. The boy's bad manners, his arrogance, Saturday night strutting, all of it in time might pass.

The night's plan, then, the minute-to-minute blueprint for survival, might be modified. Meaning that first he must take up the glass and drink the contents. Then, with the glass in hand, the self in command, recovering, he would—

A knock.

At the door, someone was knocking.

34

Hastings knocked again, exchanged a look with Canelli, who went to the ground-floor window, looked inside, shook his head. Whispering: "It's all dark, I can't see a thing." As he spoke, a car came from behind one wing of the motel, the sound of its engine low and powerful. On motel property, the all-white car, a sports car, was running without headlights. As Hastings watched its progress the car passed within a few feet of them, bound for the motel exit. The driver, a man wearing a leather bomber jacket, looked straight ahead, ignoring the two detectives. Beside him, in the darkened interior of the car, a young woman sat rigidly, also staring straight ahead. On instinct, both detectives followed the progress of the white car until it turned into the Lombard Street traffic and disappeared. Speaking softly, Canelli said, "It looked like they were pretty uptight."

Hastings nodded thoughtfully. "Did you make the license plate?"

Canelli shook his head regretfully. "Not the plate. But I made the car. It's a Toyota Supra. My cousin's got one just like it, only red."

Hastings turned again to face the door of unit 5. He unbuttoned his sports jacket, loosened his revolver in its spring holster, put his right hand on the walnut grip. He waited for Canelli to turn, stand to his left, ready. As the two men exchanged nods, Hastings used his left hand to slowly, cautiously turn the doorknob. The latch clinked; the door opened one inch—two inches. Hastings drew a deep breath, exchanged a final nod with Canelli, whose hand also gripped the butt of his revolver. It was during these moments, both men knew, that their lives were most at risk. Taking a single step backward, clear of the doorway, Hastings fully extended his arm, cautiously pushed the door open wide.

"Mr. Johnson . . ."

As, overwhelmingly, the odor came so strongly that Hastings swore, stepped back. It was the odor of violent death: blood and urine and excrement. Dimly revealed in the outside light coming through the open door, the victim lay as he'd fallen: on his back, one arm flung wide, the other arm lying across his stomach, his legs slightly spread, both toes pointed outward. His eyes were open wide, staring at the ceiling. His mouth gaped. His torso was blood-soaked, one side of the skull was blown away, just above the ear. The blood was still fresh, glistening in the dim light. An empty highball glass lay on the carpeting beside his hand. Gritting his teeth, Hastings stooped, touched the victim's neck just below the ear. Yes, the flesh was still warm.

He straightened, looked carefully around the apartment's small living room, listened attentively for whatever might stir in the other rooms. Nothing. He spoke softly, an involuntary acknowledgment of death's dominion. "You call it in from the motel office. I'll wait here."

"Yessir."

As Canelli turned away, Hastings stepped back from the body, drew a long, shallow breath, let the crime scene slowly, meticulously register. Even in the dim light, it was possible to see that nothing in the apartment had been disturbed. There was no sign of a struggle, no sign of robbery. With a drink in his hand, Johnson had opened the door to his murderer and been shot twice in the chest. He'd fallen back and taken another. The murderer had holstered his gun, closed the door, and walked away—probably within the previous ten minutes. Automatically Hastings checked the time: ten minutes after midnight. Rivak lived near Chinatown, no more than ten minutes by car. Dietz, near the Daly City line, was at least thirty minutes away.

Hearing footsteps, Hastings turned to see Canelli walking toward him. At a distance of ten feet, Canelli suddenly stooped, examined the concrete driveway.

"Hey, Lieutenant. Guess what?" Kneeling on the concrete, Canelli raised his head, smiling.

"A shell casing," Hastings said. "Twenty-two caliber."

35

When Johnson's body was discovered, and the police were called, then the detective—Hastings—would arrive. Thus did the world end: with a knock on the door. *Not with a bang, but a whimper*, the poet had said. First the knock, then the whimper. His whimper, so long ago. It was an accident, the policeman had said. The policeman was sorry. The policeman had lost his own mother to random violence. Then, regretfully, the policeman had turned away. Mobs were everywhere, he'd said. The night was on fire.

For that encounter, that knock on the door, he hadn't been prepared.

But for tonight's encounter, he would be prepared, with four of the six already dead and decomposing and the fifth still lying in his own blood on the cheap carpeting of the motel, he would be prepared. Of the six only Mr. Fields, the best of them, had been spared.

All debts collected, but one debt yet to pay.

His essential self had died when the first policeman had come to the door. Leaving the remainder of himself, the husk, yet to be offered up, payment in full.

He rose from his chair and walked to the table. Still in its holster, the pistol lay on the table, the holster's strap neatly wrapped around the makeshift holster that had served him so well. He withdrew the pistol, laid it on the table, went to the closet, and put the holster on the top shelf, out of sight. Tonight he had dressed as he always dressed, in his own clothes. Therefore, tonight the holster was all that must be concealed. When Hastings came, he would find everything else he needed, all of it hanging neatly in the garment bag. Hastings would understand, then, that he meant to cooperate. Hastings would realize that, before the last of them died, he could easily have destroyed the disguises he'd first used.

Had it only been weeks since Tony Frazer had died? Six weeks? Was it possible?

But with the thought came the instant's correction. Even though the end was in sight, he must not indulge himself. Not now, not at this moment. To do what he'd done, discipline was essential, both the beginning and the ending. Great men were the masters of their minds. Images appeared as great men called them to consciousness. The images served their purpose and then, on command, submerged again, like prehistoric fish that dwelt in the depths of the sea. Some of those fish, he'd once read, had no eyes. They lived in eternal darkness.

Thus, with time running out, he must order his thoughts, must consign this final departure to the lower depths. Then, alignment achieved, equilibrium assured, everything made ready for whoever must surely come for him, he would command the other departures, as he'd come to call them, to make their consecutive appearances, each one emerging from the lower depths according to his will. Tony Frazer, Gerald Manley, Bruce Carr, and Brandon Phillips were the first departures, each enhancing those that had gone before, the ultimate distillation, all of it culminating tonight, when Johnson had fallen to his knees and begged for absolution. He'd died with a prayer on his lips.

Amen.

36

Driving with one hand, Hastings keyed the microphone, called Communications, asked for Harold Peirce, code "C." Peirce responded immediately. The Communications director was tracking the Johnson homicide; the adrenaline was pumping.

"I want to give you an update," Hastings said. "I'm just leaving the Tides Motel. I'm going to interrogate Anton Rivak at his apartment. That's on Sacramento, just—"

Ahead, a Jaguar sedan suddenly came speeding through the intersection, running a red light. Hastings braked, turned sharply to the right, his left front fender clearing the Jaguar's rear fender by less than a foot. Brakes locked, the cruiser slewed viciously. Swearing, Hastings fought the wheel, cleared the curb on the far side of the intersection, straightened the car, found the microphone on the floor of the car. "Sorry."

"Problem?"

"Drunk driver, probably. Anyhow—" He drew a long, unsteady breath. "Anyhow, Rivak's place is only a mile or two from here, so I'll be there in a few minutes. I left Canelli in charge at the Tides Motel. He'll do everything. Clear?"

"Yessir."

"The murder probably went down about twenty minutes ago. So I want to alert the Dietz stakeout. Immediately. If Dietz is our suspect, then he'll be arriving at the Le June place. Soon. In minutes. Do you copy?"

"Yessir."

"Okay—" At the intersection of Van Ness and Sacramento, Hastings made an illegal left turn onto Sacramento Street. Coming from the opposite direction on Van Ness, a driver was furiously sounding his horn, angrily gesticulating. "Okay," Hastings repeated. "So get hold of the stakeout team, make sure they've got the Le June place covered front and back. Then— and this is important—I *don't want them to apprehend Dietz.* They're to make no contact whatever. They're to let him inside the house, and they're to continue the surveillance." As he spoke, he saw the intersection of Sacramento and Hyde just ahead. Rivak's apartment was less than a block away, on the left.

"If Dietz is spotted, if he enters the house," Hastings said, "call me, obviously. If you can't get me, call Canelli. At the same time, I want you to double the Dietz stakeout, my authority. Got it?"

"Yessir. Got it."

"Okay. Do it."

"Yessir. Good luck. Be careful."

"Always." Hastings replaced the microphone on its hook beneath the dash, slowed the car to a crawl, began looking for the

229

stakeout: a man slumped low in an unmarked car, only the top of his head visible, parked just close enough to see the entrance to Rivak's building. On the second pass he saw the car: the standard middle-age Chevrolet with the telltale communications antenna mounted on the lid of the trunk, always a giveaway.

But, inside the car, in the dim light from a nearby street lamp, he saw a woman. Not a man's head, but a woman's head.

Did Peirce know he'd assigned a woman to the Rivak stakeout after Whaley had gone home with stomach flu?

Or had Peirce simply contacted the duty officer, filled him in, told him to make the assignments?

Either way, someone should have told Hastings, briefed him.

He parked in front of a fireplug, the only slot available. He switched off the engine, set the brake, and keyed the microphone. Should he call Peirce and complain?

Complain about what? About a woman assigned to back him up, protect him if Rivak was the one and came out shooting? In hours, it would be all over the department that he'd objected to serving with a woman.

But in the clutch, when the shooting started, a shaky backup was worse than no backup.

And a female backup . . .

Hastings angrily secured the radio, secured the unit, stepped out into the street, walked along the sidewalk to the Chevrolet, on the passenger's side. He looked up and down the block, looked at Rivak's apartment building, then tripped the Chevrolet's door handle and slid into the car. As he did, he recognized her: Janet Collier, newly promoted to the Inspectors' Bureau, in Bunco. Time on the detail: less than six months. Time on patrol: perhaps five years.

Janet Collier, about thirty, divorced, with two children. She'd never been known to drink an after-work beer. Instead, she went home and cooked for her children.

Janet Collier—beautifully built and serious-minded, by all

odds the most desirable, most aloof woman in the department.

Sitting behind the wheel, Janet Collier greeted him with a restrained smile. Then, all business. "I think your guy went into the building just a few minutes ago, Lieutenant. At least, he fits the description." She pointed ahead, toward the intersection of Hyde and Sacramento. "I'm assuming that he came by car and parked out of sight around the corner. Anyhow, he arrived on foot."

"Did you call it in?"

"Yessir."

"Who'd you talk to? I just talked to Peirce."

"I talked to Sergeant Hathaway."

Grudgingly Hastings conceded to himself that, yes, Collier followed correct procedure, calling the duty sergeant.

"Is the back covered?"

"Yessir."

"Who's back there?

"It's Pomeroy, Safes and Lofts."

Gritting his teeth, Hastings nodded. In less than a year, Pomeroy would retire, draw his pension. During his entire time on the force, Hastings happened to know, Pomeroy had drawn his service revolver only once, a bluff.

Collier or Pomeroy . . . it was an impossible parlay. But he'd brought it on himself. Instead of calling Communications, he should have taken the time to track down Friedman.

Canelli—should he get Canelli?

No. To take Canelli off the murder scene at the Tides would compromise the chain of evidence. And in Homicide, keeping the evidence chain intact was the first commandment.

Pomeroy and Janet Collier—both of them untested, one of them over the hill, the other one a woman.

Don't go in alone, Friedman had warned. It was the second commandment.

As Hastings stared at the entrance to Rivak's building, making his decision, he heard the sound of voices coming closer. On the sidewalk beside them, a young Chinese couple was drawing abreast of their unmarked car. Hastings watched them as they passed one apartment building, then another. As they approached Rivak's building, the man was reaching in his pocket for keys.

"Here's our chance," Hastings said. "Let's go." Quickly he swung the door open, stepped outside, said over his shoulder, "Secure the unit." As he began walking, half trotting, he withdrew his shield case, held it in his left hand, ready. About to open the door to the small, dingy lobby of the building, the Chinese man suddenly straightened. Startled, instinctively crouching, he turned to face Hastings. The woman, too, was facing him. As if to protect herself, she raised both arms, palms outward. Eyes wide, she spoke in Chinese: a plea, or a protest.

"Wait—please—" Hastings stood motionless, raised his right hand, a gesture of reassurance. In his left hand he held the badge at shoulder height. Now the man's eyes shifted to the badge. Yes, the man was relaxing, muttering something in Chinese to the woman. Hastings heard footsteps, sensed that Janet Collier was behind him.

"We're police." Hastings pointed to the door. "When you go inside, we want to go with you."

Anxious, the woman moved closer to the man, touching his arm. Her eyes hadn't left Hastings's face. Now displaying her own badge, Janet Collier was shoulder to shoulder with Hastings. Then she moved a half step in front, spoke directly to the woman. "We're friends. Police. Friends." Then, with her eyes on the woman's face, she said, "*Pung yow.*"

Instantly the woman's face cleared. She said something in Chinese to the man, who nodded, said something in return to the woman. Then the man nodded to Hastings, smiled, and turned to the door. Moments later the four of them stood in the lobby. The Chinese couple was looking expectantly at Janet. After slipping her badge into her shoulder bag, Janet smiled, gestured to the stairway. "Okay—" As if to boost them up the stairs, she made a seat of her hands, gestured to the stairway. "Okay. *Cyra low tay.*"

In unison, the man and woman smiled, nodded, obediently began climbing the stairs.

"Impressive," Hastings murmured.

"My first duty was in Chinatown, walking a beat."

"Hmmm." As he spoke, he glanced at his watch. The time was twelve-forty A.M. Approximately forty minutes since Gordon Johnson had died, approximately fifteen minutes since, according to Janet Collier, Rivak had entered the building. In the small, dimly lit lobby, except for the front door, there were three other doors. Two of the doors were designated 101 and 102, and were apartments. The third door, in the rear, unmarked, doubtless opened on a utility area, and led to the building's rear entrance. The stairway, also dimly lit, its carpeting threadbare, was set against the rear wall.

Gesturing for Janet Collier to follow, Hastings moved away from the stairway, spoke in a low, cautious voice. "Rivak's apartment is on the third floor in back. I've talked to him, and I don't consider him dangerous. But—" Suddenly aware of what he was about to say, he smiled spontaneously. "But there's a chance he could've killed five men." As he said it, he looked directly into her eyes. She blinked. Then, suddenly, she smiled in return.

This, Hastings decided, was a first. Never before, to his knowledge, had Janet Collier been known to smile—such an open smile, so engaging, momentarily so intimate, just the two of them together, standing close, their voices low, conscious of the danger they might face together.

For an instant the moment held between them. Then, in unison, they both looked away.

"What I meant to say—" Once more, frowning, Hastings broke off. What *did* he mean to say?

"What we'll do," he said finally, "is go up there."

Straight-faced, she nodded solemnly. But was there the suggestion of a smile lingering in her eyes, touching the corners of her mouth? What did Janet Collier do most Saturday nights? Was there a man in her life? A lover?

He cleared his throat, pointed to the staircase, began again. "What we'll do is go up to the apartment. Have you got a radio?"

She was wearing a leather bomber jacket, blue jeans, and running shoes. Her hair was caught in a ponytail, as if she were about to go running, or to an aerobics class. Her eyes, Hastings realized, were hazel. She wore no makeup. For a moment she held his eyes with hers, as if she were deciding whether to ask a question. Then she pointed to a pocket of the jacket and the bulge of a surveillance radio. Two wires from the pocket were looped around her neck beneath the collar of the jacket. One wire was attached to an earpiece, one to a tiny microphone.

"Call Pomeroy. Tell him to stay put, keep his eyes open. Tell them we're going in."

"Yessir." She put the Lucite earpiece in her ear, switched on the radio, spoke into the microphone, small enough to be concealed in the palm of her hand. As she talked in a low, cautious voice, Hastings went to the staircase and looked up. The rectangular cage of hand railings and spokes rose four flights above him. There was no sign of movement from the stairwell; the only sound was muted rock music and distant laughter. Janet had come to stand beside him. She, too, was looking up the stairwell. She'd moved her large leather shoulder bag in front of her, opened the flap, loosened her revolver in its holster. Hastings studied her face surreptitiously. Could she pull the trigger? In her face, he could read nothing. She was simply standing beside him, her head raised, listening and looking. No more, no less. She was—

From behind them there was a sound: one click of metal against metal. And another click. Hastings crouched instinctively, unbuttoned his jacket, began a cross-body draw as he pivoted to face the sound that could be a gun cocking. Beside him, Janet was already in a crouch. Her revolver was almost clear of her shoulder bag.

Through the plate glass of the lobby door they saw a tall, stooped, gray-haired man who was fumbling with his keys at the lock.

"It's okay," Hastings whispered. He straightened, seated his revolver in its spring leather holster—left the jacket unbuttoned. In unison, he and Janet Collier moved away from the stairs to stand together at the back wall of the lobby. Acting on the same impulse, they turned to face each other, pantomiming a couple in quiet conversation, saying good night to each other.

As, still, the newcomer worked at the lock, finally succeeding. Letting the door close behind him, the gray-haired man began walking toward the stairway. His progress was unsteady, his eyes were bleary. It was Saturday night, and the newcomer was drunk.

Putting his back to the drunk, Hastings leaned closer to Janet, who stood with her back to the wall, facing him. Surprisingly, the top of her head was hardly higher than Hastings's chin. How, he wondered, had she fared on the Academy's obstacle course? They stood close together, as Saturday night lovers might.

No, not Saturday night lovers. If they were lovers, they would—

"Evening," the drunk said. Then, looking at them closely, frowning, he said, "You live here? I don't remember seeing—"

"What floor do you live on?" Hastings asked, putting an edge of authority on the question and staring hard at the drunk. "What apartment?"

"Well, it—it's two oh four. But I want to know—"

235

Hastings showed him the badge, jerked his head aside, jerked his chin up. "Get up there and lock your door. This is police business." He spoke softly.

"Well, Jesus—" Aggrieved, the drunk drew himself up, a lame imitation of righteous indignation. "Well, Jesus, I was just—"

"You've got thirty seconds," Hastings said. "Either get to your goddam apartment, or you're going downtown. I mean it, asshole." As he spoke, he saw Janet, too, with her shield in her hand. Fixed on the drunk, her eyes were blazing.

"Aw, stuff it, why don't you? Both of you." The newcomer turned away, took a firm grip on the handrail, began climbing the stairs. As he disappeared, the words "*lady cops*" came clearly down the staircase, followed by a string of indistinct obscenities.

"Okay." Hastings turned to face the woman. "Ready to do it?"

"Ready." As she said it, she met his eyes squarely, fully.

"His apartment is in the back," Hastings said, his voice soft and low. "Third floor. I'm not positive, but I don't think there's fire escape access to his apartment. So if he's up there, he's all ours." He broke off, kept his eyes steady, locked with hers. Even though the clock was running on the operation, time to make the decisions that couldn't be wrong, a part of his consciousness was still registering her woman-to-man nearness as they stood so close together, speaking in hushed voices, sharing the particular intimacy that the prospect of danger could confer.

Against the distraction of the wayward thought, Hastings frowned, shook his head, dropped his voice to a different note: the officer in charge, instructing a subordinate.

"I'll go up first, you come right behind me. I'll go to his door. There's a buzzer. I'll ring it, then I'll step back. I'm not going to draw my weapon. I'm going to try and do it the easy way, talk my way in. So—" Without meaning to do it, he realized that he was smiling. Again. "So you'll be the muscle. The door'll open from my left, I'm almost sure. If it does, you stand to the left, back against the wall. You'll have your weapon drawn. You'll be ready to shoot." He stared at her deliberately, the final test. Then, in the same crisp voice of command: "Have you got that?"

"Yessir." Steadily. Calmly.

"Have you ever done this before?"

"No, sir, I haven't." Then, defiantly: "Never." Her voice was precisely clipped. Yes, she was ready. Now, at least—in the lobby, safe—she was ready.

"If he cooperates," Hastings continued, "and it looks all right—if he'll let me in, no sweat—then that's what I'll do. I'll go inside. He's a strange little guy, but I have the feeling that he'll talk to me. If that's the way it works out, then I'll let him talk, see what he says. He might not be our guy. It's fifty-fifty, I'd say. No more. We don't want to lean on him until we know what we've got. Clear?"

She nodded. "So you want me to stay out of sight."

"Right. Hopefully, I'll back him into his apartment, get him to sit down. I won't let him lock the door on the inside. You hold your position beside the door, out of sight, until it's closed. If I want you once I'm inside, I'll yell. And if you hear anything that indicates I could be in trouble, obviously, you come on in, your decision."

"Right."

"Maybe you should get Pomeroy." He said it tentatively.

"Why don't you let me decide?"

He looked at her—and smiled again. Saying: "Okay, Janet. You decide." As he said it, the smile widened. Was he offering encouragement?

Or something else?

37

Hastings pressed the bell button beside the door, stepped back. Nodding, he smiled at Janet—one last smile. Then, jacket unbuttoned, .38 loose in its holster, he faced the door again, intently listening for the sound of movement from inside the small apartment. No light shone under the door; the door's peephole was dark. He pressed the button again, stepped closer to the door, listened.

Just as the latch clicked, and the door began to open.

In this moment—this instant—it could happen. From the darkness inside, the invisible muzzle of a gun could be tracking him. The touch of a finger on a trigger, and—

"Ah, Lieutenant Hastings." As the door opened wider, Rivak

238

materialized, silhouetted against the dim light that came from the living room. Both his hands were visible, both empty. Hastings drew a deep, grateful breath. As he looked covertly at Janet Collier, almost imperceptibly nodding, the first hurdle cleared, he spoke to the man.

"Mr. Rivak. Can—" He broke off, swallowed, began again. "Can I come in? I'd like to talk to you."

"Certainly. Come in." The door opened wider. "I've been expecting you."

"You have?" In the narrow hallway now, Hastings moved to stand against the interior wall as Rivak swung the door closed— and quickly turned the dead bolt.

It was another make-or-break moment, the second hurdle. Could Janet kick in the door if something went wrong? The odds were against it. Two, three minutes would elapse before Pomeroy could get to the third floor.

I've been expecting you.

Signifying what?

Signifying, certainly, that this small, wizened little man was cooperative. Suggesting, then, that Rivak's confidence must be encouraged. Suggesting, therefore, that the door should remain bolted, a demonstration of faith, of goodwill.

Don't interrogate these guys alone, Friedman had ordered.

They were standing face-to-face in the narrow hallway.

"Would you—" Rivak gestured to the living room. "Would you like to sit down?"

"Yes. Thanks." Hastings smiled, gestured for Rivak to precede him. Rivak shook his head, gesturing Hastings inside. It was, Hastings knew, the reflex action of the dedicated waiter, the eternal servant. With a last glance at the hallway door, all hope of surreptitiously unbolting it abandoned, Hastings decided to take the chance, walk first into the living room. They took the same well-worn chairs they'd taken earlier in the day, Hastings with his back to the room's only window, Rivak with his back to the empty fireplace. Even though the apartment was warm, Rivak still wore the shawl, clutched close to his chest. He was fully clothed and wore a neatly knotted tie.

Except for a card table set up beside Rivak's chair, the room was unchanged. The dim light from a single lamp shone on the card table, scattered with vials, cotton balls, surgical instruments, small ceramic dishes, and fragments of paper. A high-tech extension desk lamp, unlit, was clamped to one edge of the card table. A large rectangular display board covered with cotton was propped on the table at a forty-five-degree angle. The board was dotted with small objects. A picture frame was on the floor, resting against a leg of the table.

"Working on your beetle collection?" Hastings gestured to the table.

Rivak touched the table with his right hand, a subtle caress. "Yes . . ." He nodded, smiled benignly. "Yes. This afternoon I got twenty-six specimens from Thailand. And one of them might be unclassified." With his left hand he gestured to a stack of thick books and notebooks piled on the other side of his chair, on the floor. "It's too early to be certain, of course. But so far, I'm encouraged. *Very* encouraged." The benign little smile remained in place as he turned his attention fondly to the table and its contents.

"Unclassified? Does that mean it's a new species—or whatever you call it?"

Rivak nodded gently. "It's possible. But the confirmation process can take years."

"Have you ever discovered a new beetle?"

Rivak nodded. "One. It was five—no, six years ago. But the mandible was missing, and part of the skull. So—" The benign smile faded, the eyes hardened. "So I couldn't get it certified. I appealed. If I'd had a degree, been an academician, it would have been different."

"It's a closed shop, then. Politics."

240

Rivak made no reply. Instead, with his right hand, he reached behind the table for the electrical cord attached to the desk lamp. Reflexively Hastings moved his hand closer to his revolver, holstered at his belt. The switch to the lamp was in the cord. There was a click, and the high-intensity desk lamp came on. The beam was focused on the tabletop and the display board. As Rivak's hand reappeared from behind the table he picked up a small plastic bottle, which he held delicately between thumb and forefinger. "This is it," he said, his manner hushed, reverent. Then, as if remembering his manners, he extended the specimen jar toward Hastings. "Would you like to see?"

Hastings got to his feet politely, took the few steps to stand in front of Rivak, who remained seated, slowly rotating the bottle to give Hastings a better view of the beetle. It was orange, with dark green markings.

"Ah—" Hastings nodded. "Yes. Well—" He gestured encouragement—lamely, he knew. What was there to say about a beetle in a jar? "Well, good luck with it." He stepped back, resumed his seat. Now he glanced at his watch. Time to do business.

"It's almost one o'clock in the morning, Mr. Rivak. Am I keeping you up?"

"No, not at all. I sometimes don't go to bed until two, three o'clock." As he spoke, Rivak studied the beetle in the bottle close up for one last, lingering moment before he placed it carefully on the table. Then, again, his hand went behind the table to the cord of the lamp, and switched it off. Once more, a conditioned response, Hastings moved his hand closer to the butt of his revolver. But, passively, Rivak brought his right hand into full view, resting now on the table beside the new beetle. His gaze remained fixed on the beetle.

"Have you been out of the house tonight, Mr. Rivak?"

Rivak nodded dreamily. "Yes, I was. I got back after midnight. Just a little after." He spoke without inflection, without conscious involvement, as if he were in a light trance. Then, suddenly, he coughed, at the same time drawing the shawl closer.

"Where were you tonight, Mr. Rivak?" As he spoke, Hastings watched the other man's face for some reaction, some indication that contact had been made. There was nothing. Had the question registered? Should he try to—

"It's ironic, isn't it?" Rivak's voice was hardly more than a whisper. His eyes were still fixed on the beetle—his eyes, and his whole self. Everything. As before, Rivak's arm rested limp on the card table, close beside his chair.

"All my life," Rivak was saying, "I've been searching for that beetle. That beetle, or something like it—something that would make me feel like—" Searching for the phrase, he broke off. Then, in the same disembodied monotone: "—like other people must feel." He sat silently for a moment, looking at the beetle. Then, heavily: "I don't think you've ever felt like that, Lieutenant." As if great effort were required, with his arm still resting on the card table, Rivak took his eyes from the beetle, looked directly at Hastings. "Have you?"

"You're wrong, Mr. Rivak. I *have* felt like that. Everyone feels like that, sometimes."

With his eyes fixed sadly on Hastings, Rivak shook his head. "To say that, Lieutenant, you make the assumption that you know how I feel. But I submit to you that no one knows how I feel. Not unless—" A final pause. Then, as if he were surrendering to a burden too heavy to bear, Rivak's gaze fell, his head sagged. "Not unless they're locked up." As he said it, finally pronounced the fateful words, Rivak's hand moved slowly on the card table. This one last time, all hope surrendered, the little man with the deformed body and the dark, tragic eyes picked up the small specimen bottle containing the orange and green beetle. For a long moment he looked at the beetle, as if in farewell. Then, carefully replacing the bottle on the table, he moved his hand slowly behind the propped-up display board . . .

. . . and withdrew the .22 automatic with the silencer attached.

"I know why you're here, Lieutenant. Didn't you realize that I'd know?" Vaguely incredulous, perversely vexed by the detective's naïveté, Rivak frowned fretfully. The pistol with its six-inch barrel and five-inch silencer was pointed at Hastings's chest. Dead center.

Hastings sat motionless, frozen, his hands locked to the arms of his chair, his feet flat on the floor. It was, he realized, the position the condemned man took in the electric chair, before the switch was thrown. His gaze was fixed helplessly on the round black maw of the silencer, the abyss. The pistol was a Colt Woodsman, a long-barreled target gun, a semiautomatic. At close range, loaded with the high-speed hollow-point cartridges that left no ballistic fingerprint, the .22-caliber handgun was as effective as a .38. Fully loaded, with ten cartridges in the clip and one in the chamber, the gun was deadly. File down the front sight, fit a silencer, and the target pistol became the hit man's favorite weapon. In that, at least, he and Friedman had guessed right.

How loud would the report be? In the hallway outside, would Janet Collier hear? If she heard, and called Pomeroy, would . . .

"What I want you to do," Rivak was saying, "is tell me exactly how it happened that you first suspected it was me. I want you to be very precise. Will you do that, please?" With his forefinger on the target pistol's hair trigger, holding the pistol as steady as any professional killer might, Rivak was still the polite, self-effacing servant, always asking, never demanding.

What had he felt, this strange little man with the hot, feverish eyes, when he'd seen his victims die? What did he feel now? Would he . . . ?

"I'm quite sure," Rivak was saying, "that you have people with you here. 'Backup,' isn't that the word?"

Aware that he must make no sudden movement, Hastings nodded slowly, carefully. "Yes," he said. "There're two people here. And more on the way." He broke off, considered, then decided to say "You were right to bolt the door. That was smart. Very smart." As he said it, he ventured a cautious smile. Here—now—it was necessary to make contact, get inside the head of the man who would decide whether he lived or died. Only dialogue could save him, there was no other chance. He could see it in every movement Rivak made, every word Rivak uttered. A gunman holding hostages—a potential suicide poised for the final step-down to oblivion—the only hope was to get them talking, keep them talking, make them believe that you cared.

"And, of course," Rivak was saying, "you have a gun."

Hastings nodded again. "Yes." And, to himself, the desperate admission: *But I don't have a radio that might pick this up.*

It was an oversight that could cost him his life. Three years ago, in identical circumstances, a veteran detective named Markham had been able to use a surveillance radio, undetected. Friedman and Company had lowered a willing volunteer from the roof of an apartment building on a rope. The volunteer—Hardy, a rookie just out of the Academy, gung ho—had shot the suspect once in the back of the head. The stunt had made network TV, made Hardy an instant hero. But, less than a year later, addicted to the headlines, Hardy had volunteered for another dangerous job—and died.

"Show me the gun, please. Carefully."

Hastings drew back his jacket to reveal the short-barreled .38, holstered at his belt on the left side.

"Will you please put the gun on the floor beside your chair? As far as you can reach, please."

"Certainly."

"Use your thumb and forefinger, please."

As if he were watching someone else do it, Hastings saw his right hand moving in slow motion, withdrawing his revolver, laying the revolver on the floor three feet from his chair, then returning to its previous position, gripping the arm of the chair—still the prisoner, about to be executed. A wayward image from earliest childhood flickered: a glassed-in penny arcade machine, a miniature grappling claw that could be manipulated to pick up prizes lying inside the glass cube. Somehow the movements of his own right hand were just as mechanical, just as nonhuman, utterly removed from him.

After the fatal shot, only a high-pitched *pfft*, would Janet and the others break down the door to find him dead in the chair with his gun three feet away, on the floor? For a policeman, there was no more grievous humiliation. *Never surrender your weapon.* From the earliest days in the Academy, the refrain echoed and reechoed.

"And now, please, move your chair about two feet to the left."

Hastings obeyed awkwardly.

"Thank you." Rivak nodded. Then: "Now, I'd like you to tell me how it was that you first suspected me."

Hastings was compelled to clear his throat—once, twice. Then, speaking very deliberately, he said, "It was only this morning that I first suspected. It was something Louis Fields said. He'd been out of town for two or three weeks. He came back either Thursday or Friday. He'd only known about Frazer and Manley. He didn't know about Carr. Then, this morning—yesterday morning, Saturday morning, really—he heard that Phillips had been killed Friday night. And then his wife told him about Carr. And, of course, he immediately knew that someone was killing the Rabelais poker players. So he called me."

"Mr. Fields—" Rivak nodded gravely. Even in the light from a single dim table lamp set across the room, Rivak's narrow, pinched face was so pale that he might have been made up for the theater, a grotesque, his face painted a chalky white, with contrasting red lips, exaggerated dark eyes, and a hank of dark hair falling over his forehead. "Mr. Fields was the best one of them. I've often wondered how I would have felt, when he died."

"And Gordon Johnson," Hastings ventured. "He was the worst of them."

Once more, very seriously, the little man nodded. "Oh, yes. He was an evil man—the only one, really, who was evil. I always knew that."

Was, he'd said. Past tense.

An hour since the Johnson murder, and Rivak had said *was*.

Had Rivak looked this composed, spoken this softly, in the moments before he watched Gordon Johnson die? Was that, for Rivak, the addiction: smiling, nodding as he watched them die? Was . . .?

"Go on," Rivak said. "Tell me what happened next. Tell me everything, in detail. It's important, you know—important that you tell me everything." For emphasis he moved the pistol, a gesture of urgency, politely delivered. The meaning: time was passing.

All the time? Eternity?

"Well, as—as I said, after I talked to Mr. Fields, everything fell into place. I knew it was probably either Mr. Dietz, or Johnson—or you." As he said it, Hastings looked covertly at Rivak's face. Was it pleasure that he saw? Satisfaction? Something else? If the murder was premeditated, the psychologists said, one of the motives was recognition. *Will my name be in the papers?* It was a question Hastings had heard more than once, snapping on the handcuffs.

Hastings considered, then decided to say "You were the first one of the three that I decided to interrogate this afternoon. Then I talked to Mr. Dietz. And then Johnson—he was going to be the last one of the three. I think I got to the motel just a few minutes after you left."

"And so when you discovered Mr. Johnson, then you came here."

Mr. Johnson. Even now, Rivak spoke respectfully of the man he'd once served, however resentfully. Even with the gun in his hand, he was still the servant.

"You were the closest. Dietz lives almost to Daly City."

"Ah . . ." Once more Rivak nodded. There was a shadow of satisfaction in his mannerism, as if Hastings were giving him pleasure. Then, speculatively: "I suppose that, once you suspect someone, focus on him, you have ways of finding out that truth. Scientific tests, things like that."

"Yes." Hastings decided to nod, decided to pitch the single word to a regretful note, as if he were admitting to something regrettable, yet inevitable. Repeating: "Yes, that's true. We—"

Suddenly Rivak was racked by a spasm of coughing. Instantly Hastings gathered himself, his eyes on the gun, calculating the life-or-death odds. But the gun did not fall, did not falter. As the spasm passed, Rivak blinked, wiped his eyes with his free hand. When he spoke, his voice was steady. "I've been home less than an hour." He lowered his eyes to look down at the Woodsman. It was a fond look, vaguely nostalgic. "I didn't even take time to clean the gun. I suppose because I knew you'd be coming." He raised his dark eyes to look at Hastings. It was the same look of vague fondness that he'd fixed on the gun.

"It's surprising," Rivak said, "how much one thinks about, alone in a dark room waiting for a knock on the door. It's been amazing, really. Some say a man's whole life passes in front of his eyes during those last moments before he dies. And I suppose—"

He broke off, frowned. "I suppose that's what's been happening to me, this last hour. Except that it's as if—as if—" He broke off again. Then, with his eyes still fixed on Hastings, studying him now, looking for something hidden, something secret, Rivak's expression turned quizzical, vaguely puzzled. Finally: "It's as if my thoughts were tied to you—tethered to you, as one would tether an animal that would soon be slaughtered. I'd think about something—my childhood, in Budapest, for instance—and I'd remember something that happened to me when I was a child. But then my thoughts would turn back to you. 'Where is he now?' I would wonder. 'Has Hastings found Mr. Johnson?' Then I might think about how seasick I was on the ship to America. Then, once again, I'd come back to you, wonder where you were, when you would come for me. Because I knew—absolutely knew—that you would come. If not tonight, then surely tomorrow. Because, really, you're my destiny, Lieutenant Hastings. We're connected. Do you understand that? Do you understand how it happened, that the two of us are connected?"

"I—I'm not sure, not really." It was, Hastings realized, a meaningless answer, dangerously ineffectual. *We're connected*, he'd said. Signifying what? Would they die together? First him, then Rivak, a one-sided suicide pact? At the thought, the barrel of the silencer once more began to expand, the maw of eternity. Deep down, he felt the trembling begin, the first ragged edge of terror. Never had he faced death like this: helpless, witless, disarmed, the captive of a polite, articulate, psychopathic little man who was incapable of regret or remorse.

"I can see," Rivak was saying, "that you don't understand what I'm trying to tell you. But how could you, if you don't understand me? And I can see it in your eyes that you don't understand me. You're an experienced policeman, that's obvious. Death is your business. I can see that in your eyes, too— that, and something else, something that allows you to see things other men can't. You've suffered, I think. Perhaps it's because

248

you've killed men and can't forget. Yes . . ." Rivak nodded thoughtfully. "Yes, that must be it. You can't forget, so you try to understand. But for people like us, you and I, it's impossible for us to understand. A year ago—perhaps two years ago—I would never, *never* have believed that I was capable of executing five men. To take a life—any life, except for an insect's—was unthinkable. And even when I found a beetle and decided to keep it for my collection, I killed it humanely, with a drop of chloroform. So, the very first time the thought entered my mind . . ." Plainly reliving the moment, cherishing it, Rivak nodded fondly to himself. Now he was speaking from deeper inside his consciousness, exploring.

"I remember that moment very clearly. I was sitting exactly as I'm sitting now—sitting in this chair, working on my collection. I'd just gotten specimens from the Congo—wonderful specimens, and very inexpensive, too. And, in the same mail, I'd gotten a sizable check from a British collector, for five beetles I'd sent him. One of them was a Dynastes Hercules, an unusual variation. It was at night, I remember that, too. Just after eleven, I think. It had been a little more than a year since I'd been fired from Rabelais. By that time, I'd realized that the memory of it, of being disgraced, would never leave me. Not until I'd exorcised it would the memory leave me in peace. It became a disease—a cancer. It began as cancer does, with a single infected cell. It's difficult to describe how I knew the infection had begun. I suppose the critical time came when I was unable to make the memory go away. One moment, if I concentrated, I could clear my mind of it. But then the time came when I lost my free will. Whatever I was thinking, I was aware that the memory was there. It was a second presence. It became entangled with all my other memories, even from earliest childhood. All the humiliations, all the tragedies, even the random moments of sadness—whenever they came to the surface, bubbled up, they were infected with the virus: Mr. Johnson, accusing me. And the others—all the others, passing judgment—their faces were part of it, too." As if he were back in the game room of Rabelais, stricken, searching for some sign of compassion, some hope, Rivak's eyes moved from side to side, unfocused, inwardly traversing the impassive faces sitting in judgment. Then, softly, almost dreamily, he began to speak again.

"I'm sixty-three. And at that age, one begins to look back. Because, you see, one begins to realize that we're shaped during those first years. We might fight it, might protest, might beg for some dispensation. But we can't change the truth. And the truth is—*my* truth is—that my father couldn't bear to look at me. I suppose he tried, when I was a baby. I have no knowledge of that. But, from the time I was four years old, or perhaps five, I was aware that he would never look at me directly. In my memories I see him with a newspaper, or a magazine, or sometimes a book. I don't remember him talking, or laughing, or even smiling. I only remember him reading. He was a very precise man, very proper. He began working at the customs office in Budapest when he was nineteen. And he stayed there, at that same office, even under the Communists, until he died. He was meant to be there, you see. It was his destiny. Probably he should never have married. Or, if he'd married, it should never have been to my mother. Because neither of them could bend. My father could break, though. And so, when I was ten years old, and he was forty, and my mother had gone to church, I was in the tiny garden behind our apartment building. There was never any grass in that garden, I remember. And no flowers, or shrubs. There was only dirt, and a high brick wall with broken glass set in the cement along the top of the wall. I hated it, I remember, when I was sent to play there. With the high walls and the broken glass, it was like a prison. But I never would have thought to disobey. I was a very obedient child, I'm sure of that. And so I was sitting on the dirt and playing with

250

my toys when I heard a sound from inside our apartment, which was on the ground floor. It was a thump. Not a very loud thump, just a thump. I knew my father was in the apartment—in the tiny living room, reading his newspaper. I remember thinking that he'd dropped something, or knocked something off a table. But then I heard another sound. It was a human sound, or so I thought. After some time—a few minutes, probably—I decided to go inside the house. And as soon as I did, went just into the kitchen, which was in the back of the house, I knew something was wrong. It was the smell, I suppose. Excrement." Rivak blinked his eyes back into focus, fixed on Hastings. "You know what happens when someone dies."

Hastings nodded gravely, at the same time glancing covertly at his watch. It had been exactly twenty minutes since he'd entered the apartment. Once he'd heard a click, almost certainly Janet Collier, cautiously trying the door. How much could she hear if she pressed her ear to the door? What would she think? Almost certainly she would decide that the interrogation was peaceful, nonthreatening. Instead of being alarmed or suspicious, she would be reassured.

"And then, in the living room," Rivak was saying, "I saw the dog lying dead in her basket, covered with blood. Fouchette—the dog—was the only living thing my father could love, I'm sure of that now."

"Ah—Jesus—" It was, Hastings realized, an unpredictably heartfelt response. Murdered humans were, after all, his stock in trade. But murdered animals were—

"My father was hanging from a hook in the bathroom," Rivak was saying. "His tongue was protruding, like Fouchette's. My father's eyes were open, of course. They were bulging, and his face was very dark. He was dressed in his bathrobe. He'd been reading the Sunday paper. Later—years later—I discovered that, two days before, he'd lost his job at the customs office. And, of course, that explained everything. Without his job, his

251

life had no meaning. None. So he killed Fouchette. And then he killed himself. Quietly. He lived quietly, you see. So that's how he died. Quietly."

"I—" Hastings cleared his throat. "I'm sorry. I'm very sorry."

"Yes . . ." Rivak nodded, then sighed. "Yes, I really think you are sorry. Somehow I really think you are." For a moment, intently, he looked deep into Hastings's eyes. Then, speaking tentatively, almost shyly, as if he were admitting to something shameful, Rivak said, "Do you have any idea what it is to be alone, Lieutenant? Utterly alone—no family, no friends, no one in whom to confide, no one but grocery clerks and ticket takers to talk to?"

"I—I guess I don't, Mr. Rivak."

"You've experienced sadness, though. I can see it in your face."

"Yessir, I have. Anyone has. It's inevitable."

"What a shame . . ." Rivak ventured a smile, a timid offer of friendship. "What a shame, that it should end like this. Until now I've never confided in anyone. Even my mother, when she was alive—I never confided in her, not really. But now—" Once more he smiled. "But now—tonight—you're here. You want me to confide in you, tell you what I did, and why. Do you see how ironic it is—that you're my only confidant? It's—" Rivak smiled again, wistful now. "It's the perfect ending, really. The perfect circle. You came to arrest me for murder. But instead—" He raised the pistol an inch, then lowered it to its previous position, perfectly aimed at Hastings's heart. "Instead, you've become my confidant—my only confidant."

Hastings tried to smile, a failed effort. From the hallway he heard the faint sound of voices, quickly gone. Was it Janet and Pomeroy? No, they would whisper. Not until the door came crashing in would they reveal themselves.

Would they try it, make the move? No, not Janet Collier or

Pomeroy, not on their own authority. That would come from Friedman. It would be a life-or-death order.

Hastings's life.

Hastings's death.

Was it in *The Arabian Nights*, the story of the woman who kept death at bay by telling stories to a king? As long as she talked, amused the king, the desperate woman could live—but no longer.

"Your mother," Hastings ventured. "How old were you when she died?"

Rivak's eyes sharpened; in the old leather armchair, the room's only comfortable seating, his slight, narrow-chested body tensed.

"Why are you asking about my mother?"

" 'When she was alive,' you said. So I gathered she's dead. We've talked about your father. So I thought . . ." He let it go unfinished. But he must think ahead, anticipate. The longer a suicide talked, the less likely he was to jump. Hostage negotiating was the same: get them talking, keeping them talking.

And then pray.

"There's an expression," Rivak said, "that 'he's a saint,' or 'she's a saint.' And I suppose that described my mother. She was Catholic—a devout Catholic. There were only two parts to her life. There was the church, and there was me. If she could have kept me under glass, protected from everything, she would have done it. She *did* do it, really. She was my only refuge. All my life, I was an object of ridicule. Almost every day after school, I would be chased home. Children are like that, you know. In nature, if one of the litter has a deformity, his litter-mates kill him. It's called natural selection. It's cruel, but it's necessary. Absolutely necessary, for the species to survive. 'Nature is bloody in tooth and claw,' the poet said. And children instinctively know that. Therefore, children are savages. If imperfect babies weren't protected by their parents, the other children would destroy them. Or the members of the tribe would cast them out of the cave, to be killed by predators. Later, a few rungs up the evolutionary ladder, the witch doctors would pronounce the banishment. To this day, in some primitive tribes, the priest takes the deformed baby from its mother and places it where it will be destroyed by animals. And there's logic to it, of course. It's necessary. Absolutely necessary. How else could the tribe survive?" Gently, benignly, Rivak smiled. "You wouldn't know about any of this, Lieutenant. Not really. You're one of the strong ones, blessed by nature."

"Did you have brothers and sisters?"

"Oh, no." As if Hastings should have known better than to ask, Rivak promptly shook his head. "Oh, no," he repeated. "I suspect—strongly suspect—that my parents coupled only once in their entire marriage. And I was the result. Even though I was imperfect, I was nevertheless the product of their union. Which, in my mother's view, I'm sure, was the only purpose of marriage. Or, rather, it was the Holy Father's view. They were one and the same, of course—her views and the church's." On the thought, Rivak broke off, seemed to ruminate. Then: "I was ten years old when my father died. I was twenty-nine when my mother died. It was in 1956, during the uprising. A runaway army truck that had been firebombed by the insurgents killed her when she was leaving church, after Mass. It was two weeks, because of the uprising, before I could get her embalmed. And it was more than a month before I could get her buried. She—for a week—she was in her bed. There wasn't anything else to do. I was helpless. Utterly helpless."

Deciding against a show of sympathy, perhaps an intrusion, Hastings decided to ask "Did you live with her?"

"Oh, yes," Rivak nodded primly. "Of course."

"Were you working then?"

"I did odd jobs—small, menial jobs. Under communism, you know, most jobs were like that. Especially for Catholics. But then, after my mother died, I was allowed to leave Hungary. Of course, I wanted to go to America, and after I sold my possessions, I had enough money, just enough money."

"And you became a waiter."

"Yes . . ." With increasing gravity, he nodded. "Yes, I became a waiter. I came to San Francisco, you see, from Hungary. I'd heard that San Francisco was the most cosmopolitan city in America, so I came directly here. I was thirty. I worked hard for ten years—from 1957 to 1967. And then I got the position at Rabelais. But then, three years ago, they fired me." As he said it, his eyes hardened grimly, his voice grew tighter. "It wasn't an economic problem for me. I've always saved my money. And, working at Rabelais, I kept my ears open. You'd be surprised how much waiters hear. In fact, for the first month or two, I thought it was all for the best that I got fired. I was, after all, sixty years old.

"But then I began to think about it—about the injustice. And I began to realize that I must resist. Somehow, I must make them pay. That's the way I first thought of it, that I must make them pay. But who was 'them'? Finally, of course, I focused on those card players—Gordon Johnson and the others. And then, having made that decision, I began to speculate on the kind of punishment—the manner in which it should be meted out. And, of course, once I began to consider the kind of punishment—well—there was no other punishment but the obvious." As he said it, Rivak gestured with the pistol, an explanation.

"Death."

Once more, this time a disclaimer, the other man gestured with the pistol. "What else could there be? I couldn't blackmail them, not really. And I certainly couldn't ruin them financially. So death—execution—was all that remained."

"Ah—" Solicitously, Hastings nodded. "Yes, I see." As he said it, he heard a faint click from the hallway. Someone—a locksmith, probably, rooted unceremoniously out of bed—was trying to open the door, unaware that it was bolted from the inside. Hastings's glance fled from the hallway to Rivak. Had the little man heard the click, the faint scrape? If he had, there was no sign.

"The truth is," Rivak was saying, "that, incredibly, after I'd killed Mr. Frazer—after the first few hours, when I finally quit shaking—I realized that, at age sixty-three, I'd finally come alive. Can you understand that, Lieutenant?" With the question, Rivak's entire persona was hard focused on Hastings. This was the moment. On the answer, everything depended. Everything.

"I—ah—" Suddenly Hastings's throat closed. Compelling him to clear his throat, a definitive admission of weakness. "I— yes, I think I can understand. You—" He drew a deep breath, took the inevitable gamble. "For a lot of your life, you were a victim. You were cheated, really. So that, when you finally struck back, you felt alive. Maybe for the first time."

"Ah . . ." As if he'd been relieved of some terrible burden, Rivak nodded, let himself sink back in his chair. "You *do* understand, then."

Hastings made no reply. In the silence, there was no sound from the hallway. The room's only window was behind Hastings. If they were lowering some volunteer from the roof, another hero, it would be Rivak who saw him. Not Hastings. And if the sling or the rope went under the arms, the feet would come into view first—and the head and eyes last.

"Each time I did it—killed one of them—there was a release. A euphoria." Rivak waited expectantly for Hastings to make the required reply.

"Yes . . . I understand."

"I know now," Rivak said, "that my mother destroyed my father. Or perhaps his mother destroyed him. I have no way of knowing. All I know is that, in later years, I came to realize that my father had grown too weak to live. And so he killed himself. And then I realized that it could happen to me. And then I realized that it could already have happened to me. Do you understand, Lieutenant?" Once more, it was a hard-focused question, no margin left for error.

"I—yes, I do."

"His mother destroyed my father. And—" A final pause, the final explanation: "And my mother could have destroyed me. Do you see?"

"Yes, I see."

And, in that instant, yes, he *did* see. For Anton Rivak, there had been nothing left but murder. To come alive, Rivak must kill his tormenters: all those faceless tormenters, past and present. All of them, incredibly, reincarnated around a poker table at Rabelais, a club for rich, spoiled men.

Without realizing that he meant to do it, Hastings was saying: "You had to kill them. You didn't have a choice."

Once more, projecting infinite gratitude, Rivak nodded. Saying almost prayerfully "That's right, there was no choice. None. Not even now. There's no choice now, either. Thank God." As he said it, he was staring down at the pistol, which was now slightly lowered. When he spoke again, it was almost in a whisper. "You wouldn't have ridiculed me, Lieutenant. You wouldn't have chased me home from school."

"No," Hastings answered, "I wouldn't have done that." With his eyes on the barrel of the gun, he gathered himself. Because now all the time had gone; only the final gamble remained.

But now, slowly, the pistol was coming up—up.

Hastings's muscles had locked, immobilizing him. In despair, he closed his eyes, gritted his teeth, made fists of both his hands, tried not to whimper so loudly that, in the hallway, they would hear—

—and then cried out with the muted explosion—

—and opened his eyes to see the pistol falling away from Rivak's temple as the blood began flooding from the wound.

38

"This," Janet Collier said, "is incredible. My God. *Beetles. Look* at them."

Seated on Rivak's bed, his head low, eyes downcast, Hastings said, "Do you know how many different kinds of beetles there are?" His voice was dull; on the neatly made bed, his hands were listless at his sides. It was a posture of utter defeat.

"Ten thousand?" As she asked the question, she turned to look at him. Frank Hastings, co-commander of Homicide. Did he realize that, in the Inspectors' Bureau, he was a star? He looked the part and, yes, he acted the part: conscientious, fair minded, and modest. And, yes, brave.

And, yes, Hastings was a hunk: big, broad-shouldered, light on his feet, smooth when he moved. He had the body of an athlete and, sometimes, the eyes of a poet. For as long as she'd known him, always at a distance, she'd been aware of him as a man.

But never—ever—had she expected to find herself alone with him. Not like this, together in the small, meticulously kept bedroom of a serial killer, a dwarf of a man, a table waiter who'd forced Hastings to watch while he'd blown his brains out. Some of the blood had spattered on Hastings. In the bathroom, she'd helped him sponge off the blood.

For the past two hours, while the technicians had made their measurements and drawn their diagrams and taken their pictures and lifted their fingerprints, and while the ME had taken the body's temperature and cataloged its wounds, she had stood by while Hastings directed the show. He hadn't excused her, and she hadn't asked to be excused. The reason—one reason—was that, like every inspector in the SFPD, she hoped for an assignment to Homicide.

The second reason was Frank Hastings.

After the shot was fired—after Rivak died in a cascade of blood—Hastings had called out to them that it was all right, that he was safe. Then he'd come to the door, and drawn back the bolt, and let them in—she and Pomeroy and two uniformed officers.

For more than thirty minutes the three men had crouched soundlessly in the corridor while she'd stood with her ear pressed to the door of Rivak's apartment. When the shot had sounded— no more than a sharp spit, because of the silencer—she'd recoiled, sprung back, instinctively crouching, her revolver trained on the door. It had only been a split second, she knew, before Hastings had called out, and only seconds before he'd opened the door. Yet, in those few seconds, deep in some secret recess of herself, she'd experienced a pain so sharp that it could have been the thrust of steel.

Never before had she heard a shot meant to maim, meant to kill. Never before had—

"I'm sorry," Hastings was saying. "I—" Slowly, as if he were in acute pain, he began to shake his head. "I can't get it out of my mind. That—that poor little guy. Him and his—his beetles." He gestured helplessly. "That's all he had, really. Those goddam beetles. And he was happy, too—as happy as anyone, probably. He had a hard life, you know. He—Christ—he never really had a chance when he was young, with that deformity. And his father was a suicide—hanged himself while Anton was playing in the backyard. But—still—he pulled himself out of it, made something of his life, even though it was a pretty—" He broke off, searching for the word. Finally: "—a pretty narrow life. But it was all he needed, all he asked for. And then some—some asshole lost a hand of poker, and—" Once more he shook his head. Then, in apology: "I'm sorry, Janet. I—Jesus—I've seen so many bodies, seen so many people dead or dying. And most of them deserved to die. But this—" He broke off again helplessly, drew a deep, shaky breath. He blinked, cleared his throat, finally said, "I've been shot at, and I've—I've shot back. I—I've killed three people." As he said it their eyes met, and she could clearly see the pain. "But this," he said, "somehow this—it's so—so sad."

Without realizing that she'd meant to do it, she was sitting beside him on the bed, both of them looking at the little man's framed collection of beetles, each beetle impaled, pinned forever to a backing of snow-white cotton.

"I—I can't think of anything to say." Her voice was hushed, somehow intimate. "I—I've never even heard a shot fired, except on the range, to qualify. So I—there's just nothing I can say."

He made no reply. From the next room someone laughed: a technician, cracking a gallows joke.

"It's all right," Hastings answered. "That you don't say anything, I mean. Most people, you know, they say too much."

"Yes," she said, "I suppose they do."

As, without conscious forethought, she realized that she was touching his hand with hers.

As—yes—he was responding.